Blaze

By

Rayna Noire

BLAZE
Rayna Noire
Copyright © 2018
Print Edition

Chapter One

Easter Sunday 1916

THE ICY, DARK waters closed over Meara's head as she clutched the horn box against her chest. Shouts penetrated the water, but they were mere sounds without words. Even with her eyes open, she could see little. Where was the wagon? Hercules, the horse? Rosemary? Jane? Ronan?

One of the nuns at the convent told her that people often had their lives flash in front of them when they came close to dying. She went on to add it was supposed to help a person realize the evil of their ways and give them a chance to repent before they died for real. No images of her escaping the convent after it was bombed appeared in the watery dark. If she was going to see anything, it should have been the sweet kiss she'd shared with Braeden before he left to fight the Germans. Nothing.

This wasn't her first time in the water. How did she survive before? She kicked out with her booted feet, glad she'd dressed like a boy for the trip. A dress would likely tangle around her legs, trapping her. All she had to do was make it to the surface any way she could. The few seconds before they plunged into the water came back to her now. There had been gunshots. Ronan was certain they were meant for them. Hercules must have thought so, too. He galloped faster than she'd ever witnessed the old horse run. Ronan tried to stop him, but they hit the water at full speed.

Something bumped up against her arm. A hand grabbed hers and pushed her upwards, up into the blessed air filled with smoke, gunshots, and screams.

The gypsy wagon bobbed in the water not too far off. Jane swam beside Hercules, guiding him toward land while Rosemary peeked out the wagon window and shouted, "Is she okay?"

Ronan's voice sounded loud near her ear. "Believe so! Time will tell." Her cousin wrapped his arm around her as he kicked to get them above water a little more. "Should I assume you can't swim like most lasses?"

Jane had made a point of teaching her. She felt there were things a woman needed to know to survive in the world—swimming being one of them. Another was how to throw a knife with deadly accuracy.

"I can, a little. Not that I ever had much time to practice, but I know the basics. How to kick with the legs and paddle with the hands, but it will be hard to paddle holding the box and all."

"Aye. Why don't you grab onto my belt while I swim and float along beside me?"

Her fingers scrabbled for purchase on his thick, homemade belt. Some of the belts the village men wore were so wide Rosemary joked they could serve as a corset. The weathered leather made it hard to get a good hold. Her fingers curled around it like a hook. No way was she letting go after coming so far to finish a mission her parents had started so long ago. She'd not be the one who failed to perform her duty. No matter how cold or wet—a shot sounded close by followed by a bullet skimming the water—or scared she was.

A masculine voice called out from the dock. "Could you use a hand?"

Ronan answered, "That we could."

Meara wanted to remind him that they could trust no one. Many a person had been taken in by someone pretending to be a friend. Their mission was a delicate one in an unstable time, which made it more likely an unexpected helper could be a spy or an assassin. Her gaze traveled over Ronan's shoulder to the unknown helper. It would take a great deal to get both Hercules and the wagon ashore.

A splash sounded nearby, and the head and shoulders of a man appeared near them. Smoke laid low near the water making it hard to distinguish much about him, except he was human. He paddled close to Ronan and angled his head to the wagon, which was floating.

"You be travelers?"

They had painted the wagon to disguise it, knowing how some felt about the *travelers*, which was just another name for gypsies. So far, Ronan hadn't followed directions well enough before and could say something that might land more calamity on their heads—as if that were possible.

She answered before he could. "Oh, no, we bought it fair and square."

The man pointed toward the wagon as he treaded water. "A gypsy wagon is a good thing to have, especially considering you drove it into the bay. Most tar the bottom of their carts to float them across when needed. Still, strange you having one."

He struck out for where Jane struggled with Hercules. The woman had to be freezing. Meara's toes were going numb inside her boots, and her hand on the belt stayed, probably due to being frozen there. She couldn't feel the arm gripping the box. It took a glance to be certain it still remained. It did.

By the time the three of them reached the wagon, Jane had managed to turn Hercules toward land. His flying leap hadn't taken them too far from shore. The stranger made his way to the horse and took the other side of the bridle. "You did well to turn it."

Instead of accepting the compliment, Jane answered in a gruff voice. "I'm not an eejit."

"Did I say you were? There's a ramp by the pier. It's not the first time an animal has gone into the water. Usually, it's a cow or a sheep, though."

Ronan neared the wagon. Between noisy swim strokes, he gasped instructions. "Scamper up on the wagon as soon as you are able."

He made it sound as easy as if she were going to break into a skip on a sunny morning. It would help to have feelings in her hands. "I'll need help with the box. I can't chance dropping it. I'm half frozen and can hardly feel anything."

The wagon shifted as Rosemary crawled through the open window behind the driver's seat. She gave a small shriek and latched onto the seat.

"Jaysus!" the stranger cursed.

Rosemary put up one hand. "I am fine." She directed a smile at the unknown man, always on the lookout for a husband since she felt at nineteen she was already a spinster. Oddly, she forgot she was attired in boys clothing and had shorn her hair before embarking on the trip. "I can help Meara up."

Meara wasn't all that sure, but there wasn't a multitude of options to choose from. "I need you to take the box and place it in the wagon. Put it in one of those locking cabinets before bothering with me."

The last thing she needed was for two-thirds of the device that would supposedly stop the war to tumble to the bottom of the muddy bay, possibly never to be seen for another hundred years. No one knew how old the horn was. The parts could have rested hidden for a millennium or two considering the faeries conversed with humans on a regular basis well before Christianity forced them into hiding. Some say they sunk into the ground and live in each plant, rock, and animal.

"Show care," Ronan added as if none of them understood the necessity.

To be fair to her cousin, he was a man raised in a traditional household where men were expected to look after women as if they were newborn kittens. She'd overlook his remarks when he reminded them of the obvious, but Jane didn't.

As if hearing her thoughts, Jane shouted back to be heard over the noise from Dublin's streets. "We need to hurry! Cold isn't good for Hercules. We gotta keep swimming, and we need to get ashore. Billy says shallower water is near."

At least they now knew the man's name. As an actual traveler, her friend had a strong distrust of everyone who wasn't a traveler, which was ironic since most felt the same way about her people. Her general attitude was to expect the worse from someone until they proved otherwise. It made her wonder how Billy was doing as far at proving himself.

The wagon rocked as Rosemary leaned into the window to locate something. She mumbled as she looked and returned, brandishing a rope and a basket. She tied one end of the rope to a metal ring near the window. Jane had once told them they sometimes tethered their children with a rope to prevent them from wandering off. Since she never saw any tethered children while she was in Red Sasha's camp, she assumed it was a joke.

After tying the knot firmly, Rosemary knotted the other end firmly around the basket. "Put the box in the basket!"

Ronan paddled close enough to grab hold of the wagon side with his free hand as he snagged the basket. All she had to do was loosen the box and place it in the basket. It sounded simple, but it felt as if the hard corner of the box pressing into her side had become one with her skin. *Let go of the box,* she mentally urged herself.

"Meara, you've got to put it in the basket," her cousin urged. "You'd be the first to say we can't stay here where all and sundry can see us."

She would. "I'll need to balance myself a little more than holding onto your belt. The wagon might help."

A few sidekicks with one leg brought Ronan parallel with the wagon, pinning her between his body and the hardwood side. A twist and a backward throw landed the basket on Ronan's back and within reach. Her Irish cousin had made himself into a type of table, floating on top of the frigid bay. Her free hand touched the slack rope and drew the basket closer. Using one hand, she tipped it on its side and opened the top. A slight bob in the water brought the box level with the basket. All she had to do was shove it in and latch the top, but she didn't want to.

Meara, don't let the magic make you forget your purpose.

Her deceased father didn't always speak to her, but when he did, she knew he'd not lead her astray. With some strenuous effort, she pried the box from her side and pushed it into the basket. At the last moment, she gazed at it, fighting the need to have it in her hands again. "Soon," she muttered the words, latched the basket, and pulled on the rope.

A strong wind blew out of nowhere and tossed the basket to and fro. The sounds of people screaming in agony swirled around Meara. The blood-chilling screams and hopeless groans would have frozen her blood if she wasn't already sure the icy water had done about as much. It could have been the fighting in the street or it could have been those who died eons ago in a constant struggle for greed and power.

The wind vanished as fast as it arrived, making Meara doubt it had happened at all. The basket went up, there was some movement, then Rosemary called out. "You're next!" She threw down a rope that had a loop formed at the end.

"Smart lass," Ronan commented and helped ease the rope over Meara's head and tightened it under her arms. "I'll give you a nudge from my end, and you do what you can."

The rope tugged, while she batted at the side of the wagon with her frozen fingers. This must be how seals felt whenever they tried to go anywhere on land, using only their flippers. Ronan wrapped one arm around her hips, held onto the wagon with the other, and groaned as he boosted her. It was enough for her to grab onto a metal bar at the edge of the wagon lip. When driving, the driver usually rested his booted foot on the rod. It was also the right size to grab.

Her body hung suspended for what seemed forever until she managed to flop onto the wagon with Rosemary pulling hard on the rope. Once she managed to get both boots on the wagon, Ronan swam toward Jane and Billy.

Rosemary, despite them being similar ages, had appointed herself as Meara's guardian. It may have been the only way she could justify running away from Hogstead, the tiny village that held no future for either girl. As guardian, her job was to battle anyone who would do Meara harm. So far, her record in that department was lacking, although Meara knew her friend meant well. Some of the dangers they had fled as opposed to fighting were new to them and pure evil. A person doesn't hang around to exchange words with the likes of that. So they hadn't.

Rosemary helped Meara into the cabin area of the wagon. "You need to change clothes and get dry."

"The others are trying to get us ashore."

"That they are. You and I are not exactly strong swimmers. There's a good chance we might end up drowning. Then, everyone would have to stop and rescue us."

Meara smoothed the wet hair from her face. "I hate to agree with you…"

Before she could finish her statement, the wagon lurched. Jubilant cheering sounded outside. She could pick out Jane and Ronan's voices. She cut her eyes to Rosemary, who shoved a pair of pants and a shirt at her. It was helpful that her aunt had kept Ronan's outgrown clothes. She probably wasn't expecting to lend them to females for masquerading as men as they traveled the country, though. Still, it was awkward changing clothes with everyone pushing on the wagon.

Rosemary moved closer, keeping a hand on the wall for balance. "You need to change before you catch a chill. Don't be missish."

Easy for her to say since she had on dry clothes. Meara slipped off her wet shirt and pulled the dry shirt over the wet strips that flattened her chest. Cutting her hair would have been pointless without obscuring the main thing that identified them as women. No extra binding strips were to be had, since none of them had foreseen taking a dip in the water. The boots were even harder since the laces were tangled and interlaced with something slimy she didn't want to identify. The more she struggled the tighter the knots became.

"Here, try this." Rosemary passed her a crochet hook.

"Where did you get this?" She took the proffered tool and inserted the small hooked end into the knots. It didn't miraculously undo the knots, but it did loosen them, making it possible to pick the knots apart, and she handed the hook back. With her boots off, she shucked her pants, socks, and underpants. Once she toweled off, she redressed in dry clothing.

Rosemary opened one of the drawers where Jane kept her belongings and dropped the hook into it.

"I can't believe Jane would own something so traditional and ordinary," Meara stated in surprise.

"Maybe we see it as a crochet hook, but she has discovered a way to use it for a different purpose, possibly fighting."

"That makes more sense than Jane crocheting."

The wagon lurched again, then shuddered. A voice shouted something about hitching another team to the wagon. There was a whinny, then an answering call. Someone shouted instructions, and then the wagon started sliding. Rosemary grabbed Meara in a tight hug. "It's been an adventure, and I'm grateful for that. Perhaps I expected it to last a little longer."

A loud rap sounded on the side. "No worries! We're changing teams."

There was a jingle of harnesses and a deep throated, "Go on."

The wagon jolted and rocked back at an angle causing them to fall to the floor. Rosemary managed a grin. "Still, adventure. I wouldn't trade it for anything, especially to being back in Hogstead married to some farmer with five kids to look after."

It was a brave speech coming from a woman who made it clear that all she wanted to do was to get married and have a child or two. Still, Meara wouldn't call her friend on it.

"It *is* an adventure, and I have the feeling this is only the beginning."

Chapter Two

PLUMES OF SMOKE crowded the sky. The scent of burnt wood indicated someone had lost a business or possibly a home. Shots were still being exchanged. The warehouses along the water provided a barrier of sorts against whatever chaos had taken to the streets. Every now and then, someone would run between the buildings, huddled over, trying to make a smaller target. At one point, a mother tried to herd her children to a safe spot. Wherever that might be, it certainly wasn't there. Whatever was happening on the other side of the buildings may not involve them, but evil had a way of taking out everyone in its path, which she had experienced more than once.

The wagon rested on a pier, muddy, but not any worse for the wear. Hercules was draped in packing quilts, and Jane fussed over him, rubbing his nose, trying to get him to eat.

Ronan popped out of the wagon, dressed in dry clothing. "Billy and his da will take us across on the ferry, but he wants to go now. He should be back in a few shakes of a lamb's tail."

Since their original plan had been to get to Scotland, it seemed fitting they cross and the sooner the better. Before she could answer, Jane's head went up, and she stepped away from her beloved horse. One fist found purchase on her hip as she walked toward Ronan. "Who died and made you God?"

Ronan held out his hands. "I'm only telling you what is. Billy's da is convinced there's a donnybrook. Either you're in it or you get out of the way. Figured we might want to avoid the fight."

"Oh, you did, did you?" She pivoted to return to Hercules but threw her voice over her shoulder. "You're right this time, but don't go making a habit of thinking for us. Sounds like the fight is going strong, and we'd do well to leave."

Their impetuous helper, Billy, returned with an older version of himself in tow. Gray was just making an appearance in the man's hair, and time had curved his shoulders in a bit. Before Billy could introduce his father, the man clapped his hands together. "Know you had a bit of an accident. We have to go. Waited too long as it is. Are you coming or going?"

"Going," Jane answered.

The man cut his eyes to Ronan, who gave a slight nod of the head. Satisfied with the response, he gestured to the wagon. "Your horse up to pulling it?"

Ronan knew better than to answer for Jane. She shook her head. "It's been quite a shock for him. He needs to rest."

"He can rest on the way over," the ferry master said. "We can push the wagon onto the ferry. No problem with all you hardy young lads." He said the last with a wink.

They pushed the wagon onto the ferry, Billy's da, whose name was Bill too, decided to make use of all the hardy young men. They helped load supplies. Jane and Rosemary tossed heavy bags over their shoulders without too much trouble, demonstrating how they'd both had experience with hard work on a daily basis. Meara found herself wrestling with bags she knew good and well didn't want to be picked up or so it seemed. She'd wrestled one into her arms only to have it slither back to the floor.

Ronan picked it up for her. "Save yourself. Your work is the magical kind. Only you can do it. I can carry, as can Jane and Rosemary."

"I should do something…" It wouldn't be right for her to stand by while everyone else worked.

"Go take care of Hercules. He needs someone to stand at his

head in case he decides to bolt."

The possibility of Hercules bolting was right up there with lightning striking in the same place twice. Hercules probably couldn't even remember the last time he bolted. Still, it could happen, so maybe she should hold the lead.

Her fingers wrapped around the rough rope attached to Hercules's halter. The horse closed his eyes and emitted a blustery sigh that showered her with spit. He showed no signs of making a mad dash anywhere. Might as well make some use of her time. Meara opened her senses as Grandmother Biddy had taught her, listening for any information that could aid them. A wave of hatred rolled in and smacked her hard. So much hate, so strong, and directed at the English. It knocked her into Hercules, who opened his eyes to give her an offended stare.

There was more hatred directed toward the Irish. Whoever it was regarded the entire population as a worthless waste of air. While she knew there was hate in the world, she never had the ability to read it—until now. No wonder Bill's da wanted to leave immediately. At least none of the hate was directed at her. She was ready to shake off the experience when something dark came slipping through. It wiggled into her thoughts and stared out through her eyes.

Her father's voice resonated in her head. *Block it. Block it now. Hold onto your amulet and forbid its entrance. Be gone.*

She patted her chest, feeling for the outline of the amulet under her shirt. It was there. Her fingers wrapped around it tightly, holding onto it as if her life depended on it. "You're not welcome here. Begone!"

The feeling that something had entered—left.

Meara exhaled audibly and watched as everyone loaded the barge, not even bothering to glance her way. They had no clue what had just happened. She didn't, either. Was the evil they were hoping to outdistance and finally put an end to by finding the third section of the horn and blowing it, close?

Not as close as you might think, but close enough. War, hate, and death feed it. Please hurry, daughter.

Her fingers loosened around the amulet as she opened her eyes. Her gaze landed on her friends who scurried back and forth, bent underneath the weight of their various loads. Leaving this place, which was engaged in a battle, didn't seem like such a bad thing. Still, this quest was more of a family thing for her—a legacy of sorts—the only tie left with her parents she'd never met. How fair was it to take the others on this mission?

"Meara!" Jane shouted to be heard over the fighting in the parallel street. "Bring Hercules."

She led the tired horse, which moved about as slow as an animal could. Once on deck they cross tied and hobbled him to limit his movement. The ferry was more of a barge than a boat. Waist high railings edged the deck to prevent cargo and passengers from falling over. A small cabin in the middle offered passengers a place to hide from the wind. Atop this structure was the wheelhouse where Bill or Billy would keep watch. There was a mechanical cough, then a *cha-cha* as Billy labored over one engine. Finally, it caught, and he moved onto the second engine and repeated the same procedure. Coal bins resided next to the engines since they would have to be fed continuously throughout the trip.

They traveled through the bay without talking, hoping that the violence spilling out on the streets wouldn't touch them. Once they got to open waters, Billy joined them. He angled his head back in the direction they came.

"Tricky bit back there. My da told me the rebellion will start tomorrow."

"The what?" Meara asked. Her convent education had left out a great deal. When it came to battles, God always favored the winners.

"Rebellion. The Irish are tired of being told what to do by the Brits. Not only do they tell us how to run our own country, they tax us for that privilege, too."

Ronan murmured his agreement. "The Irish Republican Army have been recruiting back home. Plenty have joined. As a homebody, I knew nothing about a rebellion."

"Aye, makes sense." Billy continued. "Seeing as they did most of their recruiting at local pubs, it might be hard to touch a homebody. Both Da and I were invited. The leaders thought with England fighting the Germans, it would be the perfect time to take back what's ours."

"The country?" Meara hazarded a guess.

"That," Billy expanded on his answer, "and our way of life and our pride at being Irish. A British soldier manages to say the words *Irish* and *cow pie* with the same amount of disgust."

"I don't understand why." Meara's limited exposure to both Irish and her own native people found the Irish more hospitable. "I found the Irish to be very kind—most of the time." She didn't include escaping from outraged citizens, convinced the travelers had taken their money or dallied with their wives. As to the money, plenty of housewives or single women came to the camp to have their fortune told. Some may have lied about where the money went.

"We are kind, especially to the lasses." He gave her a wide wink.

Maybe their disguises left something to be desired. Dry and at a distance should serve. She wouldn't put it past her cousin to tell all, being the trusting soul that he was. She was never that trusting, although most people would have thought anyone in a convent would have been. Instead, she was told everyone and everything outside the convent was evil. The truth was some were evil, but most had different motivations than the sisters. Their goals as opposed to having pure hearts were more about taking care of their families, paying bills, and occasionally, besting their neighbor.

Jane chafed her arms for warmth as the breeze picked up. "Never known any other place than Ireland. I'll be glad to be stepping on Scotland's soil."

"That will take more than a day or two, especially traveling by horse."

Before Billy could elaborate, his father called. "Son, you need to stoke the engines to make Holyhead before dusk."

Rosemary's eyebrows lifted with the request, and her mouth dropped open. Finally, she spoke so softly Meara almost missed what she had to say.

"That's in Wales."

"Why are we on a ferry that is going to Wales?"

Ronan shrugged. "It was the only one leaving today."

He had a point. No good would have come out of staying. Taking an impromptu swim wasn't in her plans, either. When it looked like Jane would object, she held up her hand. "Remember, Grandmother Biddy told us that fate had a way of making things work out?"

Jane acknowledged her remark with a look.

Meara continued. "Maybe we are supposed to go this way. It might be a way for us to avoid danger. Perhaps it will put us nearer to where we need to be. It could confuse whoever is following us."

She listened to the words pouring from her mouth and marveling at the ring of truth in them. Maybe a higher force was guiding and protecting them.

Chapter Three

AFTER ESCAPING THE trouble in Dublin, the ferry ride was uneventful, bordering on monotonous. The cold air whipping off the water kept the trip from being pleasant. That, and Bill Sr.'s constant narrative of what was happening back in Ireland.

"It's a good thing your sainted mother is not around to witness this."

Billy grimaced. "Yes, I know. Do we have to talk about that?"

The older man grumbled something unintelligible under his breath before saying, "It's only fair that these young people know what's happening."

"Ah, Da."

Most of the trip, Meara had been reacting to everything. It would be nice for a change to be informed. "What's happening?"

"As you guessed, the Sons of Ireland are taking back their country from the power-hungry Sassenachs."

"Who?"

"The Brits."

Meara nodded, not knowing what to say. Technically, she was British.

Bill didn't need any encouragement to keep talking. "I'm not saying that our boys aren't right to fight back. More power to them but can't see it coming out well. That's why we left. British forces are better organized and armed. They have no problem with crushing the rebellion, and in doing so, they'll stomp out others who did nothing more than being born Irish. Figured it would be best for me and my boy to stay in Wales with relatives until everything is sorted out."

Bill's plans surprised Meara, but not as much as it did Billy, who stared at his father slack jawed. "Da, you never told me. I would have at least met up with my mates before leaving."

"Those mates of yours." Bill made a derisive sniff. "They'd have you fighting with them. Your blood would be emptied out on Sackville Street."

Instead of answering, Billy crossed his arms and turned his back on his father.

The tension between the two men was palpable, which may have been the reason Jane checked on her horse. Rosemary remembered something she needed in the wagon. Ronan caught Meara's eyes and motioned to emerging scenery in the distance. "I think I see land. Is that Holyhead?"

There were some rocky outcroppings, a bit of green, and seabirds circling overhead.

Bill Sr. acknowledged them with a nod. "That it is. I'll need to steer us in."

With that pronouncement, he hurried up to the captain's house. Billy went to the aft of the craft to shovel coal. The rest stood and watched Holyhead grow closer. Buildings sprung up on the land and watercrafts hovered near the shore. Their ferry gave a few toots of the steam whistle as they motored in. They sounded friendly but were probably more for navigational purpose to warn folks that the ferry was headed in and to watch out. The wide bottomed craft probably had very little maneuverability.

Ronan pointed to a castle on shore. "I heard about that one. Wouldn't mind doing a little sightseeing since it's my first time in Wales. What's our next stop?"

Their next stop was something she should know. The dreams and visions had simply told her to go to Scotland. She remembered a majestic mountain in the background, which could be anywhere with mountains. She didn't know the country at all but assumed it must be the highlands because of the name. It didn't feel right, though.

"First, we need to replace the supplies we lost."

"Aye. You're a bright lass. We only lost the things that weren't tied down and flew out the open window."

All she remembered was being flung into the air like a rock from a slingshot. For a moment of flight, she'd felt free, scared, but free. Then there was the cold, dark water. Can't say she paid much attention to what went catapulting out beside her. "What's missing?"

Ronan shrugged. "My attention was elsewhere. Let's ask Rosemary."

The smell of coal smoke filled the air as the various vessels lobbied for docking space. Shouting men wrestled cargo off their ships. Some shouts were in accented English, a few Irish, and the others she had no clue. They drew closer. Meara scanned the busy dock, curious if she'd recognize whomever or whatever had been following them. One thing she could be sure of was it didn't ride over with them. That should give them a day or two head start. It would help to know where they were going.

They made their way to the wagon and Hercules, only to find out Rosemary was clueless about their supplies. "You expect me to catalog items as they went flying past me? I did my best to hold on."

If they headed out in the general direction of Scotland, not knowing what they lost, they'd discover the missing item when they needed it the most when there were none to be found. Jane joined the group, propped her leg on the front rung that ran up to the wagon seat, folded her arms, and said, "I know what is missing."

Since it was her wagon and traveling the country as she did, it made sense she would have immediately inventoried the items.

"What?" Meara had to ask, since it didn't seem like Jane would announce it. The woman's expression made her think it might remain her secret.

"A bale of hay. The basket with all the food Ronan's mother made for us."

"Oh. That's a loss since Aunt Erin is a grand cook."

"And the shotgun."

Ronan groaned. "That stings. No way an Irishman can purchase a firearm."

"Maybe not. This is Wales." Jane reminded. "Besides, one of our fresh-faced English boys can do the job. On the docks, everything is for sale, and there are no questions asked. We'll get another one."

Sometimes, Meara found it was best not to ask about specifics, such as how would Jane get a gun. She would get one, which was the important thing. They needed some way to protect themselves from whatever was coming. Everyone from Eleanor to Grandmother Biddy had given her some magical amulet to wear. Often, the magic felt heavy almost as if she donned a heavy coat that had coins sewed into the lining. The one time she put the charms aside to bathe, she had experienced a sense of vulnerability that had her rushing through her bath.

The others had nothing. Aunt Erin insisted on saying a prayer, then reciting a protective charm, determined to call on all the options. It may have saved them since they were all safe and on their way to Scotland.

Her friends chattered about what they would do when they landed. Jane's voice sounded over the others. "I must get some oats for Hercules. He deserves a treat after what he's been through."

"I wouldn't mind a treat, either." Ronan patted his stomach. "My stomach is shaking hands with my backbone."

Rosemary's hand went to her hair She tried to run her fingers through it but only had a short crop of it since she had shorn it before the trip. A heavy sigh escaped her lips. "I was going to say ribbons. Little good they'd do me. I'd settle for a hot bowl of cawl, especially after our chilly journey."

Before anyone could ask, Rosemary continued. "I have a bit of

Welsh in me, and my momma used to make cawl, which is a cross between a soup and a stew filled with vegetables, herbs, and meat, with just a bit of juice broth. None of the gravy, though. I'd imagine most of the pubs would have some and the restaurants, too."

"No fancy restaurants for us. We need to save our money."

Meara's eyebrows went up at the thought of their Irish coinage. "Will we be able to use our Irish money here?"

"Maybe. I have some pounds that I exchanged for Irish money. Most Irishman are anxious to get a pound out of their hands. So, we have some pounds, but not a great deal. That's why there'll be no fancy restaurants for us. Heard they used the same in Scotland. We have to make it last."

"We could pick up some jobs on the way," Rosemary volunteered.

Jane tapped her cheek, then lifted her leg from the wagon. Finally, she cleared her throat. "I don't have much experience outside of Ireland. These people might not be so quick to trust people passing through." Her gaze lingered on Meara, who held up her hands, then went back to Rosemary.

"Having lived in a small town, I am sure most of the world doesn't know exists, there were no strangers. Meara was our only stranger of late, and she was running *out* of town. So, hoping to catch work on the way would not be a good thing."

They finally reached the pier where Bill Sr. expected them to unload the cargo, which they did. He agreed to forgo payment for their help. They offloaded the supplies onto skids that would possibly go into the warehouse or be bought outright by agents checking the goods. A one-armed soldier with an empty uniform sleeve stood nearby watching. It reminded her of the war and Braeden. She exhaled deeply and stopped in the process of lifting the bag and closed her eyes.

Braeden, are you out there? Still alive? Did you ever come back to Hogstead to look for me? It wasn't that I didn't wait for you. I couldn't stay.

She waited a few heartbeats, hoping to hear or feel something. *Nothing*. It wasn't like he could speak to her like her father or mother did. Their ability may have been the result of blood ties, magical powers, and the fact they were dead. Most people knew there were times when spirits could make themselves heard. With that being the case, it was good he didn't speak to her in her head, but only in her dreams.

Once they finished with the cargo, they unloaded the wagon and Hercules. They harnessed the horse but made the decision to walk to give the horse a bit of a break. As they drew nearer to the soldier, Meara called out. "How goes the war?"

The man spat on the ground. "It's bad, very bad. Hell on Earth."

Not the news she wanted to hear. If things could resolve themselves, there would be no point of wandering through various countries in search of an ancient relic. Whatever they were after might vanish once the fighting started.

They found a livery which would feed Hercules. Jane insisted on staying with the wagon to make sure nothing happened to it. Surprisingly, Ronan volunteered to stay with Jane to make sure she was safe, possibly unaware of her deadly skill with a knife.

Rosemary managed a smile and hooked her arm with Meara's. "It's just us English lads, then."

"Um, what's your lad's name?"

"Rod. You're Mark, remember?"

"Can't say that I do. I'm thinking lads don't walk around with their arms locked."

The arm lock was released, and her friend grumbled. "Some do, especially if they've had too much to drink."

"We're tough lads, though. We'll get our cawl at one of those takeaway places and bring some back to Jane and Ronan. What's Jane's boy name?"

"Jay."

"She's the lucky one. She might even answer to it. We have to start calling each other by these names so we don't slip up."

"You got it, guvnor. I mean, Mark." Rosemary delivered a playful elbow to Meara's ribs.

"I don't think boys elbow each other."

"Come on. You're talking like you're an expert when you lived most of your life in a convent."

"What do I know then?" She threw her hands up. "Still, I think we should try not to attract attention."

Her friend's lips pulled down into a frown. "Rod…" Meara tried out the name. It felt awkward. "Are you mad at me?"

"Just trying to look like the rest of the blokes. Not a happy expression on the lot of them."

"Got it." She shoved her hands into her pockets and scowled. Her gaze stayed on the buildings, looking for the elusive cawl shop, if there was one. She didn't want to chance making eye contact with anyone, unsure if someone might take her scowl the wrong way. Rosemary was right, she was no expert on men. She did know they engaged in fighting at every turn of the corner. Her knife was strapped to her calf, but she didn't want to use it.

They passed a group of men. One of them called after them, calling them *country green*. Rosemary turned as if she'd say something, but Meara hissed between her teeth. "Don't do it. Might be an excuse to start a fight."

Her friend grumbled. "You're right. The man back there was right, too. We *are* country green. We might think our ride across the pond made us somehow wiser, but we're still two innocents."

"As a slightly seasoned individual, I know enough to keep my head down." She pointed at a sign ahead of them. "Looks like we found what we're looking for."

"None too soon." Rosemary punched her arm. "Before you say anything, I've witnessed plenty of boys trading punches."

Night had fallen while they strolled, and gas lights flickered to life, illuminating small patches of street. The shadows crowded the rest of the street, making it difficult to see much.

The skin right over her heart heated. Meara reached for her mother's locket. Destiny, the fortuneteller, told her it would warm whenever she was in danger. It was burning up. A shadow detached itself from the shadows.

A certainty that evil had found them had her grabbing Rosemary's arm and pulling her into the lit shop. The problem with evil was she could never be sure what face it would take. All she could do at this point was take advantage of her early warning system and flee. The bell rang at their entrance, and a grandmotherly woman looked up.

"Two lads. I bet you have hearty appetites."

Meara looked over her shoulder, out the lit window. The bright light made it hard to distinguish the exterior or anyone that could be following them. "Do you have a back door? We have an unpleasant sort following us. We'll be back for cawl and have a little something for your trouble if we can fool the great bully."

The woman raised one eyebrow and gestured to a door that led into the kitchen. They hurried past a young girl at the stove, attending to bubbling pots. The back door opened into an alley, stinking of rotted food and stale urine. The old woman gave them a wide smile exposing her missing teeth. "I bet there's a woman in this tale."

"You bet right!"

Meara eased into the alley waiting for the shadows to shift. The woman called after them. "I'll want to hear the tale when you come back!"

Chapter Four

THE TRIP THROUGH the slumbering city of Holyhead felt more like a waking dream. A mist grew on the ground. The farther they got from the docks, the quieter it was, and the uneasy feeling of being watched fell away. Businesses were shuttered, and families were fast asleep in their beds. An occasional dog bark broke the silence. That and the creak of the wagon and clank of Hercules's shod hooves on the cobblestones were the only sounds. None of them spoke as to not to draw attention.

They had bid a friendly goodbye to Billy who had helped them harness Hercules, then stood watching with obvious reluctance as they headed away. Rosemary joked that he reminded her of a stray dog, acting hopeful and waiting to be invited along. It would be hard to imagine someone wanting to put themselves in harm's away. Still, thousands of young men enlisted every day in England to protect their county. They viewed their actions as the only honorable option. Was that what she was doing—the only honorable option?

Meara chafed her arms, fighting off the evening chill and an impending sense of dread. Fate had thrown her into her present situation. Though she would have chosen otherwise, something would eventually propel her in the direction of using mystical power to stem the wave of hate and violence sweeping the world. Personally, she would have been content staying in Hogstead and being Braeden's wife. As appealing as the prospect was, she knew it wouldn't have happened in as easy manner as her daydreams portrayed.

Adelaide, Braden's would-have-been fiancée, made sure that no one would accept Meara in the small village. Burning Eleanor's home where Meara had been staying was a clear message. Each time Meara and Rosemary landed at a different destination, she felt that maybe the new locale provided a better, different future. Then, the other boot would follow, pushing them out of the comfortable niche they'd made for themselves. Even if she had no intention of following cryptic clues given by her deceased parents, it didn't stop whatever was determined to stop her from following them or even killing her. Only weeks ago, she'd recovered from a coma where she wandered in an endless forest, hearing voices and seeing shadows, but never catching up to anyone. What she thought had been a night had been months.

Aunt Erin told her she'd been engaged in a spiritual battle that she'd overcome. Jane and Rosemary joked that cinnamon was deep in their pores since they burned it every day to ward off evil spirits. Chimes had hung near the door that jingled whenever the door had open or closed. The sound would confuse any malevolent entity hoping to enter the house. Each of her friends and relatives took turns sitting with her. While doing so they often chanted protective prayers or even sang familiar songs in hopes of drawing her back. She could remember a reedy soprano singing about the hills of Ireland.

She was here now. Her hands tightened on each other. All she knew was her life was in danger as were her friends since they'd made the decision to come with her.

The structures became farther and farther apart, and Hercules's horseshoes no longer created an eerie symphony on the paved road. The cobblestones ended abruptly giving way to a dirt road while the fog thickened, causing Jane to stop the wagon.

"I'll do better to lead Hercules. You take the reins. When we get a little farther, we can light a lantern."

Ronan answered from his place inside the wagon. "I'll have it ready."

For whatever Jane had against her cousin, the stubborn traveler would have to admit that he could be helpful. The stalled wagon jerked into movement. As the wagon wheels continued to roll, she mulled over what could have happened. The leather leads rested loosely in her hands.

A prodding had her turning in response as Rosemary maneuvered her way through the window and onto the bench seat. "What are you thinking about?"

Possible torture before inevitable death didn't feel like the right answer. She searched for one that might be more acceptable. "Braeden."

"Ah. That's understandable. If I had a lovely man like yours in love with me, I'd be thinking about him, too."

Meara sighed heavily. She hadn't been thinking of Braeden unless it was the constant question in the back of her mind. *Was he alive or dead?* Knowing the truth would not serve her, she forced a smile. "You know me so well."

"I do." Rosemary nudged Meara with her hand. "Traveling together. Crossing continents. Almost drowning. All those things tend to bond people together."

"Yes, they do." It would be hard to know, since Rosemary and she were the only females she knew who had done such things. Jane would have to be added into the calculation, too, but as much time as she spent with the former traveler, the more enigmatic the woman grew. Maybe Jane resented her decision to throw in with them. At the time, Jane thought her traveler group would break up due to the death of their monarch, Grandmother Biddy. Then again, she could have said that to justify her leaving. Jane didn't have to press on without them, but if she didn't, they'd be without transport and a place to lay their heads.

The forced smile melted and pulled south as she considered letting her friends go. It would be dangerous for them to proceed, but it would be impossible without them, too. What right did she have to allow them to run into danger? Even though they made it to Holyhead with a minimum of trouble, she should allow them the chance to leave. When they stopped next, she'd announce it.

An owl hooted in a tree as they left the city behind. The unexpected sound sent a shiver down her spine. Many still considered the call of an owl a death omen. Eleanor, who rescued her after the convent was bombed, didn't believe in that old wives' tale. She explained almost any animal or bird could be considered a death omen since so many folks died back in the old days. The only way they could explain it was by nature omens. Occasionally, they thought someone put a hex on you if you got sick, since they knew nothing about germs or viruses.

Ronan climbed out of the window behind the driver's bench, forcing Rosemary to squeeze to one side to accommodate him. He perched on the bench and announced, "I'm going to relieve Jane."

He jumped to the ground. His jogging footsteps sounded as Rosemary clicked her tongue. "Looks like someone has an admirer."

Her friend must have missed all the fights between the two. "Those two?" Meara gave a derisive snort to underscore her words.

"Yes." She scooted closer on the bench seat possibly to avoid being in the way in case Jane wanted to enter the wagon the same way Ronan exited. "I know you haven't witnessed a great deal of wooing while you were in the convent, but it isn't that unusual for men and women to spar when the sparks start flying."

"I'd say they are doing more than sparring."

"True." Rosemary chuckled. "Sparks *are* flying."

"Nothing will come of it. Jane is a few years older than Ronan."

"You're thinking of traditional relationships. The fact we're all on a quest to find the fairy horn pieces to assemble and put an end to the war makes us a bit out of the ordinary. Don't you think?"

"I do. Still, one thing doesn't naturally lead to another. I didn't fight with Braeden."

"Maybe, maybe not. Didn't you say you tried to discourage

him?"

"I did. I thought he was engaged to Adelaide, and I didn't want anything to do with breaking up an engaged couple. As far as I knew, he might not be for breaking up, but more was for having some fun on the side."

"Braeden isn't like that."

"I didn't know that then. We may have argued a tiny bit. I told him I wasn't interested but that didn't stop him from coming around or trying to explain his side of the story."

"In the end, you believed him."

"I did. He joined the army in the belief that it would put distance between him and Adelaide, causing the girl to move on to another likely target."

"It was a decent plan considering how vengeful she could be. Since her father is mayor, there could be unwelcome pressure put on Braeden's family. I've felt Adelaide's sting on more than one occasion. It's the reason I'm still single. She always had to have all the boys' admiration despite the fact she could only marry one. Whenever some bloke looked my way instead of hers, her friends started spreading rumors about me. They called me round heels, a layabout, and even implied that I had some horrendous birthmark that would disgust any man if he had to look at it."

"A birthmark?"

"There is no birthmark. I thought you were smarter than that."

Meara cleared her throat. Thank goodness she hadn't asked about the other two. "I was only teasing you about the birthmark. Not sure why any man would care, unless the birthmark was on your face."

"You're right about that. We're all usually covered up from neck to toes. The implication was that other men who had seen me naked knew I had a disfigurement. That was the real issue. It could be in a sensitive place."

Meara tried to imagine a sensitive place. Somewhere a bee might sting that could complicate healing. "Between your fingers? Inside your ears?"

"No. *Sensitive.*" Rosemary emphasized the word.

The nose could be sensitive as well as the back of her neck. Then, she got it. "Oh, *sensitive.* I got it. No wonder such a rumor was off-putting. People would have thought you played at being Lady Godiva riding through the streets stark naked with nothing but your hair to shield your body."

"Not exactly Lady Godiva since she did what she did to get her husband to reduce taxes on the people. Supposedly, he told her as a joke if she would ride through the streets without clothes he'd reduce taxes. He probably assumed she wouldn't. Women at the time were examined by doctors with their clothes on and often bathed while still wearing a shift. Doing something so bold was unheard of. The story goes the people initially lined the streets to see such a sight, but then turned their backs on the lady to preserve her dignity."

"Did her husband lift the taxes?"

"He did." Rosemary gave a chuckle. "How could he do otherwise when his wife took such a bold action?"

"I guess from then on, he never underestimated his wife."

"I suppose not. The stories spun about me were not so noble as that. Most folks question tales that come directly from Adelaide's toadies, but then, there are thoughts in the back of their minds that maybe it could be true. Most gossip starts with a spark of truth even if it is a misunderstood action. That's what really hurt my marital prospects."

Her friend had made no secret she wanted to leave the tiny village of Hogstead and start anew. "Was there ever anyone you fancied in the village?" Maybe that one person turned away from Rosemary to the gossip.

There was a silence between them. The sound of Jane whispering encouragements to the old horse drifted back. Even Jane's voice stopped, allowing the night chorus of insects to swell around them.

Just when she was sure her friend decided to pass on the painful subject, she spoke.

"I told you I had my eye on Braeden at one time. Then again, most of the village girls did since he's a handsome one. Your beau was nice to me, and that was all. He wasn't Darren." She gave a long-drawn-out sigh. "I had hopes for him. He was as blond as I was dark. His great-grandparents were Dutch and had a pottery company in one of the nearby cities. His dad broke with the family tradition after he met a Hogstead girl on holiday in the city."

"Did Darren feel the same way about you?"

"I thought so, at first. We often walked to school together. He was a few years older than me but didn't treat me like a little child the way some of the older students did. He even made a point to dance with me at the village shindigs." Rosemary opened her mouth as if she'd say more, then promptly closed it.

"What happened then? I never heard any mention of a Darren in town."

"That's because there wasn't one when you arrived." Her shoulders slumped, and she placed her hands on her knees as if to hold herself up. "I thought he cared for me. He went to the city to help his grandparents with the business."

"That's understandable. What I don't understand is why you never mentioned him?"

A small catch sounded in her voice. "It's painful to talk about him. He left without telling me. The only information was the town gossip. I tried to ask his mum." She shook her head. "For all the good it did me. All I got was that he was gone, and now I couldn't get my hooks into him."

"That's harsh."

"Indeed, it was. Later on, I heard he married up with a city girl." Another sigh escaped. "That was a good two years ago."

"You're better off without him if he could be scared away by a nasty tale."

"I told myself the same. Still, it does nothing to stop the hurt."
Her hand flattened over her heart. "It's easy to say the man should
have listened to his heart and not rumors. It's the others who do
listen that can make your life miserable. Obviously, his mother
believed what she heard and was anxious to get him out of the
village. It explains why I was more than eager to join your quest.

"I wanted to talk to you about that. This mission could be dangerous."

An elbow found a soft place between her ribs as the owner
laughed. "I noticed the dangerous part already. It beats staying in the
village and feeling sad about my lot in life. Don't go trying to get rid
of me. I'm not going."

Well, that was one down. Only two more to question. Meara
allowed herself the tiniest breath of relief. Whatever happened—at
least she wouldn't be alone.

Chapter Five

A CHORUS OF birds announced the dawn with song. Even if she wanted to sleep through it, she couldn't. A cheery whistle came from her left. *Ronan*. The owner of the whistle squatted and peered under the wagon where Meara had made her bed. Sleeping in the wagon did not appeal. It would be so easy for someone to trap her in there as she slept. Her unease at enclosed spaces had come on rapidly sometime after leaving the gypsy caravan. The rocks that poked her in the back whenever she moved were easier to deal with than the fear that grabbed her by the throat whenever she thought of staying inside.

Aunt Erin had allowed her to sleep with the window open during her stay to provide an escape route if needed. Had the window stayed open even while she was in a coma? They probably closed it, reasoning she would have no need of it. Erin was an empathetic person and could sense what a person needed without even asking. Her son had missed out on those gifts.

"Good morning, darling. Did you have a good night?"

He was asking if she had a good night? Did he forget about their late-night escape from the city? "Still alive. I count myself blessed on that matter."

He pressed his hand against his chest. "I, too, am blessed. There was a moment when we flew into the bay that I thought I'd not see another day." His hand slipped around to his back, and he moved backward. "I can't converse while being bent double." He took a step back and continued talking. "Pleased I am to be accompanying my cousin on her grand adventure."

Before she could reply, Jane's well-scarred workboots walked by. "Better lose that Irish accent, Ro, if you want to make it back to your emerald island."

"My name is Ronan, as you well know."

No response signaled that Jane either hadn't heard or was ignoring him. Remaining silent was not something the woman did well. Ronan grumbled, possibly to himself. "Not sure what has that woman sideways."

Her cousin had been accustomed to the local girls fluttering around him, all smiles and favors whenever he was about. His good looks and height along with his silver tongue had a great deal to do with it, she imagined. As trusting as her cousin was of everyone he met, he never met a stranger, and always found new friends. It would be hard for him to comprehend anyone naturally being untrusting, expecting the worse, and preparing for it, which was generally the traveler's life. His all is well with the world attitude had him blabbing their travel intentions to anyone he met. Aunt Erin had insisted they needed a man with them after Olio, the taciturn giant who had been escorting them, decided to take a wife and plant himself in the local community. Aunt Erin had no clue how clueless her son could be on matters outside their village. Then again, he had never been anywhere else. Why should he know?

Meara rolled onto her hands and knees to pack up her bedding. Even though she may not be privy to his private conversation, she still felt the need to reply. "Your accent is beautiful, but most will regard it with suspicion. You might do better letting me or Rosemary do the talking."

His formerly light voice took a downturn. "Should I be quiet now, or am I still allowed to speak?"

"You can. Of course you're free to talk around us. It's strangers you have to be careful about. Not sure how fast the news will travel, but once they hear about the unrest in Ireland, every person with a bit of a brogue in their speech will be labeled as an ungrateful rabble-rouser."

"I was talking to Billy about that before you showed up last night. He pointed out that any Irishman caught on the wrong side of the pond would be one who definitely was not part of the IRA action."

"You and I both know that if anyone took the time to logically think this out, they would know this to be true. I've discovered on my short time on earth and our various travels that logic never enters into the discussion. People act before the wits they have get to rub against each other, and later, they find a way to rationalize their actions." She crawled out from under the wagon and shook out her blanket. "All I'm asking you to do is to mull it over."

"I will." He flashed her a smile, then headed toward the small copse of woods in the distance.

His intentions would be good, but you couldn't get a cat to stop chasing mice by simply talking to it, either. Her gaze lingered on her cousin as he strolled away. Tall, good-looking, male, which usually added up to a winning hand. This time it wouldn't. Her fingers went to her amulet chain pulling it one way, then twisting it another. Her forehead grew hot and felt as if it were being held in the hand of a giant who had a preference for squeezing puny human heads. Redness colored her vision, turning the trees and field into a monochromatic landscape. She could see Ronan in the distance and his arms were held by two burly men with firm expressions. "Ronan!"

His accented voice called back, sounding neither distressed or put out. "What is it, Meara?"

She squeezed her eyes shut to rid them of the image of the burly men. When she opened her eyes again, her cousin stood close and regarded her with a quizzical expression.

Cutting her eyes to the right, then the left, she looked for the men. *Nothing*, unless you counted the yellow flowers in the field and the sheep grazing in the distance. Whatever she saw was gone. Her mind was playing tricks on her. That's all it was.

"Oh…" She paused, trying to think of a reason for shouting his name, "I, ah, wondered if you knew where Jane went?"

He shrugged his shoulders. "Dunno. She's like the wind. She shows up when you least expect it."

As if on cue, Jane stepped out from the trees and strode in their direction. Meara smiled, thinking how accurate her cousin's expression was, but she never bothered mentioning the woman was headed their way.

Ronan crinkled his nose, always an indication that he thought whatever he was about to say would be funny or at least he thought it was. "I imagine she's hiding somewhere using a magical file to sharpen her tongue, so she can flay me with it."

Her hand went up, ready to stop her cousin before he went too far. Jane joined them and pretended to toss something to Ronan. "I'm done with my magical file. Maybe you can use it on your wits."

Instead of answering, Ronan sucked in his lips and glanced at Meara for help. No way she'd get between the two. The best thing to do would be to change the subject. "I thought we could inventory what we might need. Rosemary and I could go into the next village and barter for items. We should keep our cash for when we absolutely need it."

"You *should* barter for things…" Jane agreed. "People tend to distrust coinage from strangers. I've seen more than my share bite into a pound or a shilling I paid to see if it was real."

"I've seen you do the same…" Meara reminded.

"I was always told trust was for those who earned it, not strangers. Plenty of people think nothing of cheating travelers, then go on about how they were cheated. Disgusting." She spat, aiming at the ground, but caused Ronan to move his boot, just in case.

"Point made." Usually, by this time, Jane or Ronan would have declared what their expectations for the day were. Their reticence to speak could be due to being in a foreign country and not knowing much about it. Living in a convent for seventeen years didn't make Meara a travel guide. Still, she was the one receiving visions, even if she didn't like the content.

Both Jane and Ronan fixed expectant gazes on her. "Well, ah, I expect we should get going. I know nothing about Wales. We can't go assuming we are on common grounds. Could be some farmer might spot us and be convinced we're here to steal his sheep."

"What direction?" Jane asked, probably because she naturally assumed she'd be the driver.

That again. People always needed to know where they were going especially those on a quest. "North."

"I assumed that since Scotland is north of Wales. That much I do know from looking at the maps Grandmother Biddy passed on to me. At the time, I told her I had no need of them." Her eyes grew a little glassy as she continued. "You know her. She shook her finger at me and said, 'You will.' Right she was. It makes me wonder if Grandmother Biddy ever went anywhere else, besides Ireland."

"Wouldn't surprise me. The woman knew so much about everything and the motivations of everyone." Thinking of the old woman who had taken her in when she landed wet and bedraggled on the shores of Ireland made Meara's heart ache. She placed her hand over her chest as if that would still the hurt. "I miss her." She nodded to Jane. "I'm sure you miss her more. I'm surprised she doesn't come to you in your dreams."

"I hoped she would. Could be enough time hasn't passed. It wasn't just young girls who came to the camp hoping the Tarot cards would reveal their future husband. We had plenty that wanted to talk to someone departed. Those who showed up still wild with grief, she turned away, telling them it took time for the deceased to be able to contact those here. It may have been it took a while for the living to accept their messages. Could be Grandmother Biddy is talking and I'm not hearing."

A mental image of the opinionated crone had her shaking her head *no*. "If Grandmother Biddy has something to say, you'll hear it."

"Yes. She never muted the message."

Ronan, possibly feeling excluded, stepped back. "I'm going to start breaking camp."

"Do that." Jane added an airy wave as if dismissing a servant, causing Ronan to scowl as he moved away.

"Be nice to my cousin. I'm not sure why you have to be like that."

"Like what?"

"You know." It was hard to put in words, especially since Jane hadn't changed. She just seemed harder, sharper, when compared to her cousin who probably had always been the cherished child as the firstborn son. Jane had fought for her rights in a patriarchal society, and she didn't do it by simpering.

Jane arched her eyebrow, then smiled slowly. "I'm doing him a favor. He's been coddled by women all his life. He's grown up thinking that smile and a pretty turn of a phrase will get him his way."

"It has." Even though she felt she should defend Ronan, it was obvious things were easier for him.

"Until now. The Irish aren't welcomed here. Even less so once news of the uprising reaches the shore. The man would do well to guard his tongue."

"You could say as much."

"I could." A twinkle appeared in her eyes. "Educating him is so much more fun." She chuckled, then added, "It's good you and Rosemary can speak the native tongue."

The remark made her snort. "I almost didn't understand what the dock hands were saying. The accent is so different I thought they were speaking Welsh as opposed to English. It will help that Rosemary does have some Welsh relatives. It will make us seem a little less threatening."

"You, too?" Jane fisted her hands on her hips and gave Meara a long survey from head to toes. "I've seen hares more frightening than you. You do make a fair lad, though. Try to frown more. A boy as pretty as you would make some effort at looking fierce. As for Rosemary, she needs to stop batting her eyes at every man she sees, especially since she is done up like a boy. More than likely, she'll earn a punch in the nose."

"I'll pass it on. Right now, I need to make use of the bushes before the wagon leaves without me." Meara sprinted in the direction of the trees and could hear Jane's laughter behind her.

It only took ten minutes to load up the wagon and bury the campfire. Rosemary tugged down the bill of her cap. "It's no work getting ready with guy togs." She scampered into the back of the wagon and motioned for Meara to do the same.

"No, thank you. I might ride up front or walk beside the wagon. It would do me good to stretch my legs."

There was also no need to mention her fear of being trapped in the wagon. Sometimes it was hard to differentiate between nightmares and visions. No reason for scaring her team if there was no need. There'd be enough between here and there to turn their hair white. That, she knew for certain without having a dream or a vision to tell her so.

Chapter Six

THE FIRST TOWN they rolled into, they counted the neat buildings lining the main street looking for any purveyor of items they might need. Fresh food and milk would be much more appetizing than the venison jerky and dried fruit they had locked in the cabinets. The lovely lamb pasties Aunt Erin had made for them fed the fish in the bay. Jane reported the hammer missing, which was a major loss since they used it for setting up camp and replacing a horseshoe when needed.

A dry goods store might have a hammer—but might not be willing to barter. A blacksmith would definitely have one but would most likely want hard labor in exchange. An idea took shape that had her casting side glances at Ronan who sat beside her.

Once they located a blacksmith, Rosemary and she headed to the shop. There was only a roof over the forge to keep out the rain the area was so well known for. A large man wearing a leather apron, pants, boots, and not much else sweated as he shaped a piece of iron. The metallic clang of a metal on metal caused Meara to wince. Not the sweetest sound she'd heard, that's for sure. They waited, not sure if they wanted to bother such a muscular man swinging a heavy cudgel.

After hammering for what felt like forever, he turned and frowned at them. "Wha' you wan'?"

At least that is what she thought he said. Rosemary apparently got more from the sentence. She held up her hand and grinned. "It's more what we can do for you."

They came for a hammer. She wasn't sure how her friend would work that into the conversation. "Hammer!" She hissed the word through clenched teeth.

The blacksmith repeated the word. "Hammer. Ha!" He shook his head. "Two of you no could lift it."

That she understood. "We want to barter for the hammer. Work for a hammer. Just a plain hammer. Nothing big."

His bushy eyebrows met as his scowl deepened. "You no help." He pointed to their thin arms, then gestured to his sizable muscle.

Rosemary waved her hands frantically to get his attention.

Meara made a mental note to say something to Rosemary about excessive gestures. Even though she was no expert on men, she'd noticed they gestured and talked as little as possible. Those who did otherwise might not only be memorable but regarded as a little strange, too.

Having gotten the man's attention, Rosemary spoke. "Not us. Our brother. He's much bigger…" She bent her arm and patted her bicep. "…and stronger."

The man looked around as if he somehow missed the third brother. Meara stepped away to retrieve Ronan. They decided against calling him by his name that might sound too Irish.

Ronan came around the corner with his head down. His role was to play the mute brother, but somehow her cousin acted more the part of the village idiot.

Rosemary gestured to Ronan as if showcasing a horse. "He's a good worker and will follow instructions."

The blacksmith gave him a once-over, then nodded. "How come…" He hesitated and pointed to his own mouth.

Rosemary and she disagreed about the explanation if anyone would ask. The simplest answer would be he was born that way. Rosemary wanted something to elicit sympathy, such as a war injury.

Before she could say anything, her friend pantomimed an explosion. "He couldn't fight in the war after that. They sent him home."

The story didn't appear to impress the smithy who narrowed his eyes. "I'll try him out today. Come back at lunch to see if he earned you a hammer."

Food was the harder item since any excess food was bought by the government for the soldiers. Rosemary and Meara finally got work clearing fields for a woman whose husband and son had left for war. For their work, she gave them a loaf of bread, a few eggs, a half pail of milk, and a small wedge of cheese. They made plans to come back the next day to plow.

Since they were late checking on Ronan, the blacksmith continued to work him in an effort to finish the many requests he had. They left with a hammer and a red faced Ronan. He waited until they got to the wagon, which was outside the village, to complain.

"We should have had a dozen hammers for as much work as I did today."

Jane rubbed his cheek. "I thought you were just red with anger, but your skin is actually chafed, probably due to the heat. There's some ointment to help with that." She vanished into the wagon to search for it.

Rosemary placed a hand on her back. "I feel for you. Still, Meara and I spent all day clearing a field. Last year's crop must have been stones because they certainly had enough of them."

"That wasn't all of it." Ronan crossed his arms and leaned against the wagon. "Every word out of the man's mouth was something bad about the Irish."

"Did he say anything about the war?" Meara was hoping to hear the war had ended on its own, and her help would not be needed in this matter.

"Yes, he did. Said the Irish started the war."

"That's no help."

Jane reappeared and gently smoothed the salve on Ronan's red face. "I think you don't need to go back to the blacksmith now that we have our hammer."

"Wasn't planning on it. The sooner we get the relic the better off we'll be."

Well, maybe. That wasn't exactly her thoughts. Meara assumed the sooner they got the second relic, the more difficult things would be. "Rosemary and I have work tomorrow and maybe the day after, too."

Ronan grumbled, anxious to leave an area with at least one Irish-hating resident.

Rosemary held up the food they brought back. "At least you can have something easy to chew tonight. You're also getting a taste of what it felt like to be English in Ireland. Then, people would add on that it didn't matter much since we were gels. Did that make us less English? Less powerful? Less dangerous? Less smart?"

"Stop! You made your point. My ears hurt from all the banging and clatter. I'd appreciate it if you could speak softer."

Rosemary winked at Meara, and they both mouthed their words, not bothering to use their voices at all, which caused Ronan to glare at them. Jane unexpectedly scolded them. "You two should be ashamed of yourself. You know what it is like to be picked on for something you had no say in. This is Ronan's first time."

They both apologized and got busy making omelets for dinner. After eating, they sat around the campfire and speculated on their day.

Rosemary was the first to speak. "I had no clue that the two of us working all day would earn so little. We did better in Ireland."

"I figured as boys we might get paid more." Meara stared into the fire as she spoke. "It's war time, and people don't have much. They're afraid to part with what they do have. I imagine the woman was generous with us. Those in Ireland haven't felt the pinch of war as much."

As Jane reflected on her day of inventorying what they had, Meara continued to look into the flames. If she stared hard enough, she could see images. Soldiers fighting. They were all flame-colored so it was hard to determine who was who. One of the soldiers turned and stared back at her. *Braeden.* Her breath caught. That meant he was still alive. She squinted to see more, but the images were gone.

A masculine voice called out from a distance. "Hello, camp!"

It was customary when someone walked into someplace uninvited to call out a greeting. Not everyone was welcoming, a few might shoot, while others would just loose the dogs on the strangers.

Ronan was the first to speak, "Hello, yourself. Your voice sounds familiar."

"As it should."

There was the sound of horse hooves on the grass as the man drew closer leading his horse. The firelight did more to shadow his features than pick them out.

Rosemary recognized him first. "Billy! What are you doing here?"

He laughed and stepped into the circle. "Looking for you. Luckily there weren't too many strangers traveling through town. People remembered a pair of scrawny brothers, one with brilliant red hair. The third brother was mute." He waggled his eyebrows. "Heard it was due to a bomb or something, which makes no sense. I could understand someone going deaf or even blind, but never losing the ability to speak due to an explosion."

Meara's gaze met Rosemary's, and she gave a small nod. It helped if someone explained the holes in her war accident story.

"Anyhow," Billy held out his hands, keeping a hold on the reins, "here I am. Might you have a bit of supper left?"

"I could make you something. We have some bread, cheese, and an egg left," Jane answered and reached for the skillet. "Hobble your horse and let him graze."

Billy followed her instructions and squatted by the fire. It was obvious he hadn't simply stumbled across them. He had deliberately searched for them even to the point of renting a horse. It made her wonder about his motivation. She closed her eyes and stilled her senses, closing out the voices and the crackle of the fire. No evil or trickery emanated from Billy. She enlarged the circle searching for the evil they fled. It was one person or one thing. From what she understood, it was more like a free-floating cloud, looking for a person to possess. Apparently, it found many willing hosts within the war. *Nothing.* She heaved a sigh of relief coming back to the circle. Even though they might be safe now, it didn't mean they would be safe in the morning.

They were teasing Billy about sounding less Irish.

"This isn't my first time on this side of the pond. I know when to pull in the brogue. After you left, I hung out at one of the pubs to get a feel for how things were. One fellow told me the Germans were winning the war while the bloke next to him swore the British sent the Jerrys packing with their tails between their legs."

"You hear anything about Dublin?" Ronan asked.

"No and didn't ask, neither. Da thinks it is better to keep a low profile. It will be a couple of months before we go back. He has been courting this widow woman who owns a boarding house. It's all gravy for him. I can't stand watching the two of them act silly. I asked Da for my share, bought this horse, and decided to join whatever adventure the four of you are set upon."

Adventure. So that is how he saw it. Meara wasn't sure how much Jane and Ronan revealed. Probably Ronan since Jane never gave out information. It may have been part of the Traveler culture or maybe it was just Jane or more likely, a combination of the two. What could she say to discourage him?

"It's more than an adventure. Not sure what you were told."

Billy ducked his head, then turned the slightest bit to give a knowing smile. "I suspect there will be danger. The fact Ronan drove the horse into the bay was proof of that." He straightened his shoulders, pulled up his chin, and pointed back to himself. "I am a fair hand at the ferry but am even better with a team. I wouldn't have driven the wagon into the water."

"Neither would I," Jane asserted with a flash of anger in her eyes. "Unfortunately, I wasn't the one at the reins. For that, I will never forgive myself."

Rosemary mouthed something Meara couldn't decipher. More likely it was a plea for her to do something. Even though she didn't want the job she *was* the group leader. She cleared her throat for attention but could not be heard over Ronan and Jane's bickering. Hand clapping fared little better. Finally, as a last resort, she wrapped her fingers around the amulets she wore and squeezed her eyes tight. *Help me powers that be. Mother Earth, Faeries, Universe, Mother, Father, Grandmother Biddy, anyone listening. Calm these hotheads and bring peace to our group.*

With her eyes still closed, she noticed a lack of raised voices. There were no voices at all. Her eyelids fluttered open to see if everyone had suddenly vanished and found everyone staring back at her. "Oh, you stopped fighting."

"No choice," Jane admitted, "with Grandmother Biddy yelling at me in my head."

"I had no clue." She directed her gaze to Ronan. "And you?"

"Grandda Felix. He's been dead these past two years. Even told me how ashamed he was of me fighting with a woman."

"Oh, he sounds like a good man."

"He was." Ronan nodded. "I didn't know you could sic the dead on us."

She had no clue, either. Meara casually scratched an eyebrow as she considered the matter. "I did try to stop you."

"She did." Rosemary was quick to confirm. "Neither one of you would listen."

"Aye…" Jane agreed. "Even so, I could have stopped Hercules."

Meara winced, not wanting a repeat of the argument. It didn't help that Jane just lobbed a verbal grenade into the temporary truce. Her gaze switched to Ronan who heaved a massive sigh, then shook his head slowly. "I imagine you could have stopped Hercules. I've witnessed your way with him. My stupid male pride got in the way of you driving as you should have. When my mam told me it was my job to help shepherd the women to their destination, I may have gone overboard. There are things you are better at than me." He managed another sigh, but not as long. "I felt there were things men did as opposed to the ladies. Driving being one of them. Truthfully, I'm not much of driver. When we use horses in the field, I usually lead them, since we don't have a cart of our own. We usually walk everywhere or get a ride from a neighbor. It was wrong of me to insist on driving."

A derisive snort sounded, causing Meara to glare at Jane. She held her hand up. "It wasn't me."

"Rosemary." Meara scowled at her friend. She was the last person she expected to react.

She held up her hands and shrugged. "It just came out. Besides, I can drive a team, too, but Ronan never lets me."

Before she could think of something soothing to say, Billy interjected his own feelings about the matter. "You mean to tell me that you had two experienced drivers and you insisted on doing it yourself?"

Her cousin merely nodded, then stared at the ground.

"Devil mend you!" Billy exclaimed and spit. He sat back and eyed Ronan. "If I had two friends who knew their way around the horses, I'd not be breaking my back doing what I wasn't good at. Give it a think, then put your shoulder into what you know how to do."

Meara figured she should jump in and say something. So far, the man appeared to be doing the job. Ronan wrinkled his nose as he answered. "I'm not that good at anything."

"You're strong..." Rosemary pointed out. "Not only did you help out the smithy all day, but you managed to keep your mouth shut, too. That means you can act and follow directions."

"Playing the part of a mute is no great skill." Ronan planted his elbows on his knees and cradled his head in his hands.

Billy held up one finger. "What about an Irishman's most basic skills? Can you weave a tale? Keep your word? Hold your own in a fight?"

"That I can." The corners of Ronan's lips lifted from a frown but didn't quite make it to a smile.

Jane cleared her throat, then spoke. "You're overlooking your most valuable skill."

"What is that?" His eyebrows went up, and he turned to direct his comment to Jane. "Making you so mad you practically glow with pent-up passion?"

She gave a nervous laugh, then waved the remark away. "No. It's your good nature and likability. You are able to put people at their ease. You know *no* strangers."

His brows came together as he considered it. "Grandda Felix always said strangers were unknown friends."

Chapter Seven

THERE WAS NEVER an official meeting where everyone voted on Billy staying with them. It was more like he was a visitor that never left. He joined Meara and Rosemary in helping prepare the widow's farm for planting. They explained Billy's presence as a shy cousin since he was able to cobble together words with no trace of his birth origin. It helped to have a third person to ready the land. The widow came out and helped them plant barley. The spring weather, with the chilly mornings and the occasional breeze turned sultry, forcing Meara to wipe her brow. Her back ached a little from walking at a slight angle, trying to plant seeds along the edges of the field. Both Rosemary and the widow followed the plow furrows, kicking the dirt over the new seeds.

The brilliant sun made her squint to view the surrounding farmland. Along with her aching back, her nails were ragged. Those were little things in the scheme of things. As far as she could tell no evil forces were lurking, waiting to spring out and put an end to their party, but a slight ripple in her psychic senses let her know something was about. The birds warbled in a nearby tree while a cat sat off at a distance watching them, his tail slowly sweeping from side to side. Nothing was coming from that direction. She brought her cupped hand up to her forehead to shield her eyes as she slowly pivoted.

Not too far from the road stood the heavily built horse Billy had bought. The animal appeared to be a variety of several different horses with his patchwork coloring, feathered forelocks, and a refined head that was out of proportion to her body. Billy had nicknamed the horse *Wind Racer,* which had to be a hopeful name since she barely managed a trot. The horse wasn't fast, pretty to look at, or quick to obey. The mare's specialty had to be eating, which she did most of the time. Her thick sturdy body allowed three of them to ride her at once, although Billy often walked beside the mare since there was little chance of being left behind. The horse couldn't be the reason behind the tiny touch of magic she felt.

A glance backward revealed her friends working. Rosemary noticed her and commented. "It's not quitting time yet. Not even lunch. What are you doing?"

The tingle came again. Instead of answering her friend, she held up a hand and turned slowly toward a small outbuilding. Whatever it was had to be there. A flash of red had her staring at the edge of the building where the grass was a little taller. No red flowers, no abandoned scarves, nothing that would account for the flash. It could be the sun was getting to her. Black spots were the usual result of being in the sun too long, not a red triangle of sorts. She knew she saw what she saw. More proof was the hairs on her arms stood up, and the day was far from cold.

The red came again and underneath the peaked hat was a small round face with a brown, curly beard. Below that was a small torso, but she couldn't tell much more since the grass obscured the rest of the creature. It was a tiny person of sorts. Something she'd never seen. In Ireland, they spoke about leprechauns, but she'd always heard they had red hair.

Not sure what to do, she wandered back to where Rosemary and the widow walked. Meara made sure to step over the completed rows not wanting to disturb the newly planted seeds. Not sure how to introduce the subject, she indicated her limp seed bag. "I was running low on seed."

"Here." Rosemary dipped her hand in her bag. "I have plenty. I noticed you were gaping about nothing."

The description made her sound lazy and chafed a little. "I was not gaping. I thought I saw something." She pointed toward the shed, unwilling to elaborate. Her friend turned to look while the widow didn't look up from seeding, but still answered, "The nains. You must have seen one. They are all over the place. Or at least they were, once my neighbor dropped the cat by to help with the mice. Yonder cat is not the friendliest creature. I am glad the nains are still around, though."

"Nains?" She said the word slowly, unfamiliar with it. "What are nains?"

The woman looked over her shoulder as if expecting someone to pop up. No one did. She cleared her throat. "Some say they are the devil's children, but I don't believe it. How could anything that helps out with plants and wildlife wish anyone harm? In the garden, they help plants to grow. I'm glad to have them here. Last year when we had the drought, my crops kept growing. Some whispered I put some spell on them, but I suspect it was the nains. In the forest, they release any animal that has been unfortunate to be caught in a trap."

Rosemary, who had been listening, chimed in. "That sounds like the gnomes my granny told me about. She mentioned house gnomes could even talk to you."

"That's not happened to me," their hostess concluded with a nod. "I do put out a bit of bread and milk for them. Some tales say they like a bit of ale, too. Not sure if it's my cat that licks it all up. I do know in the morning it is gone.

Gnomes sounded right to her. "Do you know where they come from?"

A shrug of the shoulders announced Rosemary's cluelessness while their hostess pursed her lips before speaking. "It's never been clear where they came from. All I know is they were here before we were and are attached to the earth. Some say they are very strong and others comment they are fast. Never heard about them hurting anyone, but they do love a good joke."

"Did one ever play a joke on you?"

The woman's lips lifted into a smile as her eyes twinkled. "I like to think I am decent enough of a person to avoid the joke-playing. They only work their mischief on those who deserve it. All in all, it's not mean. A village priest who takes most of the offering to suit himself and not the needy might have a purse full of money spill out from his robes, letting the people know where the money goes. Sometimes, they'll settle for a pail of water or flour spilled on the head for all to see."

"I would think you have nothing to worry about. Maybe the nains or the gnomes are looking out for you while you're alone."

"That they are. They sent me *you* to plow the fields."

Meara nodded her head, not willing to say it was their decision to knock on her door seeking work that sealed that deal. Had it been their decision or had something influenced them? The smithy they picked because he would naturally have hammers and would make hammers. They wanted someone who would look kindly on them and allow them to work for their dinner.

Many houses they bypassed in their search, because everything from scowling faces to vicious dogs made them rethink walking up to the house. It would be natural for people to be put off by strangers, and the Welsh certainly were. A business or shop might be better, but there was none in this small village outside of the pub and a dry goods store. Maybe they *had* been guided here.

Rosemary was nearly as reticent to speak. "I guess it was a good thing that we followed the hints the gnomes must have left."

"Ah yes." She straightened and placed a hand at her lower back. "I only wish I had more to offer you than bean soup."

"My favorite!" Billy, who had been leading the plowing horse, enthused with the tiniest bit of a lilt. "My mam, God rest her soul, used to make it for us every Saturday, so we had some left for Sunday dinner."

His Irish accent was full out. Meara snapped her eyes to their employer's face to see if any shock or fear showed itself. *None*. The woman continued to sow seeds as she spoke. "She was a smart and caring woman."

"That she was."

The day's work went on uneventfully until almost the end of the day. The jangle of harness and the creak of wagon wheels announced someone was coming. Meara stood on the porch, holding the empty seed bags, waiting to see who would come around the corner. It was Jane. Her eyes were wild, and Hercules was lathered as if he had been running, which would make no sense at all. Not waiting to call out to the others, she dropped the bags, jumped off the porch, and ran to her friend. "What's wrong?"

"Ronan has been taken for a spy and thrown in jail!"

None of this made any sense. She shook her head violently as if she could shake out the words. Aunt Erin asked him to watch over her. Maybe *she* should have watched over *him*. Rosemary and Billy joined them and asked the same question, which ended in her repeating the same thing again.

Jane's face was flushed as she tied the reins to the post, possibly forgetting the possibility of Hercules taking off on his own was zero. Her hand shot through her hair as she added more disarrangement to the wind-blown mass. Her evident distress gave lie to all the complaints she had previously made about Ronan.

Maybe Jane did have a fondness for Ronan as Rosemary had suggested previously. They had decided their daily schedule would consist of Ronan and Jane staying with the wagon and possibly doing a little fishing. "The two of you were supposed to stay at the wagon. Did they come to the wagon and arrest him?"

"I know we were supposed to stay at the wagon and told him as much." A snarl crept into her voice. "Being a man, he thought he knew so much more than me." She hung her head, allowing her hair to hang down enough to hide her face and a small sob was heard.

"You haven't told us the whole story. We need to know what he did to get arrested that caused him to get thrown in jail."

Her hand pushed her hair back as she looked up with anger still flashing in her eyes. "The stupid fool *spoke*."

Chapter Eight

THE THREE OF them thanked their hostess. Meara and Rosemary boarded the wagon with promises to return the next day. Billy tied his horse to the back and came in through the back door. He worked his way forward and opened the window behind the driver's bench to continue the discussion.

Hercules's head turned, watching something they couldn't see.

"What did you mean he spoke?" Meara asked, not quite getting the cryptic statement. It wasn't that unusual for Jane to say something that made no sense on the surface, but after reflection did have some pertinent meaning.

The reins cracked as Jane lightly snapped them over Hercules's back. The wagon jerked once as the horse settled into a plodding walk. "I don't know the details. The sun had moved to the noon position, which was really too late for good fishing. No sign of Ronan. I rode Hercules to town. On second thought, it might have been quicker to walk. Anyhow, I tied him at a hitching post once I arrived. No one noticed me because there was a crowd all in a bother about something. As I came closer there was a brawny man with a leather apron on, yelling about how he'd been tricked by a man pretending to be a deaf-mute."

"That must have been the smithy."

Rosemary interjected, "We never said anything about deaf."

It made sense the man might have thought he'd been tricked. No one likes being made a fool of, especially in front of others. "Is that all there was?"

To add his remarks, Billy nudged her, causing her to move to the side. Then he wiggled between Meara and Jane, causing them to lean sideways to accommodate him. "That's not a jailable offense. I expect the man took a swing at Ronan, and he got the worse of it. Ronan's not exactly a fighter."

Jane made a derisive snort. "That could be the problem. There was some pretty, dark-haired girl singing Ronan's praises. How he was such a kind and gentle sort, unlike the men in the town."

"That was enough to put him in jail?" Meara knew when people got emotional there was no telling what might happen. Still, wouldn't leaving town work well enough? There were plenty of men who got passed over for someone with a smoother manner or a pair of lively eyes.

"Well..." Jane hesitated and bit her lip before continuing, "That may not have been it. The smithy started talking that he must be a spy. That's why he snuck into the village pretending not to talk. He was part of a group of German spies planning on invading Wales."

"That's just poppycock!" Billy asserted.

"Poppycock it may be," Jane agreed with a nod and a twist of her lips. "Doesn't make him any less in jail."

The four of them sat and brooded on the situation as the wagon moved slowly down the road. They were passed by another wagon filled with cargo and given a curious look by the driver. Meara held up her hand in greeting, but he chose not to do likewise. "Look. We're already tainted. We *are* the gang of spies."

"It's the Welsh," Rosemary reminded. "It's not that they aren't friendly. It just takes time for them to trust people. I'm not that surprised about Ronan. I expect he was flirting with the girl, who was probably all but promised elsewhere. She placed her hand against her chest. "Being a female, I can understand a girl having her head turned by a handsome foreigner."

"All he was supposed to do was get fish hooks, not flirt with every female he met," Jane grumbled and gave an extra snap of the reins that had Hercules picking up his pace to a fast walk.

Rosemary clucked her tongue. "He didn't flirt with every female. Only the pretty ones."

That didn't help. "We can speculate on what he did later. I'm sure he'll tell us as soon as he is out of jail. Now, how do we get him out of there?"

Rosemary gave her a blank look. "If you remember, Hogstead didn't have a jail. If people had a problem, they worked it out."

"Or chased it out of town, if you recall Eleanor's and my fast departure."

"They do that, too."

Jane cleared her throat. "My people worked hard never to end up in jail, but when they did we did our best to break them out."

"Very bad bet." Billy slapped his knee for emphasis.

"Would it be better to leave him in jail to rot?" A sob sounded in Jane's voice, but she swallowed it and continued. "No telling when there will be a trial, if any. Who will stand for Ronan?"

Good question. Meara knew they didn't have any money for representation. "What can we do?"

Billy held up a finger. "Pay off the jailer. He, in turn, will swear the prisoner escaped. They might look for him, but we will be gone by then. I suspect our best chance will be for one of you to doll yourself up and appeal to the jailer, who will be a man. As a woman, he'll see you as defenseless. As annoying as Ronan might be, he could be your male relative who is in charge of your protection. You would only be passing through. It would help to say something about boarding a boat. That might discourage a chase. Most country folks avoid the city."

"This will work," Rosemary pulled on her short tresses, "since we all look more like twelve-year-old boys."

"A headscarf, a dress, maybe even a little extra padding, and Billy could play the part," Jane commented with a sparkle returning to her eyes.

"Don't be an eejit. That would never work. I'm too manly."

That made them chuckle. Any one of them, with the exception of Billy, could be made attractive enough. "What about the money? We don't have much, and we were saving it for important stuff."

"Getting your cousin out of jail isn't important?"

"It is." No need to add everyone knew the risks when they signed on or that without money, they would have a hard time accomplishing their mission.

Instead of replying, Billy groaned at the same time the same little man she had spotted earlier used him as a bridge. He scampered over Billy's head and stepped onto his thighs. He clapped his hands together and bowed. "Thaddeus T. Greenbrier at your service. Former house gnome, but I've moved out into the yard since the odious animal moved in. *Cats.* Nasty things."

"Pleased to meet you, Thaddeus. What brings you here?"

Rosemary reached over Thaddeus to nudge Meara. "I admit talking to myself, but I haven't gone and given myself a name like Thaddeus."

"You can't see him?"

"See what?"

The tiny man took off his pointed hat and scratched his head. "Oh dear. I may have made a mistake addressing you when you weren't alone. As gnomes go, I am quite young. Only thirty-four, and I never did an outside mission before. When the faeries came whispering in my ear that only I could do what they could not..." He put his hat back on, puffed out his chest, and placed his thumbs behind his suspenders. "...it made me proud to be a gnome. Most people know faeries. They get all the credit and the blame. Have you ever heard of people being grateful to the gnomes?"

Meara settled for shaking her head, aware that her friend was already convinced she might be a tad unhinged due to stress. She glanced at Jane to see if she had noticed their magical visitor. *Nothing.*

"They can't see me."

Her eyebrows went up.

"Only those that need to see me can. I knew before you arrived Ronan was in jail because the faeries told me. Some of my special gifts include being blinding fast so the human eye can't see me, and I'm stronger than any man. I have my own specialty, too."

Meara opened her mouth to ask what but closed it, remembering those around her. Jane and Billy started a discussion about where to camp for the night. They came to the decision it couldn't be where they were previously, in case someone had noticed them camping near the creek.

All it took was a look for Thaddeus to resume his conversation. "I relocate money." He held up his hand before Meara could voice any objections. "I'm not a thief, but others are. They take what is not theirs. They charge for what should be given freely. I merely move things around. My hostess has been overcharged continually by the man who runs the dry goods store because she has no male family member to object. She thinks the money she finds around the house is something left behind by her husband."

"That's a service we could use!" She placed her hand over her mouth once she spoke. Goodness, she had done it again.

"What service is that?" Billy asked, twisting his body and moving his arms, which caused Thaddeus to sidestep to avoid being swept off by an outflung arm.

"Just thinking." She simpered the way she'd seen Rosemary do. "Wouldn't it be great if there was a way to take from the rich and give to the poor?"

"Robin Hood did that. A number of highwaymen claimed they were doing exactly that before gasping their last breath."

"I'm not talking about stealing. Just taking back what is right."

"Sounds like stealing to me."

Thaddeus steepled his fingers together and reminded her, "*Relocation.*"

"It's a relocation of funds. Don't worry, *we* wouldn't be doing it."

Billy reached and twisted as something tumbled from his pocket, making a ringing sound on the foot rest. Thaddeus made a leap to Meara's lap before Billy swung his head low. His overlong hair caused the gnome to stumble and grab a hank of hair for balance.

"Ow!" Billy jerked up from his bent position, carrying the gnome with him.

Meara threw her arms out to catch Thaddeus.

"My thanks. The faeries had great things to say about you. They were obviously true. I am fortunate to be picked for such a mission."

She carefully lowered him to her lap. What mission did he mean? Was it just getting Ronan out of jail or was it more? If he intended to make the trip with them, the others needed to be told so they didn't desert her due to thinking she was barmy.

A nice clump of trees would provide a sufficient blind for the wagon. Jane veered off the road. The others grabbed onto the bench, well aware of Hercules's sudden stops. Meara used her free arm to sweep Thaddeus against her side. The wagon halted, giving a small jerk. Jane jumped down to deal with her horse while Billy scrambled into the vacant space. He turned to stare at Meara who had her arm cupped around Thaddeus.

"I would have thought you the best one to approach the jailor, but you've gone and started acting peculiar."

It was happening exactly as she feared. "I will be the one to intercede for Ronan. He's my cousin, after all. I won't be the only one. Meet Thaddeus T. Greenbrier."

Rosemary craned around her to peer at the spot where Thaddeus stood. "I don't see anyone."

"Peculiar." Billy repeated his earlier assumption. "You might end up in jail, too. Folks can tolerate their own relatives going around the bend. Strangers doing the same thing are crazy."

Thaddeus chose to appear more solid, causing Jane, who had

walked back to the wagon, to whistle. "It's a leprechaun!"

"I beg your pardon." Thaddeus flushed and puffed out his chest. "I am a gnome. I will admit to being related to the leprechaun, but they are the greedy trickster cousin of the family line. We gnomes are gentle, kind, and helpful."

Jane smiled. "Heard that about you, too. I also heard you were fond of practical jokes."

He placed his tiny fingers against his cheek and tapped. "Sounds like propaganda spread by my ne'er do well cousins. As for the jokes, we only play them on those who are deserving to be played."

Chapter Nine

THE SETTING SUN set the village aflame with reds and oranges. Shadows popped up as it dipped beyond the horizon. Meara tugged on the restrictive waistline of her dress and wished she had on her boy togs. Her own dresses were too tattered to be used. This one belonged to Jane, who was obviously narrower in the torso and taller. Rosemary put in a whipstitch hem that would keep her from tripping on the skirt. What they soon came to realize, after combing through the cabinets, was none of them had slippers that would fit. Billy pointed out that country lasses would have no use for such things unless it was a special occasion.

Rosemary and Jane had argued if she should look like a poor cousin or a seductress. Since she wasn't planning on seducing anyone, she voted for the poor cousin. This meant that the colors had to be subdued, which wasn't something normally associated with travelers, but she did find a scarf with a black background strewn with burgundy roses. Rosemary held up earrings to her ears, which Jane vetoed. "We want her to be attractive, but not memorable, which makes me wonder about your hair."

She had tugged on her bangs before pulling the scarf forward to cover her hair.

"Won't it make me look like I have no hair?"

Jane shrugged. "I think not. Plenty of women cover their hair. Why do you think we have scarves and hats? I'm sure women invented them."

Personally, she thought the hats were probably invented to keep off the sun but didn't mention it. Billy rode her in on his horse, and she tried to perch sidesaddle, which was no easy feat as she kept slipping. It was hard to believe women could ride this way. At the edge of the town, Billy stopped the horse, dismounted, and helped her down.

"I'll stay here since they are in the habit of throwing strange men into jail. From what I heard, there's only a few businesses in town. Head for the pub, which should be open. Ask there. I would be surprised if they have an actual jail. Probably locked up in a storeroom. Just ask to talk to your brother."

"Cousin."

"Brother sounds better. You are blood relations so there should be some resemblance."

She dwelled on his words as she walked past the shuttered homes. Muffled voices drifted out onto the still evening, and there were probably more than one or two villagers peeking through the slats. Her steps slowed as she made her way into the center of town. *Pub.* Billy said the word as if she'd know what it meant. None of the nuns talked about pubs and their visitors. The most she knew was that it was a place frequented by men to engage in profane activities. Aunt Erin had sent Ronan to the pub to bring back Marie's recipe for Dublin Coddle. He had returned empty-handed since Marie felt giving away her recipes would be giving away business. By that, she knew women might work inside a pub and apparently there was food, which made it a trifle less scary. Still scary all the same. She hadn't decided what profane things went on inside.

Her steps faltered to a stop and something bumped into the back of her leg. Even though it was hard to see with night falling, she would have sworn nothing was there.

"Never fear, Meara. I am here." Thaddeus shimmered into vision. He made a fist then popped a small bicep. "Keep in mind, I have the strength of five men. None will see me, which makes it all the better. Easy to get a jump on a man who knows not where the next punch comes from or where it might land." He gave her a wide wink. "The pub's up ahead." He pointed at a plain building with a hand-painted sign the read *The Majestic Lion Pub*. There was a blob of color that may have been a lion. It was hard to tell.

"Should I knock?"

Thaddeus wrinkled his nose. "It's a business. Walk on in. I'll be invisible, but make sure to hold the door open long enough for me to enter."

The aroma of onions and meat cooking reminded her of the meager supper they had shared. Meat was not an item they could afford nor was it one folks gave away even for a hard day's work. Her stomach growled reminding her of its half-filled state. The news of Ronan's trouble had them all rushing off before they received their payment in bread and eggs. There had even been talk about a dried apple pie. Instead, they toasted the stale bread and chewed on the leftover jerky.

A smoky fire indicated a chimney that needed cleaning. The windows stood open to clear the room of smoke but was not fully successful. The men gathered around the tables in twos and threes. A few sat alone at a long bar either drinking or smoking a pipe, which added to the thick air.

A woman with a tray of mugs popped out of the kitchen. When she spotted Meara, she asked, "Come for your husband, have you?"

She said the first thing that came to mind. "No, I'm not married."

A few men at the bar cursed. One turned and yelled at the woman. "What's going on here, Liz. Are you putting holes in the glasses now?"

"What's wrong with you? If you're seeing things, then you've had enough."

"I haven't had enough. That's the problem." He stood and threw down some coins. "It's time for me to leave when you start sounding like my wife."

Another patron complained about missing ale. It didn't take long for Meara to figure out the culprit as mysterious hiccups sounded where there was no one sitting. When an especially large one sounded, Thaddeus shimmered into view. Oh, no! A drunk gnome would be no help. Worse, she might have to carry him.

"Did you see that?" A grizzled patron asked, pointing his pipe at Thaddeus's last location. "An ugly boggie. The pub is crawling with them instead of them hanging out at the bogs." He stood and waved to the others. "Get out while you can."

A few other men pushed to their feet and left with some grumbling about stupid boggies, showing up to cause trouble.

She had her suspicions that the mischief might not be boggie-related at all.

The woman put down the tray and glared at Meara. "It's you. A female is bad luck in a pub."

"You're a woman." She pointed out the obvious, unsure why a woman would want to be in such a dank, odorous place.

"I own the place, and I always entered through the front door." She placed a fisted hand on her hip and lifted her eyebrows as if the dimmest of dim would know this. "What do you want?"

"I've come for my brother. Heard he was put in jail when all he came for was fishing hooks."

The woman laughed and slapped her thigh. "Oh, the handsome Irishman. I do love an Irish accent. Turns out I'm not the only one."

"What happened?" She clasped her hands in front of her, trying to appear as defenseless and demure as Jane had coached. The defenseless part was true enough. A glass almost tumbled over on the bar then righted itself at the last minute, letting her know where Thaddeus was.

"Since he's your brother..." She stopped and gave her a long stare. "He's not your sweetheart or lover? Although, you look much too young to have either.

She quelled any comments that many were married at her age

and some even earlier.

"You must have realized women like his flattering ways."

"I've heard this."

"Betty at the Mercantile is a fan. She showed more attention to your brother than she's ever shown to her would-be swain."

"Let me guess. The smithy."

"You got it."

"They locked him up for his flattering ways."

The woman snorted. "Of course not. They locked him up to save his life. Once it is full dark, he'll be let go."

She angled her head to a man sitting at a corner table. "He's at Fred's livery. You could go talk to him."

The middle-aged man had his hat pulled down shadowing his eyes and his hands wrapped around a sizable mug. "So, what's a pretty girl like yourself doing in a pub? I know you are no one's daughter else I would have seen you before."

Her eyes dropped to her hands which were tightly clenched. "It's my brother, sir. We were heading back to Hogstead. That's in England. He came to town for fishing hooks and ended up in jail."

"Your brother, you say?" The man pushed back his cap exposing two intelligent eyes, not the least bit dulled by alcohol.

"Yes, sir."

It wasn't hard to tell the man had his doubts. His hand went over his beard stubble. "Odd. He's Irish as the day is long while you sound more English to me."

This was not going the way she planned. A mug went crashing to the ground, which caused the barkeeper to shout. "You'll be paying for that!"

Before she could come up with a tale of why they didn't sound the least bit alike, the man placed money on the table and stood. "It was my plan all along to set him free. He's in my back room, repairing harnesses. I had to play along with the smithy because he's the only one we have. No one wants to make a long trip just to get their horses shod. It's more important to me since I deal in horses and tack. This has been a most peculiar night. Not sure what the cause is, but it is best to get you two out of town and any enchantment you brought with you."

Not sure what to say, she nodded as another mug tumbled to the floor.

Fred, the Liveryman, whistled. "Louise won't be happy and will probably be charging everyone extra. Let's get out while we can."

When they reached the empty bar, Meara moved her arm around trying to find the drunken gnome but got the barkeep's attention instead.

"Are you trying to wipe out my remaining glasses?"

"Oh, no." She was at a loss to explain her movements when the door blew open. Even though it looked black outside, she knew it wasn't just the wind. An ominous feeling swept over her. *It had found them.*

She touched Fred's arm and rocked up to her tiptoes to whisper in his ear. "Let's use the back door."

"Don't be silly." He tried to turn toward the front door but couldn't move. He peered down at his feet. "The floor is stickier than usual." He made another attempt, then stumbled. "Backdoor it is."

He circled around the bar and into the kitchen as Louise yelled after him.

"No inspecting my kitchen!"

A young girl was scrubbing dishes and something delicious simmered on the stove. Meara took an appreciative sniff. No time for food. No time to hesitate. A tug on her dress had her leaning over and sweeping up an invisible Thaddeus.

"What are you doing?" Fred asked as he pushed open the back door.

"Dress got caught." She almost said on the *stove* but wasn't close enough for that to happen.

It wasn't too far to the livery, but it seemed like forever with Thaddeus in her arms. Every now and then he'd burp, fanning her with an ale scent.

Fred chuckled. "To hear you, people would think you were the one drinking, not me."

Obviously, being invisible didn't mean you were inaudible. Ronan was definitely carrying Thaddeus from now on. Even though it turned out she didn't need his money finding skills, he'd been excellent at turning Fred to the back door.

"The hiccups. I get them when I'm nervous."

He stopped at an oversized barn and opened the door. The smell of hay and horses washed over her as Fred lit a lantern. "That's odd. Knew a fellow who often hiccupped when he lied. I'm sure that's not your case. There are so many strangers around that it makes folks edgy. Even today there were some rough sorts asking about a girl with a gypsy wagon."

She wasn't sure how they knew so much about her. A gypsy wagon would be recognizable enough. That's why they painted it. The sound of an Irish folk tune was audible as Fred led her past horses who poked their heads eagerly out of stalls hoping for a treat.

"Doesn't sound like he is suffering too much."

To think Jane was almost in tears while Ronan was in no trouble at all. She thought of the rough sorts asking about her and the wagon. He was in no trouble from the town folks, but they needed to leave by tonight.

"Hello." Fred greeted Ronan as he opened the inner door and spilled out the light. "I met your sister in the pub."

"That would be odd indeed because my sister…"

She pushed past Fred to make eye contact with Ronan. "Is here. Your sister *is* here."

"Oh, hello, sister!"

A loud burp sounded.

"Excuse me. Must have been something I ate." More likely

something Thaddeus drank.

Fred wandered over to a pile of harnesses and bridles. He picked a harness and shook it out. "Very nice. You do good work. I will be sorry to see you leave. I know your sister here is anxious for you to go."

Meara gave an emphatic nod, hoping they'd be gone in a matter of seconds. She waited while she shifted her gnome friend to a table top to rest her arms. Fred held up his hand as Ronan rose to his feet. "I'll get you your money."

"Money?" Meara asked in astonishment. It wasn't something people usually paid in unless they had to.

"Yes. Fred told me he'd pay me if I did a good job on the tack."

"That I did. I need to go to the house. I'll be right back." He took the lantern and retraced his route leaving the three of them alone.

Meara stepped closer and noticed an empty plate. "You ate?"

"I did. A fair shepherd's pie."

Even the name of the consumed food made her sigh. "That's more than we had. We dropped everything in an effort to rescue you. All we had was little more than stale bread washed down with water. Turns out you didn't need rescuing at all."

Another loud burp sounded.

"It sounds like you had more than water," Ronan teased and winked.

"That wasn't me. It's Thaddeus the gnome. You're carrying him back. My arms are tired. He may be small but he's heavy."

"Gnome?"

"Yes." She gestured to where she had put him down. "Everyone at the pub was calling him a boggie."

"Gnome? Boggie? Why would we need either one? Have you been out in the sun too long?"

This was getting past tiresome. "I'm fine. Thaddeus is over there. He can make himself visible or invisible at will. Show yourself."

Thaddeus shimmered into existence, swinging his legs as he sat on the table ledge. "I am tired of being compared to a boggie, which is an ugly fellow with little personality. I don't hang out with boggies. Tree spirits, water sprites, an occasional wood elf, and of course, dwarves." He pointed to himself. "Dwarves are cousins I'll admit to having."

Ronan stepped closer to inspect Thaddeus. "Sweet Mary, he smells like a brewery."

"I had a nip. No more."

Meara coughed at the obvious falsehood. "You're carrying him."

Thaddeus stood up. "No one is carrying me. I can move fine on my own. Did I not turn Fred when that thing slammed open the door?"

"You did."

"What thing?" Ronan asked, his voice swinging up in alarm.

"Not sure what it was. It was just a feeling. I think it tracked us from Ireland. Fred said something about rough sorts asking about a girl in a gypsy wagon."

He shot one hand through his hair. "Maybe they were asking about Jane?"

"That doesn't make it any better since I was last seen with Jane, as were you."

A thump sounded as Thaddeus jumped to the floor. "You do realize they can't see you."

"What?" Both Ronan and Meara asked in unison.

The gnome gestured to himself again. "I have the ability to make myself visible to who I please. When I saw Meara working in the field today, I saw she had the ability to make herself invisible to those who want to do her harm, but apparently you are not taking full advantage of this skill. Did you not wonder why whomever opened the door didn't enter?"

"The thought did cross my mind as I struggled to leave by the back door."

The gnome grinned. "I can teach you. You have a protection spell on you. Unfortunately, whoever is seeking you will not just look under bushes and in local haunts. He or it will search minds. That could be your downfall."

This brought back memories of her recent illness where she'd fought off a looming presence in her dreams. Before she could answer, Fred walked back in, and Thaddeus faded.

"Here you go," Fred walked back into the room. "Here's the crown I promised you for work done well."

Ronan accepted the coin with a smile and tucked it in his pocket. "Many thanks."

He held a cloth wrapped bundle. "And for you, some leftovers because I could see you drool as we left through the kitchen."

"I wasn't..."

Ronan nudged her. "Take the food and tell the nice man thank you, sister."

"Thank you."

They left with Meara making sure to leave the door ajar enough for Thaddeus to escape. They slipped out, keeping to the shadows. When they were close to the smithy, Ronan asked, "Is your little friend going to be traveling with us?"

Before she could answer, the smithy slammed out of his shop, glared in their direction, and slurred, "Who goes there?"

Meara swallowed. They were so close to getting out of town. If the man was mean sober, she doubted drink would improve him any.

Thaddeus called out, "Watch this!" He made himself visible for a brief moment and charged the man. The muscular smithy flew through the air, which was the break they needed. Meara pulled her dress to her knees and ran, keeping pace with her cousin. When they got to the edge of town, they waited. Soon, the sound of running feet and a swoosh of air passed them.

"I assume that was Thaddeus," Meara commented. "He's not

only fast but strong as five men. On top of it all, he's going to teach me to be invisible."

"Good thing I recommended keeping him."

Chapter Ten

THE FARTHER THEY got away from the village, the darker it was. Meara hadn't thought to bring a lantern. A sickle moon climbed into the sky as stars popped into visibility. Doves called to one another as they settled in for the night. Nothing looked that different from those times she snuck away from the convent to spend a little time outdoors in nature. At the time, she thought slipping through the hole in the garden wall to the forest was such a dangerous, wild thing to do. She had no clue.

Ronan broke the silence. "Do you think Billy is still waiting?"

"Not sure why not. He knew I'd be coming back with you." Secretly, she had her doubts but chose not to share them. Even though she sensed no evil from the man, Grandmother Biddy's instructions to trust no one came back to her. What had she done? Trusted Ronan and brought him into the circle. Even her Aunt Erin and her daughter knew of their quest but had no clue of their destination. As blood, she'd felt compelled to tell them, wanting at least someone to care if she never returned. Then there was Billy.

A restless young man, not sure of where he was going and open to chasing every rabbit that crossed his path. How could she be sure he would be there? He may decide her venture didn't meet his specifications for adventure and fun.

"He'll be there," Ronan declared in that no-nonsense tone he used when he was certain of things.

His turnabout confused her. "You were the one doubting previously."

"I know. I also know even before you made your transformation to sister for me that he knew good and well none of you were boys. Anyone who spent time with you would know that. Plenty of women who work on the farm will don boy's clothes now and then. That, in itself, wasn't mind-boggling. The short hair, while odd, doesn't mask your feminine features. Your disguise was only meant to work from far away."

She could accept that their disguises might not be the best, although the three of them had practiced male walks and mannerisms that often set them into gales of laughter but only irritated Ronan. He often scolded, telling them men weren't a bit like that, which was amusing since they based their play on his movements and speech. "True. We're getting better."

"Maybe. Not enough to fool Billy, especially considering he was in the water with you and Jane. No man I know has such a nicely rounded bum."

"Are you talking about me or Jane?"

"Neither."

"I think you are talking about Jane."

He made a derisive snort, which meant he wasn't answering. Feeling a little less stressed and definitely more playful after fulfilling her mission of retrieving Ronan, she decided to needle him. "So, you think Billy has a fancy for Jane?"

"He does not!" The words were short and abrupt. "How could anyone fancy such a sharp-tongued female?"

"She's only that way with you, and I'd say half the time you provoke her."

"I do not."

Thaddeus, who had been walking so soundless beside them she almost forgot he was there, commented. "Are you two going to talk nonsense the entire way back? You need to plan a strategy. Whatever was looking for you in the village won't stop. The smithy will be telling his tale to anyone who will listen, too."

Her very limited experience was men never talked about things that made them look bad. "I don't think so. You knocked him around soundly. Would he tell anyone that someone a tenth of his size beat him?"

"That he wouldn't. He would say your brother and his vicious friends beat him for no reason."

She mulled over the possibility. "The little I heard from the pub owner and liveryman, no one has love for the smithy. Most probably they'd think he deserved a good comeuppance."

"Maybe so. Still, if he spins his yarn well enough, the natural distrust the Welsh have of strangers and the paranoia caused by the war could work against you."

"How so? We are leaving tonight."

Ronan grumbled. "I've been working all day and now I have to spend the night driving."

Her cousin really was as soft as Jane complained he was. "You'll not be driving. Jane will. It's our only option, considering we've been tracked this far."

"I was only joking." He slapped her on the back. "Of course, she'll be driving. I've learned my lesson about driving, even a horse as spiritless as Hercules."

The wind blew, rustling the leaves on the trees. Along with the breeze came a voice sighing the word, *Hurry.*

"Did you hear that?"

She could see the shape of Ronan's head but not his expression. "What?"

"I did," Thaddeus answered. "Someone sent us a message. We need to hurry. I'll sprint on ahead." He took off in a burst of speed that they both heard and felt.

They both broke into a jog. A few yards later, a form stepped out from the shadows.

"Hello? Be you Ronan and…" Billy hesitated.

"It's us," Meara answered, knowing he was probably unsure of what to call her since he only knew her by her boy name, Mark.

"Wasn't sure. I heard something whip by me, and I wasn't sure what it was."

"Thaddeus. He went ahead since we heard whispering on the wind to hurry. There were also strangers in the village looking for a girl and her gypsy cart."

"We need to go then." He reached back into the shadows and brought out Wind Racer. The horse chewed, showing no signs of wanting to run. "We could all ride Wind, but I doubt she could manage more than a walk."

"I'd run," Ronan volunteered, "except I have no clue where the wagon is."

"Not too far from here. I'll run. I'm used to it and no need for me to get soft by riding around and all."

Some wild riding would be involved, and it was no time for side saddle or attempting to be ladylike. She squatted and grabbed the back hem of her dress and pulled it through her legs and tucked it into her belt. Billy lifted her on the horse, while Ronan vaulted behind her.

Billy took off, and she guided the horse behind him, certain he'd tire. Even with four legs Wind Racer only kept pace with him and refused to go any faster. Apparently, she was going to stay with her owner. The wagon wasn't that far away. The sounds of a scuffle and curses filled the air. A scream cut the air, chilling her blood.

"It's a man's scream," Ronan reassured her as they drew closer. "Jane probably used her knife on him."

He jumped off the horse and ran the rest of the way. Wind Racer picked up speed with only one rider and passed both Ronan and Billy. A campfire burned near the wagon, and a lantern lit the scene, throwing flickering light on two unknown assailants that were being thrown about as if rag dolls. The flames lit up the dagger in Jane's hand as she stalked one of the men. He scrambled backward.

"You're not the girl I was looking for. It's all been a mistake."

One of the men sprang up and ran off just as Billy and Ronan showed up, even to the point of pushing between the two. Sensing that he had been deserted, the remaining man looked around wildly and ran off, too.

Rosemary brandished a skillet and yelled after them. "May you be afflicted with the itch but have no nails to scratch with!"

The darkness swallowed the men up, and all you could hear were their running footsteps and ragged breathing. By the time Meara dismounted, she couldn't even hear that.

The women took a seat around the fire, while the men argued if they should go after the attackers. Thaddeus reappeared on a log around the fire and pulled out a handkerchief to wipe his brow. "Whoa. I had no idea what I was getting myself into when the faeries started asking all the gnomes if they wanted to go on an adventure that would benefit all humankind."

The friendly, little guy had been a huge help to them so far. "I bet the faeries picked you because you were the strongest and most capable."

He waggled his eyebrows in response. "That does have a nice ring to it. I like it. That wasn't exactly the case. Gnomes usually settle down by the age of forty. Most of our clan is married. So, none of those gnomes were even asked. Even the single gnomes are unlikely to leave the land they were born on."

"Why not?" Rosemary asked as she ran her hands through her hair, possibly searching for briars, twigs, or even bugs she might have picked up in the tussle.

"We're part of the land. It defines who we are. Gnomes take their names from their locations. Garden Gnome, Forest Gnome, Cave Gnome, House Gnome. Once you leave your place, you are no longer where once you were."

It sounded like Thaddeus had a bit more rootedness than the rest of them, although she would have said Ronan was firmly rooted before he decided to join them. "Makes sense. So, did the other gnomes who wanted to go draw straws or something?"

The gnome chuckled as if the idea were hilarious. He laughed so hard he had to wipe his eyes. "Oh dear me, no. No one wanted to go. I just told you that the gnomes are wedded to the land. I may have been influenced by some persistent faeries. They can be persistent and don't handle the word *no* well, either."

"Ah." She was at a loss for words. It sounded as if the faeries had twisted his arm to make him come along. "We're glad you're here."

He rubbed his hands together. "I would have expected as much the way your clan keeps getting into trouble."

She hadn't thought of her assortment of friends and cousin as a clan. They were, in a way, a family of choice.

"We are grateful. Is there anything we can do for you?" She crossed her fingers and hid them behind her back. If he asked for money, they were strapped for cash as it was. Everything had to be conserved for the time when they absolutely had to use money as opposed to bartering.

"A bit of food would work quite well. Throwing oversized humans around works up an appetite." He grinned, as his task had been fun.

Before she could answer, Jane did. "If you joined up for food, then it's your loss. You must have noticed we have precious little left."

His happy expression didn't dim at the news. "What happened to the cloth wrapped bundle the liveryman gave you?"

"Oh, that!" She'd almost forgotten about it. "I tied it to the saddle. I'll go get it."

Meara retrieved the bundle and sat down beside the fire. Curious eyes measured every movement as she untied the string and peeled the cloth back. Crusty pockets sat lined up in a roll with fluted edges made with the tines from a fork. "I'm not sure what it is."

Thaddeus snatched one before she could blink.

He held the concoction aloft. "I'll do the brave deed and taste it."

He bit into it and a bit of gravy dribbled down his chin as he demolished it in a few bites. "My professional opinion is that it was a meat pie with potatoes, onion, and a sprinkling of parsley."

"Sounds good to me." Billy grabbed one with Rosemary and Jane following suit.

The appetizing scent had Meara drooling, but she picked up the last one and offered it to Ronan.

"You eat it. I had plenty at the livery."

She was hoping he would say that, but she had learned at the convent not only to beware of gluttony but avoid the appearance of it, which was hard when you were starving as she was. Meara held the pastry up to her face and inhaled. It hadn't been all that long since Aunt Erin had made them tasty meals. It seemed like forever.

She made a delicate bite and allowed the still warm meat and potatoes to lie on her tongue. Her goal was to appreciate every bite, but hunger won out and had her licking her fingers. "I wish there was more."

"I second that." Rosemary held up her hand. "Well, I guess we need to pack up now."

"Aye, we do." Jane agreed. "Let's keep the fire going as long as we can since it's only a sickle moon.

There wasn't much to be put away. Billy rolled the logs they were using as seats back into the forest. The water bucket was attached to the wagon, and Hercules was harnessed for the ride. They discussed who would ride and who would walk. Once they had worked that out, Billy shook his head and pointed at Meara.

"Did you hear the men tell Jane that she wasn't the girl they were looking for?"

"I did."

"You were standing right there or rather sitting on Wind Racer."

"Rather frightened about the whole situation, too."

"Why didn't they see you? Or did they not recognize you?"

"Curious." Meara nodded. "Thaddeus told me someone has put a protection spell on me. It allows me not to be seen. Unfortunately, it doesn't extend to any of you. It's natural to be scared and to think about it. When I do, I alert whoever is seeking me."

She sucked in her lower lip, wondering who had put such a spell on her. It hadn't been hard for the man to spot her at the train station, so it hadn't been Destiny. It must have been Grandmother Biddy. All this time, she'd been running, and she didn't know. A small snort escaped her as she considered how she could have handled things.

"When I saw those men tumbling around like rag dolls, I tried to make my mind blank. I'm not totally sure how to use this spell. Thaddeus has promised to teach me."

"That is sure to help." Rosemary strolled over and hugged her. "We need all the tricks and potions we can get. Thaddeus has been a huge help, too."

The gnome swelled up with pride as Meara suspected he would. "Sometimes, I think it might be better to go it alone."

There was an immediate outcry.

"Absolutely not."

"That's not what friends do."

"My mam would kill me."

She knew the last had to be Ronan. "If they are looking for a girl in a gypsy wagon, then it's best not to be a girl. That part we have covered although the wagon might be an issue."

Jane called over from her spot at the wagon. "It depends." She jumped down from the seat and took a few long strides to reach Meara. "I gave this some thought. Whoever is after you is expecting a gypsy wagon. We can paint it again. Make it into something else. We'll be hiding in plain sight. Think about it."

The plan did have merit except for a few things. "We can be peddlers, although we have no goods to sell."

"True," Jane cheerfully agreed, not the least dissuaded by the obvious.

"Occasionally, a tinker would wander into town to sharpen knives and refurbish pans, but we don't have the tools to be a tinker. What else is there?"

"Ah, you missed the one thing we could do, and all we need is some black paint and a Bible."

Meara was almost afraid to ask. Her friend danced over to Billy, put up her hand to measure his height, then continued on to Ronan. "They're both equally tall. People tend to pay attention to a tall man. Don't ask me why. They just do. Billy is able to lose his accent at will. That makes him a good candidate."

"For what?" Billy asked the obvious.

"What else? The Preacher and Prophet Jeremiah's Salvation Show."

Everyone was stunned into silence while Jane beamed about her plan.

Finally, Billy cleared his throat. "Don't know much about scripture and all. Da and I were just C and E church attenders. My mam did all the churching for us."

"Don't worry." She waved away his objections. "We have Meara, who knows the Good Book backward and forward. As long as you're passionate about whatever you're saying, people will believe. My uncle ran a Salvation Wagon for a few years and couldn't even read. It was good money. We wouldn't have to preach all the time, but it would explain why we were on the road. Folks are more suspicious than back in Ireland. Suspicious folks are dangerous folks. You're Brother Jerimiah unless someone comes up with a better idea."

No one did.

Chapter Eleven

ONLY A FEW determined stars and a slice of the moon lit their path. The night birds had ceased their cooing and finally gone to sleep. Cow manure mixed with a damp green scent as silence fell over the wagon. Rosemary and Ronan were asleep inside the wagon while Billy, astride Wind Racer, kept watch behind. Their pace was slow, even for Hercules.

Meara could have walked faster if she'd felt like it. The day had taken its toll, however. Dealing with the unknown could be tiring. It seemed like when she needed to hear her parents' voices the most, they were silent. Her mother had explained that communicating was no easy task. It took immense energy she had to hoard until the veil between the planes grew thin. Meara wasn't always sure when that time was. Their instructions tended to come at night, sometimes in dreams. Ever since they landed, Meara had begged for instructions for what was next.

When she came out of her coma, she had an imperfect knowing of where to find the first section. The Clearys had sold off that part of their land to the neighbors, but she still had a visual. Now she had no clue where to head. Jane rested her back against the bench and held the reins loosely between her fingers. It made Meara wonder how Jane knew where to go.

"Where are we headed?"

"Didn't know you were awake. We're heading away from the village."

"I figured as much. It seemed like you knew where we were

going, which was more than I do, currently."

"We're taking a detour."

Her lips twisted to one side as she considered if *detour* could be code for *lost*. "Do you know where we are?"

"Not exactly. I do know we are heading back in the direction we came."

"Why would we do that? I can't remember, but Ronan may have mentioned he was heading home, which would mean we'd head to Holyhead." She squeezed her eyes shut as she tried to remember what was said. Everything happened so fast, and it changed as it went along. Nothing had gone as planned. "We might have said we were heading to England, too. I just can't remember."

"Don't fash yourself over it. The point is to confuse anyone who might follow us. Those ruffians will assume we'll head north toward Scotland."

"We will." Meara felt the need to point out their end destination even if she wasn't clear on the specifics.

Jane turned in Meara's direction. "I know that. It wouldn't serve to arrive at the same time."

Even though it was too dark to determine her expression, Meara could imagine it. Jane did not suffer fools gladly. What was so obvious to her should be likewise to others. "That much is clear."

"What is our plan in the meantime?"

Meara's shoulders went up in a shrug? "I'm not sure how long should we wait."

"I figure a month or two. Billy and Ronan could get work at the docks. Close to a city, I might be able to find a local fortune teller or medium."

Jane was capable of reading cards. Grandmother Biddy had taught her. She'd tried to teach Meara, too, not that she'd learned all that much. All she retained was the death card meant *change* and change was inevitable. "You can turn a card as well as any of them."

"I know that. I was hoping for work. With the war going on

most of the mediums will be busy trying to reach fallen sons and fathers."

The word *fallen* made Meara shudder a little. Or was it something else? She put up her hand for silence. Jane brought Hercules to a stop. Something was searching for her. She could feel it. Her arms broke out into goose pimples and not because of the cool air. It was a knowing. Her eyes fluttered shut as she concentrated on the darkness behind her eyelids. Nothing must seep out to the force that hunted her. She inhaled deeply and assembled the mental blocks that Grandmother Biddy taught her. Each wall was made of impenetrable steel letting nothing out or anything in.

The wagon stayed in place, not moving for several minutes until Billy approached them. "Why did you stop?" Jane held up her hand, then touched Meara.

She knew what she was asking. "It has left. We're good for now."

"It was a break." Jane snapped the reins over Hercules's back. "The break is over."

THEY SETTLED OUTSIDE of Holyhead since Meara was firm about not being in the city. It felt too much like a trap. The men took Wind Racer to the docks to work every day. Jane did get a job as a card reader since Madame Zelda had so many seances to conduct. Most of Jane's clientele included shop girls who hoped for a better future in the form of marriage. The rest were unhappy wives who wished they'd never married and wanted the card to at least hint at an escape. Every now and then, she'd get a male client who wanted to engage in a risky venture and wanted some confirmation that he wouldn't get caught.

Holyhead, like so many towns, had given up many of its young men for the war. Even though willing arms and strong backs were needed at the docks, Billy and Ronan were often harassed for not fighting. They couldn't exactly fight back since their harassers were bitter women who had lost a husband or a son, possibly the same people who visited Madame Zelda.

Rosemary got work as a kitchen maid at a shabby hotel that catered to sea-going men who desired a bed that didn't rock. The one thing the guests wanted besides a bed was a woman to go in it. This made Rosemary keep up her boy disguise.

Meara stayed at the wagon, which was parked on a blind widow's northern fallow pasture that consisted of spindly trees and brush allowed to grow wild over the years. They moved the wagon occasionally to have the horses graze in different places. Decency had her stopping by the widow's house to see if she needed anything done. The woman was amazingly self-sufficient. However, she did ask Meara to chop wood for her.

Even though she called herself Mark and lowered her voice, the widow knew she was female. Blame it on walking too carefully. A man just stomped around and didn't care if he crushed something, whereas a woman had a much lighter step. It was something to remember for her future masquerades. Heddy, the widow, accepted that Meara's aunt had asked her to dress as a boy for her safety.

They had developed a routine, of sorts. After everyone had breakfast and headed out to work, Meara cleaned things up and put Hercules to graze. Often, she'd slip into the wagon to consult the cards using the handwritten primer Jane had made her. Then she'd consult her pendulum. She usually asked, "Is Braeden still alive?"

He was. Still, she had her doubts since she hadn't dreamed of him lately.

Her next question was a selfish one she didn't want to ask when the others were around. "Do I still need to find the horn?"

Yes. The pendulum did not elaborate.

Thaddeus had been good company for a few days, but he left to head home. He promised to return. Meara didn't know how he would since they had no clue when they'd head out. She'd only hope that when they did, she'd have a clear destination in mind. They could use his brand of magic.

In her free time, when no one was around, she lay underneath the shade of a huge oak tree, trying to reach her parents. *Nothing.* They were mysteriously silent. On the plus side, her amulets hadn't warmed to predict danger. Still, when she was hot or the weather turned sultry, it was hard to tell if the amulet was warning her.

No one hassled them about being there, since Heddy implied they were family. You would have thought someone would have come around to check, but everyone had their own issues. A silver-haired man who used two canes to walk showed up on the porch when Meara was reading from Dickens to Heddy. She marked her place and let the man in, then excused herself to the porch.

Curious if his appearance had something to do with their squatting on the land, she lingered. The open window was almost as good as being in the room. She couldn't see expressions. Sometimes words and the tone they were delivered in were enough.

"Good morning, Henrietta. You are looking beautiful today."

There was a derisive snort, then a cough. "Cut the flannel, Jason. Maybe you thought, as a blind woman, I wouldn't have noticed the wrinkles or that my hair was thinner than it was this time last month. I have. What brings you here?"

"Henrietta, my dear, I expected you to be happy to see me. You need a man in your life."

"Not this tomfoolery again. My answer is no. You may need my land, but you aren't getting it. My name's Heddy. You could at least get that right. I don't need a man. I've got Mark to chop wood for me. Are you going to take over that job?"

"Henrietta, I mean Heddy, that is not a proper job for a gentleman of my years."

"That means you're of no use to me. I'd appreciate it if you'd quit telling folks that we are seeing each other. I haven't seen anyone for years." A harsh chuckle sounded. "It doesn't take vision to see what you're up to. My question is *why*. You're closer to death's door than I am. What would you do with my land? It won't make you any younger. At our age, there is nothing you can buy that will put off the inevitability of death. Why is it so important to you?"

There was a deep sigh. "It's my duty to my family. They used to own all this land."

"If I remember correctly, your father sold off parcels for gambling money. No one made him do it."

"Will you do me the courtesy of not speaking badly of my father?"

"Only if you do me the courtesy of leaving."

Meara hurried to the edge of the porch before the front door swung open. The canes' tips hit the floor, followed by dusty boots as the old man maneuvered down the first step. Jason grumbled loudly, unaware of Meara's presence. "Nasty piece of work if ever I saw one. Her husband up and died just to get away from her."

Meara cleared her throat before she heard any more.

He looked up and scowled. "Don't waste your time hanging around. You'll get nothing. She has no use for you or me."

Not knowing how to respond to such an unkind statement, she dropped her gaze. Just then, Heddy called out. "Mark, come back in and finish reading now that my greedy old neighbor is gone!"

The open window worked both ways, so he had to have heard what was said about him. Meara slipped into the house and picked up her book. "We were at the part where Oliver Twist had been grabbed by the policeman."

"You're right. Let's hear how he gets himself out of that fix."

Meara read longer than usual until Heddy held up a hand. "Do you think that odious fellow is gone?"

"I believe so. I can take a look around."

"Do that. Then report back to me."

It didn't take her long to walk around the house to find no sign of the annoying neighbor. At least that would cheer Heddy. She entered the house and announced, "No sign."

"Good." Heddy pursed her lips, then wrung her hands. "I hate him and his slimy ways. He means to pry my farm away from me if it is the last thing he does. Even worse, he reminded me that I'm old and not long for this world. My current goal is to outlive him if only by a day."

"Understandable." She inserted her hands into her pockets and mulled over the situation. "Do you have any children to watch out for you?"

A small moan sounded. "I did. Now I don't. My son was the first to die. Farming accident. My husband blamed himself. Always thought it should have been him. Before you ask, I am the youngest child in my family. An afterthought since my brothers and sisters had left the home when I was born. I am the end of the line. When I die, I imagine my neighbors will be on my farm like a dog on a bone. It sickens me." She shrugged. "What can I do?"

Her heart hurt as she considered the old woman's plight. "My father had something similar happen to him. There were those who wanted his farm and felt it wrong that a stranger got the land. In the end, they killed him, all over the land."

"How sad." She reached out her hand, and Meara stepped forward to take it.

"Sometimes, I think about how they could have done things differently. Maybe they could have sold the land or at least taken whatever they had, such as the livestock, and left."

"You got nothing?" She gave Meara's hand a squeeze as she asked.

It wasn't the material goods that mattered. Although she found herself coveting the piece of land that cost her father his life. "No. My mother was pregnant with me and had to run for her life."

"No mother should have to endure that. It marks the child. It's sad that the world has come to that. Mr. Hitler, in all his greed, wants to gobble up the world. I wish there was some way to avoid people fighting over my stuff. They'd rob me if it wasn't for my dogs."

The scruffy mongrels were mostly bark and had accepted Meara readily enough. "It's good you have your dogs. Maybe you should make a will and name someone to inherit. That person would take care of you to protect their investment."

"Ha!" Heddy dropped her hand. "I thought you were smart. Name someone to inherit and they might help me on my way."

"There is that. Name someone who wouldn't kill you."

Heddy rocked back in her chair. "You say it like it is something simple. Nowadays, with everything in such a disarray, it will be harder than you might think." She sighed heavily. "I might be worried about nothing. My farm might be taken over by the Germans before long. I will think on it. When I come up with something, you can drive me to the lawyer."

Germans, lawyers, it sounded like it was time to move on. The world she knew could end while she dithered about what to do. Surely, whoever was after her was far ahead or possibly returned back to Ireland. They needed to leave and soon.

Chapter Twelve

EVEN THOUGH IT was technically summer in Wales, the mornings started off cool. Meara could see her breath as she kicked dirt over the campfire. Jane fussed with Hercules, who had gotten lazy with his long break and protested the collar around his neck. It was a good chance the horse had never had that long between wagon pulls before. Rosemary and Billy stood in the shade of the oak tree with their faces turned toward each other. It didn't take a mind reader to see a relationship developing between them. They might be whispering sweet nothings to each other, urging each other to be safe on the trip even though most of the time they'd be in each other's vision. Everyone was so involved in getting ready, they hadn't asked the obvious. Where were they going?

She tried asking the cards as Grandmother Biddy taught her to do. Today, she pulled the Tower card. It was never a favorite with its crumbling base, threatening to tumble in the near future. It signaled a negative experience. Grandmother Biddy would give a sage nod and remind her that the negative always followed the positive and so on. It was all about a balanced universe. Right now, with so much conflict, the world was far from balanced. Was their leave-taking the negative experience? Even though she would have preferred to stay with Heddy, it was inevitable that she'd leave. On the upside, at least for Heddy, she came across a girl a few years younger than her sleeping in the woods. The girl explained she'd been cast out from her home for being pregnant and unwed. It didn't take much to convince Heddy to take her in. As luck would have it, the girl could read, too.

Heddy made her promise to swing back around since she had included Meara in her will. At the lawyer's office, she protested she wanted nothing. Still, the widow, grateful for the will, suggested wanting to do something positive for her. Heddy and Meara spent the past two weeks preserving and smoking food to take. Ronan had shot a deer they feasted on, then made jerky out of the rest. At least they would be one up from when they first arrived in Wales. The weird thing was, she couldn't get a sense of where the danger came from. How could they avoid it if she couldn't sense it?

Jane, in an effort to calm her, admitted she had psychic down times. Her only advice was to keep doing what she was doing, and something would come through. All she had was something bad would upset them or unbalance her. No need to mention it to anyone, but she did need to keep her senses sharp.

Ronan came out of the woods, whistling as if he was on a fortnight holiday. "Everyone ready?"

Billy and Rosemary chorused "yes" together. On one level, she knew she should be happy for her friend, but if they spent all their time staring at one another it could be the opening for the negative thing the card portrayed. Her fingers wrapped around her amulets. They were warm from her body, but not overly warm. With her eyes closed, she whispered a prayer. "Mother, Father, Grandmother Biddy, Helpful Spirits, Faeries, Elves, Gnomes, Sprites, and any other entity who could help, please do. Get me where I need to go." An image of an island came into her mind. Wasn't Britain an island with Scotland attached to it? The island in her mind was shaped more like a good-sized potato, not round, nor oval, but rather potato shape. Even though the only map she saw was the one at Eleanor's house, England had looked potato-like. If it bore any resemblance to a root vegetable, it would be more likely be a mandrake root that occasionally resembled a person.

It couldn't be England but someplace close to Scotland. *Maybe.*

It would help if she actually knew something about the country. While she hadn't learned much about geography, except what she managed to glean from Eleanor's maps, it left her at the mercy of train schedules, ferrymen, and Jane, who knew her way around Ireland. Wales was an entirely different kettle of fish. Rosemary had seldom left Hogstead while Ronan had stayed close to home. That only left—"Billy!"

The amiable fellow waved at her and came close when she gestured. There might be an island or two near Scotland. Maybe three at the most. It might take going to every single one, and if they were lucky, might be the first one they chose.

"What can I do for you?"

"Did you ever ferry to the isles around Scotland?"

He wrinkled his nose, then slapped his leg. "Are you having fun with me? No self-respecting ferryman plies those waters if he can help it. It's too far away for one thing. There are blue men who come up out of the water and pull people out of their craft. There's mermaids, and selkies, and a creature that looks like a wolf."

As he listed each creature, she hoped that the horn would not be on an island, even though it was possible the creatures were just tall tales told to keep children at home. "You don't believe those stories, do you?"

His eyebrows shot up, half-hidden under his overgrown bangs. "Don't believe it? I didn't believe in gnomes until I met one. Gnomes are kind, thoughtful folks while the blue men are not. I prefer to not take my chances."

"When do the blue men come out?" Maybe she could reason with him by saying they'd choose not to go whenever the blue men were at play. She firmly hoped they weren't active in the summer months, but usually, if something or someone was to come alive to bedevil folks, it would be the summer after everything had thoroughly thawed.

The question gave Billy pause. He rolled his eyes upward, trying to discover the needed information. "I heard they love the storms or anytime the water is rough. It makes it all the easier to pull unsuspecting sailors underwater."

Meara slapped her hands together. "We'll go when the water is calm."

"Summer should serve. Which island?"

Ah, she knew it would come to this. "Well," she placed her fingers on her temples, thinking about what she'd seen. "I saw an island like a lumpy potato. It was as if I were a bird flying above it. Does it sound familiar?"

"Do I look like a bird?"

"No."

"I have no clue what the islands look like from above. I heard a foreigner say that Italy looked like a boot. I am not sure if that was true or not. It just might be something people say. Makes me wonder how they drew the maps since aeroplanes are such new inventions."

Meara was about to ask if he'd be willing to go if the waves were still, but Billy never let her. The man had the gift of gab like so many of the Emerald Isle's other residents.

"Do you plan on going through the islands one by one until one feels familiar?"

That had been her imperfect plan. It wasn't the best, but the smirk Billy wore made her feel even worse. "You think that won't work?"

"It might. I realize we spent some time around Holyhead to confuse whoever might be hunting us. Still, I thought we wanted to be as quick as can be."

"Being fast is good. The sooner it is done, the sooner everyone can go back to their normal life."

The only problem was she didn't have a normal life. The convent was gone, and the remaining sisters scattered. After being in the real world, convent life did not appeal, even if it had survived the bombing attack. With Adelaide back at Hogstead running the rumor mill, it had no sentimental hold on her. She was as free as the proverbial bird, and it didn't please her one bit.

"There won't be anything fast about it," Billy told her.

"What do you mean?"

"Heard there's over 700 islands. Not all are inhabited, though. Was it an inhabited island?"

Goodness, she had no clue, which was embarrassing to admit. She closed her eyes and brought the image closer. She could see people looking a bit like ants scurrying across the landscape. One of the women looked up and shielded her hands with a flat hand as if she knew they were being watched. "Definitely inhabited."

"That narrows it down quite a bit."

"Do you know the inhabited islands?"

"Not really." He managed a lopsided grin. "There has to be someone who knows where they are. Surely they teach that stuff to school children. All we need to do is find a reasonably bright tike."

"We're not kidnapping children."

"Not kidnapping—ask them a few questions like a contest."

Meara shook her head, not wanting the fate of the world to depend on a random child. "There has to be a book about it."

Rosemary approached, hearing the tail end of the conversation. "You need one of those lending libraries. They have all kinds of books you can read for free."

That sounded promising. "Do you know where one is?"

"No, I just heard about it today. Some lady mentioned it. Not sure if they have one around here. She came into the hotel dining room talking about it." Rosemary pressed her hands together and leaned forward as if imparting a secret. "They trust folks to return the books."

"What happens if they don't?"

Rosemary shrugged.

What seemed promising fizzled down to nothing. "Who else

would know about the islands?"

"Ah," Billy held up one finger. "I can think of someone."

"Who?" It would be a relief to have a destination.

"He's a smuggler, but he does some trade up in The Orkney Islands."

No reason to ask Billy how he knew such a person. "Could we trust him?"

"For a price. There's no reason to tell him why you need to know. It's better that way."

An uneasy feeling started at the base of her spine and crept upward making her feel a bit like the falling tower. Intuition screamed it was a bad idea, but she didn't have any other options.

Chapter Thirteen

THEIR DEPARTURE WAS delayed by a day since Billy returned to Holyhead to scour all the disreputable dives in search of his smuggler friend. Since such places could be dicey with men provoked into fighting simply by an imagined slur, Ronan went along. The real question was who would protect Ronan? Meara gave a heavy sigh and shuffled the worn Tarot cards, hoping for an answer. She turned over a single card.

The Tower, again. Her lips pressed together as she glared at the card. Not what she wanted to see. It was only a confirmation of her pull the previous day. Maybe, if she shuffled it one more time and tried again, she'd get better. Were she there, Grandmother Biddy would cross her arms and give her a look for trying to manipulate the cards. She'd tell her the cards do not cause fate. They only predict what is. Then she'd tell her it was up to her to change the outcome if she didn't like it. The first thing she should have done was prevent Billy and Ronan from leaving.

The door to the wagon opened, and Jane stuck her head in. "It's not like you to hide in here."

"I agree." Her gaze dropped back to the cards, while wondering if one more pull would be manipulation. She flicked one card over as Jane entered the wagon and bent to stare at the card.

"The Magician." She nodded at Meara. "That means you already have all the tools you need."

"I don't. If I had all the tools I needed, would I be turning over cards for answers?"

Jane sat down and picked up the deck. She fanned the cards on the table, then picked them up and shuffled them again. "You have your cards, your pendulums, your visions, your supernatural help... What else do you need? Rosemary told me there was even a prophecy about you."

The mention of prophecy brought back the memory of being in Destiny's tiny storybook house. When Destiny spoke, it did seem like anything was possible. Somehow, she knew all about Meara without ever having met her. "About that. I think she had me confused with someone else."

Jane placed the cards on the table and fixed Meara with a cool stare. "Destiny is never wrong. Grandmother Biddy taught her, but Destiny even surpassed her teacher. Even the faeries do your bidding."

"Ha!" She wrinkled her nose, feeling like a fraud. Everyone thought she was such a great leader. She didn't even know Scotland had all those islands. "Faeries helped me. They never did my bidding. Do you see any around now?"

Jane put her hands up to her forehead, cupped her fingers around her eyes like binoculars, and pretended to peer around the small interior. "No faeries there. None there, either. Did you consider that maybe you don't need any right now? Nothing dangerous is happening. They've got fairy business to attend to. Like you said, they aren't at your call."

"Possibly." While she'd been busy feeling sorry for herself, a revelation occurred to her. "I know why my parents hid part of the horn on a Scottish isle."

"Why?"

Meara put out her hands. "Isn't it obvious? There are over seven hundred of them. So, whoever is trying to discover the horn first would have to investigate all the islands."

"Not all of them. Just until he finds the right one. Even then, he'd need the first section of the horn you found. He'd have to take it from you."

The words sounded ominous. She wouldn't be handing it over without a fight "What would he do with it without the third section?"

"That is the question. I wasn't there when Destiny delivered the prophecy. Did she even mention the horn?" Her eyebrows lowered as she placed her elbow on the table and rested her chin in her upturned hand. "This is a problem. Can anything evil use the horn?"

"I'm not sure." The thought of countless shadowy creatures popping out of the ground and lining up in formation, ready for battle was not a pleasant one. "The way I understood it, the horn was to summon fairy help. Faeries, being creatures of the earth, would not do anything to destroy it as the current war is doing."

"There is that." Jane's words were muted by her cupped hand. "Who made the horn?"

"The faeries made it before they broke with the humans. Still, I guess they wanted to help if ever needed. It would have to be a very special case. Anyhow, it was entrusted centuries ago to one particular person. Obviously, an Irishman."

"Why couldn't it be a woman?"

"It could. It was just a figure of speech. Anyhow, this person hid it, probably thinking no humans could be trusted. I'm beginning to feel that way."

"Your parents found it."

"Which is weird. They'd visited a place so many other people had visited before. It was really hidden. Why them?"

"Magic." Jane lifted her head, dropped her hand and straightened into a sitting position, ending with a mysterious smile. "It has to be magic."

"I'm glad you can be so certain. I'm still trying to figure things out. Do you think the horn has some sort of intelligence? It knew it was needed, and it just appeared."

"I do. Even more so, it had the ability to communicate and told your parents where to bury each piece. Instead of consulting the cards, maybe you need to be holding onto the horn and concentrating on it. Surely, it can tell where the next piece is."

"I will." She stood and went to the cabinet where she'd hidden the horn. Instead of leaving it in its decorative box, she'd wrapped it in a silk scarf and placed it under her clothing. A thief might take the box never bothering to look inside. If he did, he'd discovered a series of well-worn books. Most were indecipherable to her, written in an unfamiliar language that Grandmother Biddy must have been able to comprehend.

Her fingers searched under her clothes until a tingle told her she had found it. Every time she touched it, something happened to her. There was a high pitched keening in her ears as she brought the horn part close to her and cuddled it as if it were a babe. This feeling made her both possessive of it and a little afraid. The afraid part was what had her hiding it in the bottom of the cabinet, telling herself she was keeping it safe. Or was she keeping herself safe from *it*? Meara held up the scarf-wrapped object, holding it out as far as her arms would allow. "When I hold this, I feel odd."

"Odd? How? Do you feel magical? Powerful? Feeling your faery ancestry?" Jane said the last one with a wink.

"Powerful is definitely not it. It's hard to explain. You know my story. Mother birthed me at the convent and then died. Before I was born, my father, Fulmen, was murdered, although some called it an accident. I've never really had a family."

"What about the sisters?"

"Ah, the fact that you asked shows you've never lived in a convent or had much contact with nuns." Her elbows bowed out as she brought the object closer without any real intention to do so. It was like her body was under someone else's control. The horn section fit right over her heart as if it belonged there.

"No. On the whole, we stayed out of the towns. We certainly didn't go knocking on any convent doors." Jane chuckled. "What were the nuns like?"

Her first response would have been cold, distant women under the brutal grip of Mother Superior, but there was more to them than that. There'd been a few rule breakers in the bunch. "A few toadied up to Mother Superior by carrying tales. Someone would whistle in the knaves. Laughter was heard in the laundry. One sister even climbed a tree to see over the wall."

"If those are punishable offenses, then it was a dreary place."

It had been that. At least, most of the time. "It was filled with women that no one wanted for some reason or another. Widows whose husbands had died. Spinsters who'd never married. Those who might have committed a grievous sin that required them to be locked away. Then there was me, the orphan."

"Sounds sad."

"It was." She wrinkled her nose, trying to remember exactly how she'd felt. "I'm not sure I would say I was sad. I had nothing to compare it to then. Every day was the same. We had chores we completed in silence. We had prayers, which were also silent, but they went on forever. It was a trial to keep my mind on the suffering of mankind when I could hear the birds chirping outside. Every day was the same, except when we had a visiting priest. Then, we had high mass, which was even more prayers, standing, kneeling, and repeating."

"I'd rather be a nail under the carpenter's hammer. Sounds horrendous. Would you have left if the bomb hadn't dropped on your convent?"

It is a question she'd asked herself before. There was a pall that had hung over the place. It'd felt like something she could touch. Knowing more of the world, she'd say hopelessness permeated the place. Most accepted they were there for life. There were so many words not said on things they weren't allowed to talk about. Most had family at one time so even when they were tucked behind stone walls, they could still remember what it felt like to belong. It wasn't a feeling she could claim. "I don't know if I would have left. I had no family to call my own."

"You had your Uncle Simon, Aunt Erin, Ronan, and whatever other cousins you left back in Ireland. There could be people on your father's side of the family that you haven't met, too"

"Possibly." She'd never even thought about her father's side. "I didn't know any of that then. I was just a child that had been left at the convent. Most of the sisters whispered that my mother was no better than she should be. Meaning I had been born out of wedlock. This made me somehow less than the women who had been rejected by their families."

"A few may have felt a real calling."

"I suppose some did. They weren't at my convent." Her arms had tightened around the horn as if afraid it might slip from her grasp. "What I am trying to say is I never felt connected to any of them or anything. When I touched the horn, it felt right. Maybe it could have been because my mother and father touched it."

"That may be. Could be that you were in your mother's belly at the time, too. In your own way, you could be connected to the hiding of the horn." Jane tapped a finger against her head. "You could have memories of where the next two sections are."

"I wish that were true. I have thought and thought on it and come up with nothing."

"Thinking, that's the problem. Intuition, the knowing, is not the same as thinking. Do you remember your visions? Your dreams? Even a feeling that something was following us?"

Meara nodded as a warm, safe feeling spiraled out from where the horn section rested against her chest. "It's hard not to."

Jane arched her eyebrows and waited the slightest moment for dramatic effect before continuing. Grandmother Biddy taught her well. "Did you think the visions into existence?"

"No!"

"The dreams?"

"Certainly not. Do you think I'd want to dream of Braeden in danger?" Before Jane could respond, Meara did. "I wasn't thinking when those things happened. Just doing whatever I was doing. When it came to the dreams, I was sleeping."

"There you go."

"There I go what?"

"You're overthinking everything. Trying too hard. Take time to lean against a tree and relax. It will come when you least expect it."

"You're right. Sometimes, when I close my eyes, pictures form on my eyelids. Usually, it *is* places. That is how I knew it was an island. Billy asked me if it was inhabited. I closed my eyes and thought of it, and I could see people moving about. One woman looked back over her shoulder like she knew I was peeping. I didn't try too hard. Well, maybe a little. I needed an answer, and there it was."

"So, what do you have now?"

"Nothing. Why should I have anything when I have been talking to you?"

Jane could just be like that, asking questions that made no sense. She closed her eyes for a second. A red letter took shape. It was a bit vague at first, but she sharpened her focus. "I see the letter *A*. The island starts with *A*."

Jane hooted, causing Rosemary to stick her head into the wagon. "What's going on?"

"Meara was able to figure out the first letter of the island where the horn is buried."

"That's wonderful." Rosemary grinned, then her lips drooped a little. "If you knew the name, why did Billy and Ronan go to town? They'll be in the worse sort of pubs where the serving girls are way too free with their charms."

Even though the horn radiated goodness and wellbeing, Meara could still hear the distress in Rosemary's voice. It would be easy to ignore it and stay in her peaceful state. She placed the horn on the table. Unwilling to give up all contact, her hand rested on it. "They went because I think too much. I'm impatient and not willing to wait."

"What if Billy gets hurt? Or Ronan?"

She noticed her cousin was tacked on as an afterthought. Not surprising, considering where her friend's real interest laid. Was Rosemary more worried about barmaids with a tendency to wear low cut tops and flirt with the customers, or was she concerned about him getting hurt in a fight? "Both boys will come back tonight in fine shape."

"All is well then." Contented that her sweetheart would be back before the moon had climbed too high, Rosemary disappeared from view.

Jane gave her a doubtful look. "All is not well?"

Her fingers tightened on the horn. "They'll be all right *this* night. In their search for Scottish islands, they've drawn curious eyes and ears. Trouble follows them. We must be ready to head out tonight. We'll need some of your trickery to mislead the followers."

The knowing was back. She should be happy about it, and she would be if it ever revealed something good for a change. It could be if people were warned about upcoming happy occurrences, they'd no longer be happy ones, just expected.

Chapter Fourteen

THE FIRE DANCED, throwing alternating light and shadows on the women as it flickered. An occasional gleam lit up the pendulum Jane held. Instead of moving closer to hear what questions Jane might have for the pendulum, Meara paced. It would probably be better not to hear the various fears and doubts Jane had. She could only imagine. Would they ever find the other sections of the horn and put them together? Would they survive their adventure? Should they be putting so much faith in her, someone who didn't even know where they were headed?

"Where are they?" Rosemary stood and stomped her foot. "They should have been here by now. How long could it take to locate one smuggler and ask him some questions about an island?"

Meara shrugged, since the whole dealing with smugglers was out of her realm of experience. Still, what did Billy really hope to get out of this? It wasn't like the man would write down the inhabited islands. Or sketch a map for them. Good chance he couldn't even read or write. Why become a smuggler if he had other options?

The sound of tipsy singing about what to do with a drunken sailor reached them before the soft thump of hoofbeats. Jane looked up from her pendulum while Rosemary crossed her arms and tapped her foot. While Meara knew little of romantic entanglements, she did know her friend was far from pleased. Wind Racer wasn't the speediest of horses, which was just as well since the two may have fallen off if she went any faster. They should be thankful that the horse knew the way back.

Not waiting for the two to reach the camp circle, Rosemary stomped out to meet them. "Where have you been?" Her voice carried well. "Look at you? Drunk as a lord."

Jane gave a short laugh. "She already sounds like a wife."

Billy answered the accusation with a surprisingly clear voice. "And how is my sweetheart?"

"I'm not your sweetheart!" She stomped back to camp, turning her back on the approaching man, and made faces as she waited for Billy to say something. Ronan, unaware of the tension between the two or not caring, dismounted and walked over to the circle trailing Wind Racer's reins, bringing the tired horse along with him.

"You were right, Meara. We need to go now. Things are changing. If we don't hurry, we might not even get into Scotland."

Had he encountered whoever was trailing them? "What did you find out?"

"They're putting guards on the Scotland border. It is no easy matter to cross. You have to have a reason and papers."

In search of a magical horn wouldn't be considered a practical reason. It also might be the thing that would get them arrested. The knowledge almost outweighed her sense of foreboding—but not quite. "That's important information."

"That's not all we heard." Ronan glanced back at Billy, who was in a spirited discussion with Rosemary. "I would have let Billy tell you. He might be a while."

"Tell!" Jane and Meara demanded together.

Ronan straightened up, being the center of attention, and waited just long enough to earn a pinch from Jane.

"Don't you go being mean or I won't tell you."

Jane held up her thumb and forefinger, made a pinching motion, and moved closer to Ronan who jumped back.

"Give me space." He moved back another step before continuing. "Britain's parliament passed a bill that conscripts able-bodied men into the army. There were some uniformed, oversized thugs working their way through the taverns asking men if they were enlisted. If they weren't, they called them cowards and told them to be real men and defend their county. Often, it ended up in fisticuffs. We escaped by saying we'd already enlisted, and we're celebrating our last day as civilians. That's why we were singing."

"Holyhead is more than a few miles away." Jane pointed out with an arched eyebrow.

"That it is. The place was lousy with servicemen trying to rope others into serving. It was like they passed the bill and all these Tommies showed up everywhere. They're like mushrooms that pop up after a storm. Instead of rain, it was a storm of words. The thing is, there's no choice about it."

"What do you mean?" Meara was unfamiliar with the term *conscript*, but apparently, it had a great deal to do with Ronan and Billy's hasty retreat. "These people aren't your parents or your priest. How can they force you to do anything?"

Ronan shook his head and pointed to himself. "They call me country green. Even I know the government can do whatever it pleases. It's not all that different from feudal times. The Irish are Britain's serfs."

"Excuse me?" Meara knew her grasp on politics was non-existent. It was always the men who got all bothered about such things. The women were too busy trying to accomplish the basics that allowed life to go on while the men argued about this and that.

"An Irishman might be tending his land when a British soldier appears and demands he shine his shoes."

That sounded doubtful. Her eyes rolled upward on their own. "Did this ever happen?"

"Martin said it happened to a friend of his cousin."

Jane sniffed. "It's one of those friend of a friend stories. You might as well insert traveler for British soldier and get the same result. Moral outrage, an excuse to run out and do something stupid."

Ronan pressed his lips together and folded his arms. "I know it's true. We're lucky to have escaped when we did."

"Sounds like it's past time for leaving," Meara concluded. "The real question is, did you find out much about the islands?"

Whatever Billy and Rosemary had been discussing in heated whispers was over. Rosemary glowered and had one hand on her skirt, which she flicked now and then. It reminded Meara of a cat when it watched a bird. It might seem peaceful and content, but the tail told a different story.

Billy had his arm slung around Rosemary's shoulders, obviously believing the peaceful and contented façade, while he told them, "Ah, that didn't go as planned. By the time we found the man, he was well into his cups. Told me he is moving his business farther north and with the guard going up, it would mean that material, spices, and some firearms would be harder to get. He doesn't even know the name of the islands he visited. He just knows them by their shorelines."

Ronan coughed, earning a glare and a tart question from Billy. "Got something to add?"

"The man was playing you. That not knowing the name of an island was piffle."

Billy dropped the casual arm he had placed around Rosemary, and his hands fisted. "Are you calling me stupid?"

"No, but you're missing the obvious. You're a waterman. If you're asking someone who makes his living smuggling where he visits, he can only think of two things. Either, you're determined to steal his business or turn him over to the magistrate."

"I guess I never thought of it that way. You have a point." They shook hands, then clapped each other's shoulders. Before they could do an impromptu friendship jig, Meara broke in.

"We need to get loaded and leave. It would be a shame to get captured after all your creative singing."

"I imagine those who round up able-bodied men had their eyes on you." Jane stood, giving Ronan a mischievous look as she sashayed to the wagon.

"It is because we're strong and young."

"Possibly," Jane agreed. She checked the harness on Hercules. He'd been waiting for over an hour to start the trip. "More likely, they'd grab you two because you were singing Irish drinking songs. Many a British soldier regard the Irish as little more than cannon fodder."

"That, I know. We were singing British songs when we were in town. We're not stupid."

Jane said nothing and continued to check the harness. It looked like it was up to Meara to get everyone going. "Tie Wind Racer to the wagon. The pace Hercules will set will be close to a rest for her. We've lost time waiting on you two." What she didn't add was that they hadn't brought the name of any islands back. If only she could hear the *A* island names she might have a clue. It could just be a feeling, but it would be more than she currently had. "Did anyone follow you?"

Ronan twisted to glance at Billy who shrugged. Meara pressed her lips together knowing the answer. They hadn't paid attention, too busy singing their heads off. It would be easy for someone to follow two individuals singing loudly on a slow-moving horse. *Past time to be gone.* The words kept sounding in her head like a mantra. Whatever the Tower card represented was heading right at them.

She pulled a twig out of the fire and lit the wagon lanterns. It would be smarter to travel without them, but even with a horse as slow as Hercules, they could still find themselves headed over a cliff or into a bog. Most animals had a sixth sense about that sort of thing. Hercules had already proven he didn't by running into Dublin Bay. They'd have to take a chance with the lanterns.

She caught Billy's attention, even though he had his arm wrapped around Rosemary again. Meara angled her arm in the direction of the fire. "Kill it. Tamp it out well."

Aware there would be no more time for canoodling, Rosemary climbed into the wagon with a put-out huff. She'd need to get over that. It would have served them all well if the two of them hadn't formed an attraction for one another. She could imagine Billy on watch thinking about his sweetheart and not about the noise in the bushes.

Jane climbed up on the bench seat and reached for the reins. "Climb aboard or be left behind."

Knowing Jane, Meara made haste and scampered onto the seat. Even if they traveled all night, they wouldn't make much distance. "How far do you think Scotland is?"

"A couple of days at the most. Remember, I know as much about the country as you do."

"Which is nothing," Meara stated the obvious. All they had to do was grab the horn, then hotfoot it to England. She actually had an idea where it might be in England. Nothing magical. Logic determined the most probable place.

TWO WEEKS LATER they still hadn't reached Scotland. A deep hole broke a wheel and set Billy off to find a wheelwright to repair it. While they waited, Meara caved to Jane's plan to make the wagon into a salvation show. They had purchased paint more than a month ago but never used it. Painting the outside black seemed more of an insult to the wagon than the previous paint job. They discussed what to paint on it.

"I think it should say *Brother Jeremiah's Salvation Wagon*," Jane concluded with a nod. "The simpler the better. We can add stuff later on if we need to."

In Meara's experience, religion was more about scaring people. "How about repent or face eternity in a flaming lake of fire?"

"And," Rosemary's eyes twinkled as she spoke, "we could paint tiny little devils with pitchforks."

"Too wordy." Jane pointed at Meara. "We only have so much white paint. Most of the money went for the black paint. It is better to say little. That way, Brother Jerimiah is not tied down to anything, such as faith healing or speaking in tongues."

It would be awkward if someone brought their sick child to them for healing. "I understand." She held one finger up and glanced at Rosemary. "We're not going to paint little devils, either. I may not have a lot of experience on the outside, but I do know people tend to think if you mention the devil enough or draw pictures of him, then you must be working for him. I assume a simple cross would be a nice touch."

"Good one." Jane tapped her finger on her cheek. "This will work out well. With the war on, people will be anxious and wanting some religious reassurance. It should work with the border guards, too."

It sounded good in theory. "Couldn't the Germans easily do the same thing?"

The question silenced Jane, who appeared to mull it over. After a minute, she shook her head. "I doubt it. It would draw attention when that is the last thing they want. They'd also have to hold services."

"Who do you think can pull this off?" There had been no question in Meara's mind that a man should be the minister. No one had ever heard of a female priest, which was a shame. A good third of the visiting priests at the convent had misquoted scripture or failed to put together a good homily. Normally, the older sisters took turns directing the service when no priest was available. Most were as capable or better than the priests. Still, it would have to be a man, especially with a name like Brother Jeremiah.

"Ronan." Jane gave a little nod as if it were a fact.

"Why him? He's the youngest of the group." Meara announced what everyone already knew.

"Exactly. As travelers, we learned fast that the younger, attractive traveler received more business than his older counterpart. Grandmother Biddy would be the exception." Jane shrugged. "Her ability to see into the future was legendary. As for Ronan, he is the best looking one of the two."

"What?" Rosemary's head snapped up. "It's obvious Billy is the better-looking one."

Meara chose to say nothing, curious to see how Jane would handle an outraged girlfriend.

"No doubt you think he is handsome, and he is." Jane popped up one finger. "Does he have that innocence? A purity that you'd expect from a man of God?"

Rosemary huffed and drooped a bit, which appeared to be answer enough. Billy's rough and ready charm did not equate to godly.

"Have you asked Ronan?"

"I did. I explained what would be needed of him. He felt he could do it. My only question is should we continue to masquerade as boys or present ourselves as women? I thought one of you could be a sister, but three women would be too much."

Rosemary perked up, obviously over Billy not being chosen as a pretend prophet. "Any woman would be one too many."

"Why is that?" Jane asked, but Meara was equally curious.

"How many women have we seen traipsing across Wales since we've been here?"

"Not one," Jane answered first.

There had been a few, but always close to home and on their way home. It took Meara a while to come up with someone specific. "What about the woman we saw yesterday looking for her lost pig?"

Rosemary shot her a sympathetic smile. "She was looking for a lost pig, which might mean the difference between her family eating this winter or not. I doubt she was far from her own farm. That isn't traveling. Can you remember any of the women or girls of Hogstead traveling?"

Walking to the village market probably didn't count. "You told me Adelaide went to the city to find a husband."

"That's the rich. They don't count. No one will mistake Brother Jeremiah for a rich man."

"If he does it right, he could be richer," Jane declared with a wink. "Lots of emotion gets them every time. A testimonial works, too."

By the time Billy arrived back with the wheel, they decided to keep up the masquerade unless one of them needed to become a woman to be part of the audience. After hearing all the different ways to convince people they were in dire need of redemption and to chuck a few coins into the plate, Meara was fairly convinced no traveling minister was on the level. "Isn't this wrong?"

"Depends," Billy hoisted up the wheel on one shoulder. "Is it wrong to reflect on the state of your soul?"

She pursed her lips. She hadn't been thinking much about her soul. Keeping her body alive took most of the effort, leaving no time for contemplation. The only contemplation she wanted was to figure out on which island she needed to be. "The taking money for it."

"Every church, every minister, every priest, even the Pope takes money for services rendered. Why should we be any different?"

The subject baffled her since she'd never considered it before. It kept her busy trying to decide between what a priest did compared to what they would do. There was some grunting as Billy placed the new wheel back on the axle and tightened it. Rosemary crowded him while he worked as if she could hardly bear to be without him.

"A priest can forgive your sins." She knew Ronan in his religious attire would have no right forgiving sins.

"That's what you think!" Billy yelled from his prone position under the wagon. "I've met a few folks of different religions working the docks. Those I met didn't need no priests to forgive their sins. Another one didn't even believe in sin. The Protestants have done away with the priests and confession. Good riddance, I say. Tired of making up sins for confession."

His comment gathered a few chuckles since no one had any doubt that Billy would come by a sin or three the old-fashioned way by actually committing them. Meara wrinkled her nose as she tried to be serious in her reply. "It must be a hardship for you having to come up with a new sin every week."

"Good thing we only attend on Christmas and Easter. I'd count myself fashed if I had to do that every week."

"You lucked out then. As far as the Protestants deciding who can forgive sins, the sisters always said they'd burn in hell, too."

Billy snorted, then wiggled out from underneath the wagon. He refused the hand Rosemary held out for him and got to his feet under his own power. "The Protestants say the same about the Catholics. The Anglicans, of course, say they're both confused. If Ronan does it right, and I think he will, he can give hope back to people exhausted by war."

"Hope might be worth a few pence, I'll give you that." It would be nice if she could purchase some. Every morning was a blessing with more than a handful of times when she closed her eyes and did not expect to see another dawn.

Chapter Fifteen

THE SUMMER SUN dipped toward the horizon but still shed enough light for folks to find their way to the Brother Jeremiah's Salvation Wagon. Both Billy and Ronan had gone into the village to announce the evening service. They didn't call it a church service or even an evangelism meeting. In a truly inspired move, Billy insisted it would be a prayer service for all the men fighting and those about to go. It would make folks appear hard-hearted if they didn't attend.

Rosemary and Jane, attired in their boy togs, waited to see if they would be helpers or part of the audience. After much debate, they decided the one item Brother Jeremiah needed to be respectable was his elderly mother traveling with him. A good son would look after his mother. No one expected a man to cook his own meal or launder his own clothes, even though many did. Brother Jeremiah's mother would handle those less than spiritual items.

The padding Jane insisted on for Meara's disguise weighed her down and made free movement slow and difficult, which was part of the plan. People would think better of Brother Jeremiah for taking care of his elderly parent, Jane assured her, as she rubbed ash into Meara's hair to make it gray. Her lips pursed as she considered the proposed plan. Would no one consider it cruel to drag an elderly woman across an unsafe war-ravaged countryside?

When she asked, both Jane and Rosemary chuckled and arched their eyebrows. Her traveler friend adjusted the shawl over Meara's hair and wrapped it around her throat. "Remember. Don't come out until it is dark. Shadows make it hard to get a good look at your face. Keep your face down as befits a humble woman."

The mirror reflected back a shiny faced woman who bore no resemblance to Ronan at all. Keeping her face down would be her best bet. Not showing up would be even better. Still, she had a role to play. Technically, she was a shill, a person who came out and talked about all the wonderful things Ronan had done. After a much-spirited discussion, the plan of having a person from a nearby village show up and praise Ronan in his role as Brother Jeremiah was not considered workable since the current villagers might know someone in the next village or even have relatives there. Since no one knew Brother Jeremiah, no one would know his mother.

Then it came to Brother's backstory. They decided for him to have an Irish father who died young, but not too young. He needed to have been around long enough to impress a lilt in Jeremiah's speech.

Some muted conversation came from the wagon where Billy and Ronan were getting dressed. There had been enough plain black cloth to make Billy more of a smock than an actual shirt. Even though she had lived most of her life in a Roman Catholic convent, most of Britain's citizens were members of the Church of England. That might prove to be an issue. She rapped on the closed wagon door.

It opened a few inches, and Billy stuck his face into the opening. "What?"

"Is Brother Jeremiah going to be Church of England?"

Billy withdrew his head leaving the door ajar. Sounds of a spirited conversation drifted out. There were several *no's, why not?* and *that won't work* before Billy came back to the door.

"You brought up a good point. After talking it over with the good minister, we decided not to mention it."

"People will want to know. They'll want to know under whose authority are you out on the road, preaching the gospel."

Billy's heavy sigh announced how he felt about the situation. Another spirited discussion ensued. The door swung all the way open, and Ronan stepped out in his pseudo clerical tunic and cleared his throat and held out his hands as if giving a blessing. "I serve mankind, but never under any man. I serve the creator most of all."

He dropped his hands and winked. "I think that should suit. Don't you?"

"Don't know." Billy shook his head. "You forgot to mention God. They might think you're a druid referring to a creator. It's just a jump and a skip to the Lord of the Forest."

"Don't go changing it," Rosemary spoke as she exited from her hiding place in the bushes. "I have relatives in Wales, and there are plenty of Druids still about. Even better, the Welsh like to think of themselves as their own people. They are not Britain's puppet. They'd like it better if you weren't Church of England. Most curates have their own living, even if it is a tiny village chapel. Not sure you'd find a cleric roaming the roads. Maybe you could call yourself the John the Baptist of the Welsh Byways."

"No! No more names. I'll do well to answer to Jeremiah."

Billy laughed, wiggled his eyebrows, and pointed back to himself. "My sole purpose is to nudge the good brother to let him know when people are actually addressing him. We had some issues back in the village. A few people called him Jeremiah. Instead of answering, he had a blank stare. I had to explain that he was deep in contemplation on spiritual matters and managed to elbow him as I did so."

Ronan snorted, then lifted his hand to his ribcage. "I'd be surprised if I don't have a bruise tomorrow." He narrowed his eyes in Billy's direction. "I almost think you enjoyed it."

"Ah. There was no *almost*. I did." He chuckled and tried to slap Ronan on the back. Sensing the direction the hand might take, the would-be cleric danced out of the way. The sounds of conversation, other than their own, and footsteps, sent the five of them to their various spots. Meara lifted the shawl to cover her head while Rosemary and Jane faded back into the trees. It was time for the show to start.

Ronan, looking crisp and ministerial in his black tunic, greeted the elderly couple first to appear with a wide smile and an outstretched hand. "Welcome! Welcome! I assume you kind-hearted have come to pray for our boys protecting our shores."

The woman bobbed her head, but the man spoke as he took Ronan's hand. "It's the least we can do with me being too old to fight. Name's Evan Sears. This is my wife, Mary."

"Pleased to meet you." Ronan gave the man's hand a hearty pump. "I'm…"

Before he could say anything, Billy waded into the conversation with a loud voice. "Brother Jeremiah, the people know you from our earlier walkthrough the village."

"Of course they do." He shot Billy a look, allowing his aggravation to show for the briefest second before continuing. "I was just trying to be polite."

Rather than prolonging the conversation, which would cause people to speculate, Billy strolled over to the cut logs. "We have some makeshift chairs. Not as nice as your local church, I'm sure." He upturned a few foot-high slices for the couple. "I like to think of this…" He gestured to the surrounding trees. "…as God's cathedral."

The couple murmured agreement before taking their seats. They dropped into low conversation as Ronan and Billy moved on to greet the next group of arrivals. Meara stood perfectly still in the shadow of the bush watching and speculating on the guests as they arrived.

The older couple probably had a son or even a nephew or grandson in the service. Some of the young women who showed up in their best dresses with suspiciously red lips and cheeks they must have pinched mercilessly on their way did not come for prayer, unless they were praying for a husband. The war gobbled up the marriageable young men and often didn't spit them back. When it did, they weren't necessarily the same men who left full of determination and valor, determined to push back the dirty invader. Even an itinerant minister would look good to them.

It was hard to see her cousin as the young women might do. Getting past the blood connection, she did notice his broad shoulders and height. The last year had aged him more than the usual passage of time. Even though his eyes still sparkled when he smiled, his expression could be guarded. The mystery behind the shadows would only intrigue the females. If she'd learned one thing since leaving the convent, it was women were tantalized by the unknown and often the ungovernable. Too late, they discovered what they thought was mystery was pure meanness just packed down hard, usually after they swore to honor and obey for the rest of their lives.

Women really were the braver sex when you considered they put their future and wellbeing in a man's hand, not knowing if he'd treat her well. Did those girls even have a clue? Even if he did, a complicated childbirth could kill her in the prime of life.

Her hand went up and rubbed the bridge of her nose. Not so long ago, she was just like them. The memory of the sweet kiss Braeden and she had shared still lingered. The unexpected pull of attraction to a handsome face or a deep voice she understood. What she didn't comprehend was the average female's willingness to put her life into the keeping of another. Even though Braeden professed his love and asked her to wait for him, she had her doubts. In the end, it didn't matter since Adelaide had burned down Eleanor's house with the pillow shapes under the bedcovers they mistook for the occupants. It was then she gave up her promise to wait. If it was meant to be, it would be, Eleanor had assured her. Distance couldn't outpace fate.

Her eyelids fluttered closed as she tried to recall Braeden's face. All the Douglas brothers were handsome, tall, and had thick, brown hair. That, she could recall. What made him any different from the dozens of similarly appointed young men? The image of his face went in and out of focus rather like using a spyglass—a faulty one. Could she really not remember him? The possibility had her digging her fingernails into the palms of her hands. Was she doomed to forget everyone who ever loved her?

"He's starting." A voice hissed close to Meara forcing her to open her eyes. Jane had scooted up close to her, while more than a dozen people, which was about a dozen more than she expected, had arrived. As far as she knew, he had no sermon planned. "What is he going to say? He didn't write anything down."

"Think." Jane held up a finger. "He's Irish. The Irish have a legacy of being the best oral storytellers. I told him to be emphatic. Quote a few scriptures and end up with God enjoys a generous giver."

It seemed a little self-serving to bring God into the giving part, but most ministers did. While they didn't expect to linger here long, being run out of town was not the way she wanted to leave. Ronan cleared his throat, then scampered to stand on the driver's bench. It put him higher than those surrounding him. No worries about Hercules taking off since Billy had already hobbled the two horses and put them out to graze in the meadow.

Ronan's hands went up for attention. "Let us pray." The surrounding heads bowed, but Jane and Meara had theirs upright, earning a significant look. It wouldn't do to look like they weren't praying or totally on board with whatever Brother Jeremiah might say. He could talk about corn, and they'd need to hang onto every word. They bowed their heads and closed their eyes just in time to hear the start of the prayer.

"Father God, in the book of Jeremiah, you remind us you have plans for each one of our lives. Your plans are not for evil, but for good. They are to prosper us and give us hope and a future. Let us remember this in the dark time of war. When doubt creeps in, we will be safe, cared for, and triumphant!"

He said the last word on a major bellow that earned him a few *Amens*. He waited until the crowd quieted down before continuing.

"We come together tonight to pray for those who need your help the most. We ask that you bless each and every soldier, every son, every husband, every grandson, every sweetheart. Send these good wishes to our boys tonight to cheer them and give them the strength to go on. In the name of Jesus Christ, Amen!"

Someone yelled, "Hear, hear!"

Jane leaned closer, her mouth near Meara's hair. "That was a good one. He got the people on his side immediately by speaking of hope."

Meara could see that. It made her wonder why all she heard inside the convent walls were threats of eternal punishment and a lake of fire. The crowd turned avid faces toward Ronan as the evening light started to fade. Lanterns Billy had lit cast a glow on Ronan and threw a shadow out behind him so long that it made him into a giant.

"Love is the answer," Ronan declared, tapping his fist against his chest. "Not hate, not despair. We have to be strong for our young men. Sometimes, that means sacrifice. I know many of you have given up foodstuffs, especially meat so our soldiers can go to bed with a full stomach."

There was some murmuring at that. It was hard to say if it was good or bad, probably mixed. Some of them were willing to sacrifice and others were not fans. He went on to talk about the various sacrifices families had made. They were all imaginary, and all hailed from Ireland. He held up a hand as if giving testimony. "I know what sacrifice is. I wanted to fight in the great war, to turn back the Hun who wants to destroy not only our land but our way of life. As much as I wanted to go, I couldn't because I am the only son of my very precious mother."

That was her cue. Meara shuffled out of the shadows keeping her head down and wondering if she should say something. In her limited experience, mothers always had a lot to say. She tried to keep her voice old sounding by making it tremble. "That's my boy! Always a good one. As much as he wanted to go, he realized the right thing would be to take care of me." Getting into her role, she stopped and swayed on her feet. "He asked me what he could do to help out during this terrible war. As his mother, I had an answer." She held up one finger and waited for the murmuring to die down.

One boozy voice shouted, "Tell us!"

She was pretty sure it was Billy giving her a cue. Even if it wasn't, it worked just the same. "I told him the people need hope. It has been a long war, and sometimes we forget there is hope. Let us not forget that God is on our side. What chance do the Germans have?"

As she was speaking, a shivery cold feeling came over her, washing her mind clean of anything else she might say. It was here. She could feel the coldness down to her bones, along with a heaviness that weighed on her.

Her various charms and spells made her invisible to those who sought her. Could they hear her? If they heard her speaking where no one stood, it would be obvious someone was there. One step back brought her into the sheltering shadows where she peered at the crowd. Maybe it was one of them. The feeling came recently so she doubted that. If Thaddeus, the gnome, was there, he might be able to point out the culprit.

When they had returned to pick him up, he introduced them to Marlene, his sweetheart. Gnomes are homebodies who treasured their family and land ties. As much as she valued his superhuman strength, it didn't seem fair to take him away from all he loved. It wasn't his fight. She assured him that nature would find a way to replace him. Nature must be busy since no paranormal creatures had crossed their path recently. Maybe she needed to put out a psychic call for help.

Her gaze traveled over the assembled crowd. The older couple leaned against each other as they dozed. The young women were busy licking their lips and regarding Ronan with huge, cow eyes. This caused some ire on the part of three young men standing nearby. If trouble came, it would probably come from that area. Still, it wasn't them. The best they would do is hurl insults and when drunk enough, slam a fist into a resistant face. Even if the three of them were combined, it would not total the deep soulless evil she felt. It was ancient and fed on despair and anger. Perhaps it even birthed the negative emotions. She needed to leave. *Flee.* Go anywhere but here. Her eyes sought after the shadowy being without success while toes tensed, ready to run.

What if she did run? Whatever it was would stay with the others, follow them, and Lord knows what else. She couldn't leave her friends to that, especially considering they were here because of her. They chose danger over safety and routine.

The warmth of another body jostled her. What if? She turned her head slowly, muscles tensed, ready to jump away if needed. The limited light lined Jane's familiar silhouette. She waved a hand in the direction of the small crowd. "Will you look at them? Simpering. Ridiculous. That blonde floozie has pulled down the neckline on her blouse."

"Disgraceful." Meara murmured the agreement but refused to glance over. What if she saw him? Even though she'd never truly seen her pursuer, only his minions, she considered his energy masculine. After all, it was men who resorted to fisticuffs and declared war on one another, not women. Jane grabbed her shoulder and shook it.

"You haven't even looked. Ronan is even smiling at her."

Maybe she'd have to rethink her belief about women not being prone to violence if Jane was involved. "Ronan is supposed to be all loving. Remember, you decided that would work better than the hell and damnation approach."

Her remark resulted in Jane dropping her hand and grumbling. "I hate it when something I plan works out." She shook her head and continued before Meara could comment on the odd statement. "Ronan wouldn't have been able to pull off the judgmental tone or the half-crazy eyes. I knew he could do a love and hope message because it isn't that far of a stretch from where he is now."

"True." This time she turned her head the tiniest little bit and cut her eyes to the right. The blonde had pushed her top down. Any lower and she might as well not be wearing a blouse. The presence she had felt wasn't there. Or was it? She stilled the warring emotions inside of her, each claiming dominance. Glee filled her since the danger conveniently left. *Don't get too excited*, another part of her whispered. He has only changed position to find you better. The second voice she liked less. Unfortunately, it made more sense.

Before Brother Jeremiah retired for prayer and contemplation, Billy appeared in the crowd with a basket. "Remember, a Brother is worthy of his wages."

Meara grimaced at Billy paraphrasing scripture. "It's *a Workman is worthy of his wages.*"

Jane's eyebrows lifted. "Picky. People misquote scripture all the time. Many can't read, and others don't even own a Bible. The important thing is people are actually putting stuff in the basket. They not only stayed through the sermon but also brought something along to give. Oh no! Not that!"

The disgusted tone told Meara whatever it was would not be life-threatening. A side glance revealed the blonde, who caused so much anger in her friend, removing her necklace and putting it in the basket. She made a point of talking to Billy. "What do you think she is saying?"

"Her name and direction. She isn't the first one who has played this game. Woman drops jewelry into the basket probably with some mumbled sentiment about it belonging to her dead grandfather. The minister naturally returns it, which makes him look good in the villagers' eyes. That's all good. Maybe we will have a second meeting or even a third."

The village was a poor one, with war rationing making some of the basics even harder to get. It would be strange to receive coin when people had very little to give. One visitor clapped, then two others joined in, waking the sleeping elderly couple. They blinked a couple of times, stood up slowly, and then the woman reached into her bag and pulled out a jar of something. Instead of presenting it to Billy as he circled with the basket, she looked back to where Meara stood as if she knew. Somehow, she could see past the disguise and deep into Meara's heart.

Jane cheerfully chattered on about potential meetings while a strange peace settled around Meara and a sudden, inexplicable knowing. "We won't be staying, even the night. It's time to go, and I know our destination."

Her revelation had Jane's mouth hanging open, but only for a second. "What did you say?"

Ignoring Jane, she kept her gaze on the elderly woman who smiled and walked in Meara's direction. Feeling compelled, she walked forward and held out her hand for the jar, which she knew instinctively was meant for her.

With twinkling eyes, the woman handed the jar over. "I despair at times of living to see an end to this horrid war, but then I felt a disturbance in the universe. The light was gathering to make its final resistance. Too many think the old ways have vanished and along with them, the magic that accompanied it. I wanted to do my part, so I made this for you."

The smooth glass jar felt surprisingly heavy in her hand. "Thank you. It is very kind of you. Is it something you eat?"

"Only if you want to forget all you know. There are times I feel that way." She shook her head and gave a sad smile. "Shake it on the ground as you leave, and all will forget you. Shake it. Don't use your hand. It causes forgetfulness and confusion. Use it sparingly since you will need it on your journey."

"I don't know how to thank you." Thaddeus was right. Help would come when she needed it. "Will it shield us from all?"

"That, I do not know. As for thanking me," she said, placing a delicate, papery skinned hand on Meara's cheek, "succeed with your mission. Allow people to experience peace, kindness, and simple joy again. That's all I ask."

"I'll do my best." The sisters had hammered into her to never lie. Could she relieve some of the woman's fears with a simple yes?

"You're more powerful than you might expect. There are many who have kept the old ways. We will hold you up with intentions and spells to protect and guide. You are never alone, even when it seems like you are."

A heavy sigh escaped her lips. "I'm learning that. Please thank everyone for me."

The woman dropped her hand and stepped back. "You'll succeed since your heart is as pure as any I've touched. Be strong, daughter of Fulmen and Sorcha."

The elderly man appeared by the woman's side and held out his bent arm. She took it, and the two of them turned and ambled off into the darkness. She watched them, feeling the momentary break from fear vanishing with them. "We need to leave now. You get Rosemary. I'll notify the boys."

Chapter Sixteen

T HE EARLY MORNING light reflected off the worn Tarot cards, shiny with age. Snoring came from underneath and inside the wagon. Either Rosemary or Jane had fallen so heavy into a slumber that she snored, maybe both. Meara couldn't sleep so she agreed to stand watch. She shuffled the cards as she set the intention for the day. What did she need to know?

Her fingers danced across the cards until she felt the right one and turned it over. *Death*. The skeleton reaper stood beside a skeleton horse holding his scythe. Grandmother Biddy told her that her clients were so disturbed when they drew the Death card that they closed themselves off from hearing what she had to say. The eyeless skull did have an uneasy effect even though she knew it meant change or transformation as opposed to actual death. Some things were ending. Others beginning. That's all. It wasn't exactly a wealth of information. The pendulum might help. A few simple *yes* and *no* questions might serve.

She untangled the pendulum from her various charms. Since she'd tumbled into the water twice, she decided if she wanted to keep something safe, it needed to be tied to her body in some fashion. This might hold true for the horn, too.

The pendulum swung freely until she stilled it with her other hand. Remembering Grandmother Biddy's instructions, she placed her elbow against the wooden driver's seat. Too often, people used a pendulum not for guidance but for confirmation on what they wanted to do. The mind was a powerful tool and could influence even the pendulum. Also, intention was important. Inhaling, she cleared her mind of any lingering fears or doubts. "Will we make our way to Scotland?"

Instead of swinging in a circle for *yes* or in a straight line for *no*, it trembled as if constrained, unable to say. If turning the Death card hadn't rattled her enough, she now had a pendulum that refused to answer. It could have been the way she worded the question. Too many options make it hard for a yes and no answer. She'd try it again.

"Will I make it to Scotland?"

The pendulum swung immediately into a slow circle. It had no issues with answering that question. What was different? What had she said before? *We.* She had said *we.* Did that mean one of them wouldn't make it to Scotland? Her hand tightened around the pendulum not wanting to go through her companions to see who might not make it.

Knowledge was power you could use to change your future. Grandmother Biddy emphasized this when it came to the Tarot. With information, you could change the outcome or at the very least be aware of it. All she needed to do was watch over her friends to make sure they stayed safe. Currently, the only thing endangering them was whatever was following them.

She uncurled her fingers to reveal the pendulum. She held it up and took a deep breath. "Is the entity that wants the horn still following us?"

The pendulum made a strong circle. "Damn."

Jane stuck her head out the pass-through window behind the driver seat. "That's something I never thought I'd hear—a nun cursing."

"You know I'm not a nun."

"That I do. Thought I might have a little fun at your expense. You've been so dull lately."

Dull. Was that what she was? "Determined. We have a mission here. It has already proven dangerous."

A muffled complaint at the noise had Jane hoisting herself through the window and closing the shutters behind her. "Let's walk."

Jane dropped to the ground, and Meara followed. When they were a few yards away, the sounds of a chuckling stream reached them. By an unspoken agreement, they both headed toward the water. Once they arrived, Jane sat down on a large flat stone worn smooth by time. Meara sat beside her. Birds called overhead, completing the tranquil scene.

"Life is dangerous, though it may have been less so in the convent. I consider myself lucky to be as old as I am. Plenty of children die from disease. I had a cousin drown, which was why my father thought it so important to learn how to swim. Many more women die in childbirth. Then, there are the accidents. Riding, farming, even just horsing around could kill you. Danger is all around us. Plenty of men in the war are dying due to the Huns' greed. My uncle was lynched for a crime he didn't commit. So, what is a little danger? At least we're doing good as opposed to something stupid. My cousin who drowned fell off a wagon at a river crossing. He was showing off for some of the children in a neighboring wagon."

"Never thought of it that way." Meara shrugged her shoulders. "There seems to be a lot of ways to die."

"There are." Jane gave a solemn nod. "It's best to go with doing what is right. That way you have your honor. If we didn't try, we'd live with the regrets."

"I suppose." No need to mention there seemed to be no other way for her. It hadn't been her intention to head out to Ireland, until she discovered she had relatives. That desire faded a little when she found she liked living with Eleanor and going about their simple tasks. When Braeden asked her to wait for him, that gave her even more motivation to stay. Adelaide wasn't having any of it. It was certain she was a vengeful female, but maybe she was also a tool of fate, getting Meara to go where she was needed. Still, nothing was easy or maybe it *was*. She had nothing to compare it to, to know. "How do you think the mission has gone?"

"Outside of Ronan driving my wagon and horse into the drink, surprisingly well."

"Really?" The answer surprised her. "What about the fight with the blacksmith?"

"That could have been avoided if certain people hadn't been flirting. We had Thaddeus on our side, and it worked out okay. It hasn't been perfect, but when we need something in the worse way, we usually find it somewhere."

They had found themselves in various scrapes, but always found their way out of them. "I have been looking at everything wrong. I was looking at the problems and not the solutions. You're right."

A branch snapped to their right, causing Meara to jump. "What was that?"

"A deer most likely. They have no reason to be quiet since there are no bears or wolves left to hunt them."

The answer didn't soothe her, especially knowing they were still followed. The sun had grown stronger and higher as they spoke, lighting up the forest with an early morning shimmer that was magical. It would be hard to believe there was any darkness in the stretch of woods. Still, it would be ignorant to take their safety for granted.

"We've been here long enough. Wake the others. We need to go."

Jane shook her head and stood. "I've got other business to attend to. You wake them yourself and see how happy they are at the possibility of more travel. Hercules needs to rest and relax. If we could train Wind Racer to the horse collar, it would give Hercules a break."

Too bad doing that never occurred to anyone while they'd taken their break in Holyhead. The boys had ridden Wind Racer back and forth to their dock jobs, so it wasn't like she'd had free time with the horse. Jane knew about driving a team and could have possibly done it, but she had a job, too. All this time they'd spent waiting to fool whoever followed them could have been spent preparing for eventualities. Most would have said they'd done exactly that by earning money. What she needed were real answers. Maybe her mother and father could guide her via dreams since they were often silent in the waking world.

Sometimes she wondered if she'd imagined it all. Every now and then someone would show up to help, which reassured her some. It would be so much better to have one of her parents giving clear instructions, even if it was only in her sleep. After all, they were the ones who buried the horn.

The campfire was burning when she returned. Billy squatted by it tending the battered teapot. No matter how much she wanted to go, no one would leave without their morning tea. The announcement to head out would be best served at breakfast along with their destination. The fact they were moving was a foregone conclusion. That was the point—to locate the horn pieces and save the world. The easy camaraderie they had fallen into had knitted them into an awkward family unit of sorts. They had a rough sort of democracy since Jane knocked Ronan out of his self-appointed *I'm the Man thus the Leader* role. Still, it was hard for her to be the leader and possibly harder for them to accept her as such. As far as she knew, she was the only one receiving psychic insights.

She greeted Billy. "Morning. Did we net any food contributions from Brother Jeremiah's sermon?"

"We did." He grinned and rubbed his hands together. "The Lord loves a cheerful giver."

"Never took you for a scripture quoter. Well, what did we get? Anything we could use for breakfast?"

"Got a loaf of bread, small jar of honey, and a tiny round of cheese, along with a few pence, and a locket whose owner made me repeat her name three times."

The locket. Jane had predicted that. "I imagine Brother Jeremiah was supposed to return it to the girl with the slipping blouse."

"My thoughts exactly. Leaving the way we did, I managed to catch up with that surly young trio of boys and managed to convince one of them to return the necklace."

His face looked untouched, which surprised her. "No black eyes, no bruises for your trouble?"

"Not for me. The three may have battled for the right to return the necklace to its grateful owner. They even acted impressed. Called Brother Jeremiah a true prophet."

"Shows what they know. A prophet predicts events. You can't go calling him a prophet until the events actually happen. Otherwise, he's just another man making stuff up."

"That's the kind of stuff I'd expect from Jane, not you." He stood. "I'll go get the bread. At least we'll have some toast with our tea."

Twenty minutes later, they were headed for the border. Ronan had crawled into the wagon to sleep more, complaining he was drained from his sermon. Without him, there would be no Brother Jeremiah traveling evangelism show so they allowed it. There wasn't all that much to do until they reached the border, which they must be getting near.

Intent on continuing her romance, Rosemary had changed into a dress and her dark hair was growing out in ringlets that made her look both innocent and cherubic. Since they hadn't expected to see too many people on the road, both Jane and Meara had a combination of women's blouses and men's trousers. They didn't have all that many clothes and none of the women were fond of binding their breasts down. They didn't until the situation demanded it. With the exception of Rosemary, none of the women wanted to wear the heavy skirt and petticoat, which made it hard to scamper into the wagon, ride astride, or just about anything else.

War kept the road empty. The routine creak of the wagon along with the dust it stirred up created a monotonous day that stretched on without end. At one point, her stomach growled, reminding her of its empty state. "I'm not sure how much farther it is to Scotland. My stomach is telling me it's time to eat now."

Jane, who was driving, wrinkled her nose. "Don't tell me we are going to have to plan everything around your stomach?"

"I didn't say that."

Before Jane could reply, Billy rode up on Wind Racer. "I'll go check to see if we are any closer."

He shot off, leaving dust floating in the air. If he would have asked, she would have told him it wasn't a good idea. Any magical protection depended on them staying together as a group. She had her own charms, and Aunt Erin had done a protection spell for each of them and the wagon. They all had silver protection rings except for Billy. Her eyes met Jane's who looked equally troubled. "Nothing good can come of it. I saw an owl this morning. I knew then something bad would happen."

A tightness gripped her chest and squeezed, making it hard to breathe. If she had asked the pendulum who wouldn't make to Scotland, then she could have warned Billy. "Can you speed up Hercules? Maybe we can catch him."

"I can try. That was as fast as I ever saw Wind Racer go though." She cracked the whip over Hercules's back. Instead of speeding up, the horse stopped in his tracks and threw a disgruntled look over one shoulder. "I should have known he'd act like that. I'll have to lead him."

Jane tossed the leads to Meara, then slipped off the wagon and jogged to the head of the horse. It took some coaxing to get him going again. Despite Jane jogging beside him and pulling on his cheek strap, he refused to go any faster.

In the distance, they heard some yelling and the report of a pistol. This couldn't be good. The gunshot must have been the secret to motivating Hercules because he surged into a trot, almost shaking Jane free. She let go and managed to climb back on the wagon. Still gasping, she took the reins. "I'm glad you didn't try to slow him down. Not sure we could get him started again."

"What do you think that was?"

"Could be hunters. Let's hope it was hunters."

They came around a curve in the road to discover soldiers in Scottish plaids holding Billy between them. Wind Racer was off to the side grazing, seemingly unaware of the distress of her owner. Fear clawed at Meara. "They have Billy. What should we do?"

"It depends. Let's find out what the doofus has done to upset the soldiers. It could be a little thing that an apology might smooth over. Do we have anything we might offer them?"

"I suspect they aren't hoping for a Tarot Reading."

"Whiskey would be better. Money, too."

"We have honey."

"It's better than nothing."

Another soldier stepped out and held up his hand. "Halt. State your business."

This was her time on stage. "Good morning, sir. We are on our way to the Isle of Arran to see my aunt. Times being what they are, it isn't safe for women on their own."

The soldier gestured to Jane and Meara. Rosemary, who had been walking, finally caught up with the wagon. She was gasping for air and was probably ready to give someone a good tongue lashing when she saw the soldier. "Oh, I guess we are at the border."

"You are at that. I was about to tell your friends that it isn't safe for lasses to be on the road alone. Especially in these perilous times."

Rosemary dimpled at the soldier. "Ohno, sir…"

Before she could say anything else, Jane did. "We're together, and I'm a fair shot with the rifle."

The man shook his hand, causing the ribbon in his cap to swing. "Sorry times with lasses using rifles. You'll need it because you will not make it to Arran in a day."

Rosemary had edged around the wagon and caught sight of Billy, who ceased struggling and managed a stoic expression. She screamed and launched herself at the soldiers, beating them with her balled up fists. "Let my Billy go! Do you hear me?"

The sound of the window opening behind her caused Meara to hiss. "Stay low. We can't afford to lose both of you."

The third soldier managed to subdue Rosemary, who was twisting and screaming like a scalded cat. "Let her go," Billy shouted. "I'll go with you if you let her go. I was looking for a bit of adventure and fighting the Huns should suit."

At his declaration, Rosemary went limp into the soldier's arms. Her lax limbs indicated a faint and the soldier must have thought so, too. Meara eased off her seat to gather her friend, who sprang into action as soon as the soldier released her.

She ran to Billy and covered his face with kisses. "You can't leave me. What will I do without you?"

"You'll get by. I'll be back. You can count on that. I'll find you. If nothing else, I'll go to Hogstead to look."

She held her hands to her heart. "You remembered. You were listening."

The soldier, who appeared to be in charge, announced, "Saddle up, son. You got a better send off than most."

Rosemary, Meara, and Jane watched Billy ride off between two soldiers until they could no longer see them. The guard cleared his throat. "You better get going to make it to safety before dark."

Where was safety? It hadn't been in Ireland for Billy and his da. It definitely hadn't been here.

Jane, ever resilient, answered for them. "We'll be on our way directly."

Chapter Seventeen

THE SOUND OF muted crying had served as a backdrop for their travels for the last two hours. Hercules walked even slower, if that were possible. The horse could have been just as reluctant to abandon his equine friend as they were to leave their human one. Ronan squeezed onto the bench after they'd been moving for a good hour or so. Whenever he tried to open the window previously, Jane would slap it shut, insisting it wasn't time.

Rosemary crying, Jane brooding, and Meara second-guessing her actions when it came to the pendulum was a painful interval. Fear kept her from knowing more. Maybe if she had pinpointed Billy as the one likely not to make it to Scotland, she could have done something. Even sent him back to Holyhead where his father was still keeping company with an especially amenable boarding house owner.

Jane nudged her, gaining her attention, and spoke. "It's fate. It was Billy's destiny to leave us now."

Fate. She didn't like the answer. "I didn't want him to leave."

"Do you think any of us did?"

Before she could answer, Ronan did, turning to look at both of them. "I could have stopped it." He slammed his balled fist into his other hand.

"How?" Jane lifted her eyebrows. "Would you fight the soldiers? Fire on them? Call them names? You'd end up going with Billy instead of with us. Fate decided before we even began to journey who would go all the way. There will be those who come, then go away, like Olio who helped us through Ireland."

Meara could see her point. "There was Thaddeus who helped when needed, then returned home when the call of the land exerted its pull."

"Aye." Ronan agreed. "It doesn't feel right. I should have done more."

"I feel the same." Meara agreed but was not ready to admit she'd known all would not make it. She chose to keep that information to herself. What kind of friend was she?

A voice sounded in her head. *There was nothing more you could do. Speaking of it would have only caused anguish but would have solved nothing.*

Her father, Fulmen, was back! She had so many questions for him. Why hadn't he spoke to her until now?

I tried, but it isn't always easy to reach through the veil. You were too concerned about others, and for a while, I felt you were no longer focused on the quest. As you draw closer to the second piece, I can help you more. I was the one who whispered the name Arran in your ear. Did you think you came up with it on your own?

She had but decided not to mention it. The fact her father was back buoyed her spirits. It didn't bring Billy back, but it gave them a better chance of accomplishing their mission.

Don't worry about that one. The war will be the making of him. You may not have thought it was his destiny to fight, but it was.

That helped ease her mind a little. It was hard to believe in things unseen and not done yet. When everything was done and over, she'd reflect back on this time with some nostalgia. All she could do now was have a stiff upper lip and soldier on like any other Brit. Everyone had their losses. Some greater than hers, and yet they kept going, as should she.

Unaware of the inner dialogue she was conducting with her father, Jane elbowed her. "Go in the wagon and see if you can't soothe your friend."

It hadn't escaped her notice that Jane had grabbed the reins of leadership when everyone fell apart with Billy's taking leave. She didn't begrudge the woman. After all, she had more experience with these matters and would know the appropriate reaction. Later, she'd try to pull the reins back. It might be hard since she never felt she truly had them. Occasionally, her companions listened to her and did what she asked. It could be they were going to do likewise if she asked or not. They could just be humoring her by being nice to the oddity who hears voices in her head. Doubt was chewing away at her. Later, when she felt stronger, she'd lead.

Before she reached Rosemary, she felt her father fade away without a goodbye. There was so much she didn't ask him. It could be like that. Someone from the other side would pop in, say a few words, then vanish just as fast. It was often hard to differentiate between what was real and what she imagined. No wonder she thought she came up with Arran on her own. At least, they were headed in the right direction.

A little light filtered through the window shutters, leaving the interior in a hazy twilight. Heart-wrenching sobs came from the huddled form of her friend. "Rosemary." It was difficult to walk a straight line with the lurching of the wagon. Meara grabbed onto the walls, made her way to her friend, and knelt down beside her. "Dear, I know it is hard."

The crying stopped as Rosemary raised her puffy face. "Hard? Do you have any clue what hard is? Have you ever loved anyone and had them ripped out of your arms?"

Had she ever loved anyone? It was the question she asked herself when Braeden declared his love and headed out for war. If love was the aching void she felt when someone was no longer there, she had loved plenty. There was Sister Gabriella who had helped her feel not so alone. Then, there was Eleanor who had found her after the bombing. She was even gradually rediscovering her parents and learning to accept their love. There were her relatives, Uncle Simon, Aunt Erin, and her numerous cousins, including Ronan. There were her friends Jane, Rosemary, and the recently departed Grandmother Biddy. And, there was Braeden. In hindsight, she could admit to an attraction that might have had the beginnings of love if given enough time.

Rosemary gave a small snort. "Nothing to say. I thought as much. It's always been you and your precious quest. See where it has gotten us." She threw her hands up as she bellowed. "Nowhere! Nothing!"

She reached out to pat her friend who slapped her hand away, declaring, "If I hadn't decided to follow you, none of this would have happened."

Everything she said was true. Meara didn't have any words to comfort. She understood Rosemary was hurting. Still, her friend had chosen to attack Meara in her grief. "I didn't make you come. You chose to, telling me there was nothing there for you in Hogstead."

"There wasn't anything. All the good men had been snapped up. All that was left was the lazy ones. Even they looked at me with a jaundiced eye after Adelaide's stories." She sniffed and wiped her eyes with her hand.

"You wanted adventure. You've had plenty of that and then some."

"I have." She gulped audibly. "No complaints there."

It hurt to see her normally cheerful friend so downcast. "You wouldn't have met Billy if you hadn't come."

"True." She sniffed again. "How do I know I will see him again?"

Fulmen told her that Billy would survive the war. He hadn't mentioned if he'd come back to Rosemary. As far as she could see, Rosemary had been a rather demanding sweetheart. "He'll do fine. My father told me. He explained this was Billy's destiny. Often, we think all these things happen randomly, such as the convent accidentally being bombed, but there *was* a reason for it."

Rosemary shot her fingers through her hair and moaned a little.

"So many sisters died."

It may not have been her best example to use. "Not all of them. Many escaped. I counted the graves. I kept my silence, allowing them to escape and start a new life, as I did. There were those who stayed in their cells and breathed in the smoke accepting that as their fate. Maybe there is some leeway with fate. We both know how clever Billy is. He'll find you. When this is all done you should go back to Hogstead so he'll know where to look."

Rosemary dropped her hands, reached for Meara's, and squeezed them as she babbled. "You're so right. That is exactly what I need to do. Let's get this quest done so the war can be over, and Billy can come back to me."

"Yes." She gave her friend's hands a hearty shake. "That is exactly what we will do." Somehow, she had soothed her friend's heartache. It felt like she was getting better at this friend business.

JANE CALLED A halt to their travels a few hours before sunset. They couldn't always be confident that they could find a good place to camp. There was plenty of common land scattered about, especially on the roadside, but get too close to a farm or home and they'd possibly get buckshot as a greeting or have the dogs set on them. Normally, sociable folks kept their doors closed and their guns loaded. They couldn't take chances. Leave it to a traveler to know a good camping spot. So far, they hadn't been chased away.

Jane and Meara gathered sticks and limbs for the fire while Ronan rubbed down Hercules. Due to her grief, no one asked Rosemary to help.

As they wandered far afield looking for firewood, Jane pointed to some wood in the distance. "That might work. Many people must stop here since all the twigs and limbs you'd normally find have been swept clean. How's Rosemary?"

"I told her my father told me Billy would make it through the war. She seems much better."

"Seems." Jane bent to pick up a couple of twigs.

It was obvious that Jane wasn't convinced of Rosemary's turna-round. "Why did you say *seems* like that in that nasal tone you use to indicate the upper class?"

"Wasn't aware I used that tone. Grief is a funny thing. I should know. Plenty of people have died in my clan. The shock is just the beginning. Rosemary might act like she has accepted it, but it is only an act. When we were fleeing the traveler's camp and I knew Grandmother Biddy had died, I knew in a factual way, but my heart kept saying this is a mistake. Grandmother Biddy told me herself that she was going to die, and we needed to be far away. It doesn't get any clearer than that. Still, I refused to believe. If I did, the pain would rip out my heart and leave it bleeding on the ground."

The bloody visual left Meara speechless for a few moments. "When did you accept her death?"

Jane picked up another stick. "Grab some of the dried moss if you can find any. As for acceptance, I think that is a day to day thing. Some mornings, I wake up, hear a bird sing sweetly or see a gorgeous butterfly, and I want to tell Grandmother Biddy, only to realize she isn't with me. Even at the campfire, I often turn to my left expecting her to be there and to need my helping arm to get up."

"I never realized." It did explain Jane's attitude that sometimes wobbled between somber and contemplative.

"You knew her for a couple of weeks. I knew her my entire life. Technically, I guess all travelers are related. Sometimes, I treasured her more than my own parents. When I felt different than the other girls, while my mother would tell me to be more like them, I could go to her. I miss her every day."

How could she be so dense not to see her friend's pain? "I see that now. I wish you would have shared it."

Jane's narrow shoulders went up in a shrug. "Not my way. You have enough to weigh you down. We all do."

"Billy didn't die. He just went away. Shouldn't that make it easier?"

"Was it easier for you when Braeden went away as opposed to him dying?"

It had been so sudden. She barely knew the man before he was pledging his love and in the next breath revealing his plans to leave for the army. Jane's question really made her search for an answer. "It's odd. When he first left, I was bemused, uncertain what to do. As time progressed, I became even more attached to him and set on staying in Hogstead to wait for him."

"You were falling for the Braeden you created in your mind."

"What do you mean?"

"It's a common thing." Jane stopped to pick up dried leaves and put them in her bag. "I think every female does it before they marry. They make the man they are going to marry into the most perfect man. He's more handsome than anyone else. Remember Rosemary being put out that Billy wasn't Brother Jeremiah because she couldn't accept Ronan as the better-looking one?"

"I guess it was a good thing since he left us so soon. We would have had to repaint the wagon." No need to mention, they both were equally as handsome in her eyes.

"All women do this. Grandmother Biddy calls this self-wooing. The man isn't doing the wooing. The woman is by telling herself how wonderful a very ordinary man is. Once they get married and she finds out he leaves his clothes everywhere, burps all the time, and gambles away any extra money they have, then it is too late. Rosemary will not be grieving the man who likes to drink, flirt, and get into the occasional fight. No, she'll be crying over the perfect man. It's a lot harder when you lose someone perfect."

"How is it different from someone dying?" Dying had to be worse than leaving.

"Depends." She sighed, plopped down on the ground, and patted the grass beside her. Meara took a seat before Jane continued.

"When you know someone, you accept them as they are. I knew Grandmother Biddy could be harsh sometimes. She didn't have time to pretty things up. I knew that. I loved her, still, in spite of that. When someone is as old as Grandmother Biddy you come to the realization she will die. The only reason she lived as long as she did was she waited for you. All the more reason we had to leave as we did. People would blame you for her dying. Grandmother Biddy was the only person who kept the tribe together. When we left, it would have been a battle for power. Still, I could accept she would die. It's harder just having someone leave. It feels like you should be able to do so much more."

"I know that feeling. When I saw the Death card I knew I would not like what change was coming." Jane's fingers wrapped around hers.

"We mortals generally hate change even if it is for our own good. Once we get used to something it changes again. There is nothing that remains the same." Jane scampered to her feet and pulled Meara up. "We better find some wood before night hits. When we get back, you can pull another card. It might be surprising to see what it says."

It wasn't something she was looking forward to, but she would. It was hard to be prepared for the known, but even harder for the unknown. Once they got the fire started and supper going, she would. Dinner tonight would be a soup of random foodstuffs they'd throw into the water with a pinch of salt and hope for the best. With any luck, there might be some barley left.

The cards were in her pocket. Meara had gotten into the habit of carrying all she might need on her person, in case she needed to take off. Besides her charms, pendulum, and cards, she had her knife. Next thing she needed to do was make a bag to carry the horn with her. There would come a time when she'd have to leave her friends. It would be best to be ready.

The sun was making its descent as Ronan started the fire and

Jane named the items they had left to make a soup. Rosemary was conspicuously absent, but Meara assumed her friend was napping after her shock. It would be the perfect time to get out the cards. She fingered the cards, trying to draw some energy from them. How many times had Grandmother Biddy used them? How many times had she told someone's fortune? There was a slight residual energy as she shuffled the cards, delaying pulling one for the daily outcome. Even though she had learned some of the basics about Tarot, she didn't feel qualified to make a spread. Instead, she plucked one card out.

Jane stopped cutting vegetables and approached her with a beet and knife still in her hand. "What did you draw?"

She turned it over slowly. The High Priestess.

"Ah." Jane murmured, "The intuition card. It's a reminder to use your psychic senses. Don't be so caught up in the physical world. What is your intuition telling you now?"

As if it was all that simple. She closed her eyes and cleared her mind and waited for a great truth to materialize. She saw the glitter of magic emanating from the wagon. Her eyelids popped open. "Something's wrong!"

Chapter Eighteen

IT WAS MORE than a feeling. A sense of certainty propelled Meara to the wagon. The sound of running feet meant the others were following. *No.* They shouldn't. She whirled around and held up her hands to hold them away. "Stay back. It isn't safe."

Jane stumbled to a stop with a look of surprise while Ronan kept coming. *Obstinate male.* Meara managed to snag his arm before he pulled open the wagon door. Even drawing close to it had him stumbling back with a confused look on his face. He blinked a few times, then stared back at her. It was what she feared. She was too late.

"Nature Spirits, Mother, Father, protect me." She said the words as a type of prayer as she swung open the door. A lit lantern illuminated the interior. Rosemary sat holding out her hands in front of her, examining them. Meara allowed herself one long relieved breath. Something pushed at her as it squeezed past her. A feeling of tiny needles pricking her skin came over her and then it was gone. A slight confusion about her intentions made her wonder why she was standing on the wagon step, peering in.

Rosemary turned her head in her direction and smiled. "Who are you?"

An empty jar sat beside her friend. Meara wondered what was in it. She shook her head, trying to clear it, knowing there was something she needed to be doing. Finally, she leaned forward, picked up the jar, and sniffed it. Mint, a trace of cloves, pepper, and a few other things she couldn't discern. The memory of an elderly lady handing it to her and reminding her to be careful because if it touched your skin you would forget. Her confusion dropped away as the realization of what happened sunk into her consciousness.

"Rosemary!" She bolted up the steps and into the wagon, grabbing her friend by the shoulders and shaking her. "What have you done?'

Instead of explaining the circumstances that would have caused her to empty an entire supply of *forgetfulness* potion, Rosemary pushed at Meara's hands. "Let me go. You're hurting me."

The peevish tone of the request sounded nothing like her opinionated friend. "Rosemary, do you know who I am?"

"Who is Rosemary?" Her friend twisted to look behind her as if expecting someone else in the small interior.

"You are." She loosened her grip and pointed two fingers in Rosemary's direction.

No light of recognition shone in her eyes. Instead, she shook her head.

"What's your name then?"

Her friend's brow furrowed in thought. It was several heartbeats later before she spoke. "I don't know. Do you know my name?"

"Rosemary."

She shook her head. "It doesn't sound familiar."

What else could go wrong? She closed her eyes briefly and tried to calm herself. Jane's voice interrupted before she could calm or center herself.

"Meara, we have a problem."

"I know. I'm dealing with it." Not sure how she'd deal with it, but she had to try. The bigger question than what had Rosemary forgotten was, what did she remember?

"I need you, now!"

The urgency in Jane's voice had her exiting the wagon with a firm command to her confused friend. "Don't leave."

Outside of the wagon near the fire stood Jane and Ronan with their hands up and an angry man pointing a rifle at them. Had she seriously asked what else could go wrong? From her angle, she could still see the magic glimmering a few steps from the fire. If she could lure the gun-toting man into the forgetfulness spell, whatever imagined problem he had with them would vanish. She motioned for the man to come closer.

"Why do I need to come any closer?"

Meara held a hand up to her ear.

"If you're deaf, how come you answered?"

That was a very good question. A deaf person would have seen his mouth move. When in doubt, say nothing. She shrugged and stood with her hands open trying to appear as defenseless as possible. The man swung his rifle back in Ronan's direction as he backed up in the direction of the mist. It made her wonder if anyone else could see it.

"You're not fooling me." Their unwanted visitor growled the words. "I got no fears from a slip of a girl, but a full-grown man is another matter."

One more step, she mentally urged the man. He glanced back at Meara and made another sliding step, speaking as he did so.

"Can you hear…" He stopped, lowered his gun and gazed at her in confusion. "Where am I? What am I doing?"

"You're rabbit hunting." She pointed away from her to the woods. "It went that way."

He gave her a long look while Ronan and Jane dropped their hands. "Thank you."

They waited until he entered the woods before leaping into action. Jane put a lid on the pot that held their dinner. Before she could walk through the mist, Meara yelled.

"Go to the front of the wagon. There is a wall of forgetfulness potion lingering there."

"That would explain the man. Rosemary?"

She gave a nod that promised they'd discuss it later. Right now, they needed to leave before the rabbit hunter discovered he hadn't come gunning for dinner. Hercules was harnessed with some disagreement about the whole process since it had only been little more than an hour since he was released to eat. Some water and a few stomps of her boots put out the fire. Not knowing what Rosemary might do, she took a stick and shoved it through the hasp, locking the door from the outside. What had been one of her fears— being locked inside the wagon—would hopefully keep her friend safe.

Ronan had to be led to the wagon since he kept forgetting what he was doing and often stopped in the middle of it. Jane helped him up to the driver's bench, then walked to the front to lead Hercules.

Meara kept a wary eye on her cousin as she leaned forward to pick up the leads. "Do you know who I am?"

"Yes, you're Meara, my cousin."

"And you are?"

"Your cousin, Ronan. Why are you asking me these questions?"

"You acted confused like you didn't know what you were doing."

He peered around the wagon as Hercules started it into motion. Ronan pointed at himself. "I'm here with you." He pointed ahead. "Jane is there."

"Yes," she agreed with some enthusiasm. Maybe his memory loss was only for a few minutes, which she could survive. Maybe Rosemary's wouldn't be much longer, either. Ronan twisted on his seat, leaning forward to glance around Meara. "What are you looking for?"

"Billy. Where's Billy and Wind Racer?"

Maybe it would be longer than a few minutes. "What do you remember?"

"Jane made me raise my hands earlier. It was a game."

He sounded like a child. Maybe being without a memory made you equivalent to being a child since everyone had to look after you.

"It *was* a dangerous game. That man could have shot you."

"Why?"

"Good question. Not one I can answer. It *is* wartime, and people are suspicious of everyone, including Brother Jeremiah and his evangelism team."

Who would play the part of Jeremiah if Ronan stayed confused? It might not be her biggest concern, but it would ruin their premise for traveling the country. All she needed to do was get to Arran. Once the horn was secured, she'd head for England. After Billy getting taken and this last incident, maybe it would be better if she traveled alone.

The forgetfulness spell should confuse their follower, unless he had some sort of protection like Meara did. Maybe he could recognize magic and circle around it, too, or even the appearance of magic could be like a red flag waving him on. If so, she might as well leave someone along the trail, pointing the way.

Chapter Nineteen

THEY BUMPED ALONG for a couple more hours in the dark before stopping for the night. Denied the opportunity to look for an appropriate place in the light, they had to take what they could get, which wasn't much. A bare stretch of land along the road with no water and only a few trees. It would serve. Come morning, they'd have to leave as soon as the sun came up before anyone spotted them. With any luck, Ronan would be back to normal. As for Rosemary, Meara had her doubts. Still, she should check on her.

"Here, you take the reins." Jane handed them over. "I applied the parking brake." She wrinkled her nose. "Not sure why. It's not like Hercules is going to go another step. We'll be lucky to get him back in the harness tomorrow."

"You'd have thought with all the time he had to relax and graze he'd be ready for work."

"Ha! Shows how much you know about horses. It was the longest break in the old boy's life. Now that he's had a taste, he will never willingly go back to work." Jane gave a derisive snort. "A slow walk done grudgingly was about the best we ever got from the old man. I'm afraid to find out if he can actually go slower."

"I hope we don't find out. Why don't you take Ronan with you? I'm going to check on Rosemary." She eased down off the seat and let her feet touch the ground gingerly. Exhaustion weighed down every part of her body. Not only was she tired, but hot, too. Her hand went to her chest and loosened her neckline. The evening breeze cooled her some. Still, her chest felt on fire. She circled the wagon with weary steps and her hand pulling at her amulets. A person should expect to be somewhat hot encumbered with various chains and lockets. The metal from her mother's locket practically scorched her fingers.

Her hand closed around it as she remembered it would get warm whenever danger was near. Here she thought she was just warm. There were no birds calling softly in the night or even the country chorus of evening insects. It was still, as if nature held its breath or someone else had been through here recently upsetting everything. It usually took a while for the animals to settle, certain that the threat was gone. There was nothing to hear.

The traveling lanterns attached to the wagon threw out enough light to show the wood stick she'd shoved into the hasp of the lock was missing. Had it fallen out? Had Rosemary escaped? A woman without any memory wandering unfamiliar roads at night—maybe that's what the necklace was telling her. Meara stood frozen, staring at the door and hearing Jane and Ronan in the distance as they moved Hercules to graze.

A muffled cry from inside had her leaping for the door. There was some grunting, cursing and a long hard scream. "Rosemary!" She threw the door open only to have some stranger fall on top of her, trapping her left arm behind her with an ominous *snap*. A pan came flying out of the wagon to bounce off the man's head. He managed to heave himself up with a groan. The light glinted off a pair of large sewing shears sticking out of his leg.

The sound of running feet came from the front of the wagon. Jane rounded the wagon first. "What's going on?"

Meara pushed herself up into a sitting position, gritting her teeth against the stab of pain.

Rosemary came out of the wagon, clutching a skillet and pointed at the man who was hobbling down the road. "Get him!"

Ronan was a few steps behind Jane but kept going in the direction of the fleeing man. A thump and loud, vicious cursing carried as the two of them struggled in the shadows. Jane unsheathed her knife and peered into the darkness.

"If I throw now I'm not sure who I'll hit." She hesitated, not sure what to do. "I can't let your troublesome cousin get himself killed."

Meara had never considered Ronan troublesome, but she knew Jane did or at least she did until recently. Whatever Ronan said, Jane would disagree with. It hadn't been a day without the two of them getting into a fight about something. Meara used the wagon to pull herself into a standing position, while both Jane and Rosemary stared in the direction Ronan took.

"He's up. Ronan's up." She sheathed her knife.

"Did he kill the robber?"

Meara winced at the casually asked question, knowing good and well her cousin would step over an ant to avoid killing it. Obviously, Rosemary hadn't regained her memories if she didn't know that much about him.

The familiar silhouette of Ronan reached down to the other form on the ground. Only her cousin would help up someone he'd just fought. They both stumbled back to the wagon with Ronan keeping a firm grasp on the man's arm. As they drew closer, Rosemary shook the skillet at the captive, causing the individual to cringe. The lantern light picked out the sharp features and lean frame of the assailant. It was easy to deduce the man had missed more than a few meals recently. His scruffy beard, overly long hair, and a smell ripe enough to cause Meara to step back indicated his usual residence could have been the outdoors. At first, she thought Ronan had been holding onto the man to keep him from fleeing, but it may have been a case of him holding him up.

"Jane, Meara. We've encountered a fellow traveler." He kept a firm grip on the stranger and gave an easy smile.

Only her cousin would fall to the ground in a fight and stand up with a new-found friend. "Should I ask who our fellow traveler is and why he was in our wagon attacking Rosemary?"

People might think she was gullible. Next to Ronan, she was a cynic.

"Toby's my name." He shook his head hard but refused to look in Rosemary's direction. "I didn't attack anyone. I was looking for a bite to eat. I didn't know anyone was inside until I got in, then that woman started hitting me, kicking me, even stabbed me with scissors. All I wanted was a bit of bread. Maybe some cheese if you have it. It's been a while since I've had any regular vittles."

Normally, the tale of not eating would have stirred up some compassion. At the moment, Meara just wanted to sit down. Her legs complied by going rubbery and allowing her to slide down the wagon to land on the road.

"Meara!"

Jane reached her first and tried to help her up by pulling on her hurt arm.

"Ow! Stop!" She rolled to her unhurt side and pulled up her knees. "Just leave me alone."

"I think her arm is broke," Toby offered, earning a glare from Meara as he continued. "That happened to me once. Back when I was much younger."

"Can anyone get him to stop talking." Maybe she was being mean—but it was one thing on top of another. Contrary to what Destiny predicted, Meara was sure she was done. Billy was gone. Rosemary, as good as gone. The forgetfulness potion no longer a tool in her magic tool chest. Now, a broken arm, and she was no closer to finding the horn than she was this morning.

"Aye, she's right. Not been around folks too much. Gone and forgot how to act. Hate to ask but would you have a bit of bread?"

Before Jane could answer, Ronan did. "You're welcome to what we have, but first we have to make it. We'll need to get that leg sewn up, too."

Meara had her cheek against the ground. There were voices all around her. Toby and Ronan were conversing as if they were born pals as opposed to wrestling in the dirt mere minutes ago. Rosemary chanted something—it could have been a song. It was hard to tell because it sounded so far away. Jane was asking her something she couldn't distinguish. All her attention was focused three inches in front of her where a green spotted frog sat and stared at her with alert eyes.

Here I am. A sign. A helper. The way show-er. Buck up, Meara. Centuries ago when the horn was crafted, the faeries knew there would come a time when it would be used. They also knew who would retrieve it. They would not have chosen you if you weren't capable.

"I don't feel capable. Are they sure about this? Could I easily not find it, too?"

You could give up. Ask yourself if you're willing to disappoint all those who need your help. Think of your friends already part of the war. Braeden. Now, Billy. Your choice not only impacts the war but their lives.

Yes. What was she thinking? Feeling tired and sorry for herself. That's what it was. "I know what I have to do."

Jane's voice sounded next to her ear. "Who are you talking to?"

"The frog. Can't you see him? Hear him?"

She laid a cool hand against Meara's brow. "No fever yet. I need to set your arm, and with any luck, we'll avoid a fever. Not sure though with you talking about a frog and all."

The amphibian was only inches from her nose. He blinked, then vanished. His disappearance, she expected. He'd done what he came to do. He reminded her this wasn't her own personal choice, but a decision made centuries ago. It was hard to imagine the faeries who made such pronouncements, but obviously, they knew more about her abilities than she did.

MEARA AWOKE DISORIENTED, not sure where she was. Gradually she made out the shape of cabinets with doors, and sunlight outlined the shape of a window. The sway and the creak of the wagon announced they were on their way. She rolled to one side to push up and found her left arm heavy and awkward. Two short boards on either side were tied in place with strips of fabric she recognized as Jane's third-best dress. No wonder it felt so heavy. She was wearing part of a house on her body. Memories of Jane giving her a potion to help with the pain returned. Whatever it was had knocked her out good.

Voices filtered in from the driver's bench. Ronan's and another man's she couldn't quite place. Who could it be? She wasn't always her best in the morning, and having a potion slowing down her minddidn't help. Who was out there?

Ronan spoke again. "We're heading for the Isle of Arran."

Whoever it was, Ronan was telling all he knew at the drop of a hat. Didn't he know Grandmother Biddy said to trust no one? She couldn't quite recall if she ever told her cousin this or not. Her top teeth worried her bottom lip as she crawled closer to the sound of voices. There was an old saying she couldn't place that told her about secrets. A secret could only be kept between two people if one of them was dead. Her heartbeat increased as she considered everyone who knew about the hunt for the horns.

Grandmother Biddy was dead. Aunt Erin and Cousin Brigit were left behind in Ireland. Who knows where Billy was. Counting Ronan, Jane, and Rosemary, the circle kept increasing. Thaddeus, the gnome, knew. She didn't worry about him since people failed to realize gnomes existed. Still, another person would only increase the possibility of being stopped before they completed their quest.

Her hands gripped the shutters when the other man commented. "Why would anyone go to Arran?"

Before Ronan could answer, she threw open the windows to reply. "To visit my grandmother!"

Ronan shot her a bemused look as the thin man next to him nodded and replied, "That makes sense, especially if she's alone. I was raised by my dear, sweet grandmum."

Her breath caught, as she tried to process this stranger. The violent tumble to the ground that broke her arm was the result of this man. That she knew. Here he was companionably conversing with her cousin. Who was he? Better yet, why was he traveling with them?

Most Irishmen were quick with a remark, and her cousin was no exception. Except he'd had a whiff of the forgetfulness potion. He blinked a few times before breaking her gaze. Somehow, he hadn't remembered *not* to blab about Arran, which could just be dangerous. Apparently, the fact they were being shadowed and were at great personal risk slipped his mind. With very few run-ins lately, it would be easy to forget without exposure to the potion. For a while, the incidents—the near drowning, the chase, and the prolonged illness that had her fighting in an ether world—lingered in the distance becoming no more than a bad dream that fades upon waking.

She sensed no evil from the stranger, but he did break her arm. Right before it happened, her amulet grew unbearably hot, signaling danger was close. Her hand went up to grasp it for comfort and found nothing there. Where was it? She peered downward and plucked at her shirt to make sure it hadn't come loose and tumbled to her waist. *Nothing.* What had happened to her amulet, her necklaces, and pendulum?

At first, all the neckwear had felt unbearably heavy, then she got used to the weight. Now it was gone, leaving her vulnerable. Ignoring the problem of the stranger for a moment, she panicked and pawed through the cabinets using the daylight that spilled through the shutter she'd opened. Not finding it, she threw open the two additional shutters to help her look. What if she lost the horn section, too?

The wagon slowed and came to a stop. There was a creak as someone stepped up on the outside steps leading to the back door, freezing Meara in mid-action. Without the necklace, she was visible to the seekers. The door swung open as her fingers wrapped around a heavy glass sphere that was sometimes used to tell fortunes. Grandmother Biddy was not a fan, but some customers insisted on it. At least Meara would put it to good use. She threw it before she could fully focus on who was there.

There was a smack as Rosemary caught the sphere with both hands. "Jane warned me you might wake up groggy. Didn't say a word about throwing things. What have you done?" She gestured to the tossed interior.

"I was looking for my amulets." She pointed to her neck as if that would make the point clearer. "I never take them off, and when I woke up, they were gone."

"Ohhh." Rosemary stretched out the word. "That passel of old jewelry with an odd bit of glass thrown in. I took it off. Afraid it might strangle you in your sleep."

That explained the disappearance. The fact that Rosemary had done such a thing previously knowing the magical and sentimental purposes behind the amulets meant her memory hadn't returned.

"Could I have them back?" She held out her hand, expecting to have the requested items placed there.

Instead of complying, Rosemary gave a sniff. "I might consider it if you clean up the mess you just created."

The old Rosemary would never have commanded anything. She'd joke about cleaning, then ask for a hand. This new woman, without any of the previous experiences that had bonded the two of them together, acted completely different. It might be best if she just complied. "I'd love to tidy up, but I won't be able to until my necklace is back around my neck. Without it, my hands shake, and my eyes don't work as well as I'd like." Not certain if Rosemary would buy her excuse, she held out one trembling hand and stumbled into a wall, which hurt.

Her friend gave her a doubtful look, then reached into her pocket. "I think it passing strange that you are so dependent on some metal chains."

It was more than metal, much more. The amulet was the only tangible item she had of her mother and father. It was, in some ways, her family legacy. Her eyes tracked Rosemary's movements as she lifted the tangle of chains from her pocket. The pendulum hung lower than the rest, swinging wildly and spinning in a circle, possibly saying *yes* to its relocation.

A tear slid down her cheek as she reached out her hand. Once the weight touched her skin, a magical zing went up her arm, and her fingers tightened over the chains just in case Rosemary attempted to take them back. It was hard to know what this new version of her friend might do. A plan formed in her mind, not one to her liking, but probably her only option.

"I'll get right to work. Come back in an hour and the place will be better than it was. Sparkling even."

Rosemary's narrowed eyes expressed some reservations. "We'll see about that. I'll be back before an hour has gone by. You better hope everything is as it was before."

"It will be. Better." She forced her lips up into a smile, wondering about the change in her. If she ever lost her memory for some reason, she hoped she'd become a nicer person as opposed to the autocratic drudge that had taken over Rosemary's body.

She waited until Rosemary left and closed the door behind her. If no one else decided they had need of the wagon, it was time to leave since she didn't know exactly what she would need. Whatever it was, she needed to get it before Rosemary came back to check on her.

Chapter Twenty

MEARA BARELY MADE it out of the wagon before Rosemary came back to check. Knowing at least Ronan and Jane would search for her, she did the only thing she could think of to avoid detection—she climbed a nearby tree. All she would have to do was wait until they left before she came down. If for some reason, they decided not to go until they'd found her, she'd slip down at night. Luckily, the tree had a nice seat where the limbs formed a *Y*. It provided support for her back and would keep her from tumbling out if she fell asleep. It hadn't been easy climbing up that far with one good hand. Going down would be difficult, too. Worse yet, when would she know when her arm was better?

Even though she was too far away to hear, there were breaks in the leafy canopy that exposed the wagon. Rosemary marched to the wagon with a determined gait. *There goes the general to check on her one soldier.* It didn't take Rosemary long to discover the wagon interior hadn't been cleaned and the perpetrator of the mess was conspicuously absent. She left and was gone for a few minutes, then returned with Jane and Ronan. They, too, peeked into the wagon, possibly doubting Rosemary. They called her name as they moved around the wagon in circles. The stranger, who she now remembered called himself Toby, walked over and said something to Ronan he didn't care for. He pushed him away and went back to calling her name.

It was surprisingly hard not to answer, especially when anguish colored the calls. Would they think she had just decided to go for a walk and perhaps was simply rebelling against being told what to do? There weren't any wild animals to worry about since the wolves and bears were long gone. Badgers could be fierce, although she would work hard to steer clear of them. Unlike humans, animals didn't start a fight just to start one. Instead, they'd protect their family or home. As long as she wasn't invading anyone's den or stealing their progeny, she should be fine.

The calls grew fainter as the two moved farther away. Rosemary didn't go with them. They probably told her not to. No reason to complicate things. They had already lost one member of the party. They didn't need to lose two.

How long would they look? Surely Jane would realize the time had come for her to go it alone. Originally, she planned to make the entire journey on her own. Rosemary had appointed herself as a guardian while Jane provided transportation and actual on-the-road expertise. Her cousin served as their token male for those times when other males could be so steeped in tradition they wouldn't even listen to a woman. It was like women had no voice unless a man stood beside them. She'd heard as much from some of the sisters, which explained their frustration with the world and their desire to leave it. Life as a single woman had very few benefits, the way they told it.

A blur of motion through the leafy canopy caught her eye. The stranger had his hand on the wagon door as if he'd go in. No surprise there since Meara had caught him rummaging through their belongings only the night before. Rosemary charged after him holding a sturdy piece of firewood. If Meara could see it from her perspective, it was sizable.

There was some yelling that included the words *stay out*, said repeatedly. Toby held up his hands. His mouth was moving, which meant he was talking, but not loud enough for Meara to hear. He was a thief, that she suspected. Couldn't understand why the others were so quick to accept him. There was a flash of something. Meara blinked and leaned a little closer, not sure what happened. Whatever had happened, Rosemary refused to lower her firewood. She continued to yell to no avail.

Whomever the man was, it was apparent that Rosemary wasn't buying his poor, pitiful me act. Strange that. Her amulet warmed against her skin. Not that there was much she could do up there. As long as she had the amulet on, she was protected. Obviously, not protected from all harm. Her arm hadn't been spared, but at least from death. It wasn't as reassuring as it had been once. There were many ways a person could die, and some were slow and painful. The tree would keep her safe as long as no one decided to take an ax to it.

The scruffy stranger wasn't what he seemed. The knowing came to her as certain as she was sitting in a tree. The man was a shifter. He could take any form, and while he was in that form, he could fool people. As far as being in their wagon, his goal *was* to be caught. In an act of natural generosity, he would be invited to dinner and possibly accompany them. That had been his plan all along. Why hadn't she seen it until now?

Where were Ronan and Jane? Rosemary might look fierce now, brandishing the firewood, but what would she do if the man shifted into a large wolf? If she attempted to climb down with one arm, it would never be in time to save her friend. Wasn't there something she could do? All she needed was a distraction. Back when they realized they were being driven to their demise by a man who claimed he had been sent by her uncle, she called on the seabirds for help. There were some small birds chirping nearby, but not big enough to make an impact on a person. It was more likely they would be swatted away. As far as calling the animals, that might have been a fluke.

Her eyes closed as she tried to focus on the creatures nearby.

There were plenty of heartbeats inside the tree and all around it. She touched minds with them and showed them Toby. "He is bad for the forest, for your homes, for your children. He must go."

Not even sure if they understood, she opened her eyes as her fingers grasped the branch as tight as she could. It *had* to work. It was all she had. Rosemary had believed in her even before Meara ever did. Her friend had put herself in harm's way all in the name of a cause she didn't fully understand. It was enough Meara believed in it.

Holding the branch aloft was wearing on Rosemary who switched to her non-dominant hand. It would put her at a disadvantage but how much expertise did one need to swing a chunk of firewood? A pair of squirrels ran toward the clearing and were trailed by a third. More squirrels swarmed into viewing, creating a haphazard parade. Squirrels, on the whole, weren't the most amenable of creatures. Those she'd witnessed in her stolen moments in the woods when she'd snuck out of the convent were usually engaged in a noisy argument over trees or a particularly tasty nut. Now they were all joining together, not a dissenting voice, but united in one cause.

Toby circled Rosemary, sensing her tiring. She kept turning, not allowing the man to get behind her. Her friend may have lost her memory, but her survival senses were well intact. When Toby had his back to the trees and the ever-growing parade of red squirrels with fluffy tails, they chose that moment to swarm up his legs.

The shrieks she could hear just fine as the man slapped the determined creatures who must have very sharp teeth. Blossoms of red stained his clothes, and Meara could feel his struggle to change into something fierce that could gobble up the furry warriors in a heartbeat. Rosemary stumbled back, her hand up to her mouth. Meara didn't want the squirrels to kill whatever Toby was in front of Rosemary.

Run! She directed the intention to the shapeshifter, who took off running with squirrels so thick hanging on him, he could have been wearing a red squirrel coat. Several trailed him. She lost track of him in a short time, but an occasional shriek carried faintly, eventually fading out.

You forgot to recall the squirrels. Do it now. Her father's voice sounded in her head. Of course, she should have known.

"Squirrel friends, thank you for your bravery. We are all safe due to your efforts."

It felt like an acknowledgment as if they'd heard, but she wasn't sure. Slowly, the squirrels made their way back one by one. Most were bloody, but it was hard to tell whose blood it was. With any luck, no furry warriors had been left on the battlefield. If they had, scavengers would make short work of their bodies, which was how it was. The squirrels knew the cycles better than she did.

When it felt like she'd been in the tree half a lifetime and her bladder was full to bursting, Jane and Ronan returned. Rosemary ran to them. From her bold expansive gestures, it was obvious she was relating the squirrel battle and Toby's part in it.

Jane crossed her arms, nodded, and glanced in the direction of the tree where Meara hid. Could be she knew due to being Grandmother Biddy's favorite student. Even though Jane claimed the basic arts of reading Tarot, using the pendulums, creating a spell, and even a simple look away charm when needed, Meara suspected she knew much more. If she knew she was in the trees, why didn't she go looking for her?

It wasn't a question she'd have answered from this distance. Jane probably wouldn't even tell Ronan, who had most of his memories back. Forget Rosemary, who had turned into a domineering version of her former self. Meara could see Jane slapping her hands together. It was hard, but she could barely make out the thrust of Ronan's chin, which Meara recognized as his *I will not be moved* stance. Jane moved past him to Hercules. She led the horse to the wagon. They really *were* going! They would leave her! It was what she wanted, but still—shouldn't they try a little harder? Even as she felt a pang near her heart, she knew it was for the best.

All the shrieking was bound to bring the curious. It wouldn't do to be around if they found a bloodied body. Her brows furrowed.

What type of body they would find? Would it be human? Animal? No one would believe squirrels went wild and attacked him. When odd things happened without an explanation, strangers were always to blame, and they *were* strangers. It would do her well to be gone, too.

Once the wagon was ready. Jane moved to the rear of it and cupped her hands around her mouth. "I know you are out there, doing what you need to do. We'll head on to your father's farm."

How would they do that? Even she didn't know where it was. All she could do at this point was believe and snag the second piece of horn before heading to the farm, which she had to depend on her father to lead her to. It hadn't been said outright. Still, she had a feeling the third piece was on the farm, buried out there. Fulmen would have a hard time letting go of a faery crafted item. Her hand covered the bag resting on her stomach. It made her happy just touching it.

Chapter Twenty-One

T RAVELING IN THE dark wasn't easy, especially when she was unsure of her direction. Consulting her small compass to find west, she started the way she wanted to go, but somewhere in the night she'd veer off and even come full circle.

She'd been upset when she discovered she'd wasted an entire night going nowhere. Not knowing what to do, she slid down beside a tree and had a good cry. Then she proclaimed, to whoever might be listening, that she needed help. At the very least, she should be able to see her compass in the dark. With her grumpy attitude, she didn't expect much. Maybe a brighter moon or fireflies to light the way. What she received was a silver, electric torch that shot a beam of light out when she pushed a button, found while she scrounged for firewood.

Billy had seen one back in Holyhead and had gone on and on about it. The one she found had belonged to someone, but now it belonged to her. The former owner probably regretted the loss. Meara knew better than to think too much on who the owner was. It worked better if she pretended she was the only one about at night, other than the occasional owls, bats, and rodents scurrying for their lives. People was what she didn't want to dwell on.

Her first few days, she tried to keep to the former schedule of traveling by day. That hadn't worked. Too many people took an interest in her. Her disguise as a man at best came across as an innocent youngster separated from his family. There were plenty of concerned citizens who wanted to help find the missing family. A few decided he was a runaway and counseled return. A slow survey of her person by a pair of men made her feel unclean. She wasn't sure if they saw through her disguise or not, but she made certain to turn off the road and go a different route. All this was slowing her down. Even worse, it made her memorable.

If her amulet made her invisible to whoever was searching for her, plenty of folks would volunteer information on where they'd last seen her. At least, she thought they would. The common opinion was that the Scots were a closemouthed, suspicious people. They might keep their mouths shut, but it would be foolish to count on it, so she started traveling at night.

There was no one on the road at night, except those rushing home to avoid the usual inhabitants of the moonlit trail. Eventually, she decided to take to the woods to avoid the robbers, drunkards, and other questionable folks. No one in the woods—well, make that not too many—were sharing the cover of the trees with her. She'd surprised a pair of lovers who jumped up in alarm and ran, leaving some clothing behind. Even better, food and drink, too.

The sound of water lapping against the land meant she was close to her destination. A ferryman would carry her over for a price. She had a little money in her pocket and when that was spent she had no way to get more. Unlike Rosemary and Jane, she had no real skills people would pay money for. After spending more than a week traveling alone without the benefit of a mirror or a bath, most people wouldn't even let her come near them, let alone babysit their children or do their laundry. This was a problem. A big one. Where would she get the needed funds? Her plan to get back to England was to use the train. It would take money and plenty of it.

Everything she thought of put another brick in the insurmountable wall she'd never be able to climb. Overwhelmed, Meara dropped to her knees and considered stopping where she was. The piercing cry of a hawk caught her ear. They were not night birds. Why would one be out now? The call continued. What had she learned about the hawk? As a predator, he soared high searching the fields for possible prey. Eleanor had taught her that all high soaring birds reminded us to look at the big picture.

Big picture. What was it? It had been over a year and then some since a bomb destroyed the convent, sending her out into the world. Eleanor had taught her some housekeeping basics and what she knew about reading nature. From the moment she saw Braeden, she had been a little bit in love with him. She had her first kiss along with instructions to wait for him. In pretty swift order, she was burned out of her home, ran for her life, had some mystical predictions, and caught a train to the coast. There was calling the birds, the near-drowning, the gypsy camp, fleeing through a haunted land, and meeting her long-lost relatives only to fall into a coma. That was only half the year. A lot had happened. It would be foolish to give up now.

Whatever you need will be provided if you just believe.

The murmured sentiment sounded more like her mother than her father. "I'd like to believe that," she whispered. "Plenty of folks die hungry."

They don't die of hunger. They die of despair.

Meara wasn't totally convinced people died of despair. "The woman and her children who took the chicken from the convent after the bombing were much more concerned with hunger than despair."

True enough. They still persevered. They hadn't given up because they still saw life was worth living. Have you given up?

Had she? The feeling of being unable to go on came over her rapidly. Where was the woman who decided to set out on her own to protect her friends and in doing so make herself feel a little safer? It was much easier for one person to slip through the woods than Brother Jeremiah's Salvation Wagon. Jane could have managed, but now she had both Ronan and Rosemary with their missing memories. Surely Ronan would be back to rights by now.

He is.

"Rosemary?"

No.

She heaved a heavy sigh, wishing there was something she could do about her friend.

I came to you because of your despair. It isn't yours.

"Whose is it? I'd be glad to return it."

A tinkling laugh sounded. *I am sure you would. The dark one, your nemesis, the one who feeds on hate and death sent it out. He can't see you, so he tries to stop you by sending out a wave of mind-numbing despair.*

"Won't that infect everyone it touches?"

It will, and it has. It is dark days, but even darker days when a poisonous wind blows across the land.

"What can I do?"

Reject it. Push it away, but not too hard. If it feels too much of a pushback, he'll be able to locate you. Be strong. Keep going. Don't think of this as your mission. It is our *mission. I'll be with you, as will your father.*

"That helps."

Go to the ferryman at dawn and give him the token you'll find at your feet. He knows what it means and will be glad to take you across.

"Where should I go once I'm there?"

You'll know. I will not say now because even in the forest there are ears and wings to carry the message.

There was a shift in the atmosphere, a shimmering burst of light, then it was gone. She was gone, but so was the despair. Meara felt around her feet and found a round token bigger than a crown. She shoved it into her pocket. "You'd think if they can make coins appear at will, they should be able to locate horn pieces on their own."

Eergy that had been previously lacking rushed through her veins and filled up her muscles. She was ready. Using the torch, she consulted the compass and set out. With any luck, she'd be there before dawn. Not sure how many people would be crossing, but she would make sure to be the first and the only one with a mysterious token.

Unlike the previous nights, her journey was one of expectation. Almost there, with another horn part, she would be close to being done. The horn bag strapped across her torso vibrated as if it could hear a silent melody calling to it. Perhaps that is how she'd find the next piece. It also could be the way someone else could find it, too. It would involve countless years of walking the United Kingdom— or they could just follow her.

Company would have been nice on this leg of the journey. Someone she could bounce ideas off. Sure, her parents were good for the occasional direction. It wasn't the same as a flesh and blood person. She crinkled her nose as she realized she'd abandoned her companions for their safety. She couldn't go dragging someone else into this mess.

A break in the branches revealed a pink-tinged sky. It was almost dawn. She ducked out of the woods to locate the ferry stand. It was ahead about a thousand yards or so. Meara moved parallel with the woods ready to use them for cover if necessary.

A cheerful whistling floated on the wind that didn't sound like a bird. It reminded her of a tune she'd heard her Aunt Erin sing while doing the washing. It was something about a soldier saying goodbye to his sweetheart because they might never meet again. It made her think of Braeden with a pang. She shook off the thought, reminding herself she had to persevere for Braeden and all the soldiers like him.

A stout man came toward the ferry and unhitched the gate to the boat with an easy confidence signaling he had done this many times before. He must be the ferryman. Meara inhaled deeply, readying herself for what she hoped would be an easy transaction, and took a step forward only to stumble when her left foot didn't follow suit. A long vine had wrapped itself around her ankle several times. When had that happened?

With her left arm boarded up, it would be impossible to roll to her right side to untangle the vine. All she needed to do was get on that ferry. Not more than a handful of steps and she was on the ground fighting with a plant. Before Meara could get her knife out of her sheaf, a large, black dog came bounding toward her. Stuck the way she was, she'd have no defense unless she stabbed it. Its long pink tongue hung out of its mouth as it ran at her. It almost looked like it was smiling—a comical grin. Who knows what the dog was thinking? Its ribs showed through its coat. It might be hungry enough to dine on a human. It pulled up short before running over her, then bit at the vine encircling her ankle. She was free.

"Thanks, buddy." She rolled to her right side to begin her attempt to stand. When she was in a tripod position, the dog came rushing over. Was it trying to knock her over? His body pressed against her leg provided enough support for her to stand.

"Thanks, again." She'd never had a dog of her own but knew they sometimes helped their owners by guarding the house or herding the sheep. She'd never met this dog, and he came out of the woods ready to help her. It was nothing short of magic.

Meara walked toward the ferry never giving a backward look to the helpful canine. She fished the odd token out of her pocket, ready to hand it to the ferryman. When he turned, he gave her a close survey that ended with a raised eyebrow. She could read his doubt of her ability to pay in his expression.

"I have something I am supposed to give you."

Even though he looked doubtful, he approached Meara. "What would that be?"

"This." She held out the token.

He took it and held it up to the early morning light. "Never thought I'd see this again." He gave Meara a second, intense appraisal. "You didn't kill anyone for this?" Before she could answer, he shook his head. "By the size of you and with a bum arm, most could have shaken you off like a wee flea. I'd not been expecting the likes of you to come bearing this coin. Still, the blessed savior was born in the manger, fooling many."

When it looked like he had finished his dismissal of her appearance, he gave her a nod. And asked, "Going to Arran?"

"I am."

He gestured to something beside her. "Your dog, too?"

Her dog? The black dog had followed her and sat beside her wagging his tail and looking up at her with hopeful eyes. It wouldn't be any safer for him than it would be for people to travel with her. Then again, it might. People wouldn't expect a dog to talk, spilling out secrets he'd heard whispered in the night. A dog could be a great companion. When things weren't to his liking, he could leave, too. "Yes, yes, it is."

"Normally, I charge extra for livestock." He held up the token. "This will pay for both of you. I imagine you'll be wanting a ride back."

"I will."

He smiled. "Luck is with you because it covers the return trip, too. I'll take you now, and I can be back before the others arrive. It's better this way."

Not sure of what he meant, Meara stepped onto the ferry followed by the dog. It didn't have a cabin like Billy and his father's ferry did. There were a few wooden crates nailed to the surface that served as seats. As soon as she took one, the dog leaned against her. She found herself stroking its silky head and picking burrs out of his coat. Around his neck was a slim collar with a shiny tag. It read *Nole, Property of Meara.* Very odd.

There could be someone out there named Meara missing a dog. The condition of the dog meant it had been gone a long time. It might recover if it spent some time with her. "So, your name is Nole?"

The dog gave a bark as if he understood. The craft rocked a little as it was pushed a safe distance before starting the motor. This was probably a precaution to avoid getting weeds and mud on the propeller. Once they picked up speed a breeze blew over the ferry, chilling Meara. She might not know much about Scotland yet, but she had come to the conclusion that it was cooler, especially on the water.

The ferryman set his rudder, then wandered back to Meara and her dog. "The two of you are a mess." He shook his head. "Not sure which one is worse." He pointed at Meara's makeshift cast. "That has to be heavy."

"It is. I'm pretty sure my left arm is a few inches longer by now."

"Could be."

That was far from reassuring. The ferryman turned and gave her a smile with a few teeth conspicuously absent. "The name's John. No need to be telling me yours if you don't want to. I told you mine because I thought it might put you at ease. There was a man a long time ago who gave me a coin like the one you did. He promised me if I was still ferrying folks across the water that another would come. The coin is an old one from times gone by. The last coin allowed me to buy the business from the previous ferryman. This one will help take care of my aged da."

If she had known that, she would have paid him with another coin, keeping the more valuable coin.

John chuckled. "Now I see you're regretting giving me your coin. It would have done you no good. You need contacts to turn coins like that into real money. No coin shop would let you in, looking the way you do."

"Aye, you're right."

He moved easily across the rocking surface and picked up a bag. "My dear, sweet wife always packs me more than I can eat. I have some bread, a turnip, and a macaroni and cheese pie if you'd like some?"

She'd never heard of the latter, but anything that ended with *pie* had to be better than what nuts, berries, and roots she'd foraged from the forest. The food she'd packed in her knapsack vanished in a matter of days. "Sounds wonderful."

The pie was a round crusty pastry full of cheese and pasta. She could have inhaled it, but Nole leaned against her and stared at her, but mainly the pie. She broke off a piece that the dog wolfed down without the benefit of chewing. The rest of the pie went likewise. A bite for her, a bite for Nole. When they finished, John handed them a half loaf of bread and a turnip.

"This is all of *your* lunch. What will you eat?"

He patted his rounded belly. "I got enough here to hold me over. I could miss more than a few meals. Besides, I still have a turnip." He pulled a small cloth bag tied with a string from underneath his shirt. "I've got my oats, too. Any real Scot carries a bag of oats with them. Many times, a man caught in a storm survived by making a thin gruel of the oats."

"Sounds like something I should be doing."

John pulled the string that held the oats bag around his neck over his head. "You can have this."

"Oh, no." She held up her hands, ready to refuse the generous offer. "You've already done so much."

The man stepped toward her and looped the oats bag string over Nole's head. "Heard there were dogs in the mountains who had little kegs of brandy attached to their collar. Not quite the same, but you'll make use of it someday and be grateful for it."

"Thank you. I don't know what to say."

He held up one finger and went back to check the rudder, adjusted it, and returned. "If you want to do me a favor…" He paused and waited for her response.

"It depends. I could try."

He gave her a gap-toothed smile. "Let me think on it. I'll come up with something."

Meara and Nole polished off the bread together while she munched on the turnip, solo. She should have saved it since she didn't know when her next meal would come from, which was exactly why she devoured it.

Soft, rolling green hills announced Arran. As they grew closer, houses spotted some of the land. There were even a few crumbling castles or abbeys or something from long ago. John pointed to where she was looking.

"We get tourists. Those who travel around just to look at things." He pointed to the ruins of some older building. "They like the falling down buildings. There's more than a few here. Why not? Whoever lived here had the biggest moat of all."

He chuckled about his own comment as he steered the ferry in. Once tied up, he stood by the gate that allowed passengers on and off. Meara adjusted the straps on her knapsack and waited for Nole.

As they approached the gate, John gave his trademark grin again. "About that favor."

She blew out a breath because she had been certain he'd forgotten. "What is it?"

"The island is a big place—close to twenty miles long and ten miles wide. I doubt you'll get done all you want to do in a day. Before you go, check in on my Aunt Mary for me. She served in the Crimean War as a nurse. She was just a gel. Always headstrong and able to lie better than the devil. Told them she was eighteen and a widow. Only widows were allowed to be nurses. Life has become a bit dull for her of late. She'd welcome the company. Mary MacCartney, Lamlash. She lives near the Parish Church. Green Roof. There's a small dragon statue near the door. As a kid, I thought it meant a dragon lived inside. She'd appreciate a visit—from both of you."

Meara shook her head, not sure how she'd work in a visit to John's elderly aunt. It wasn't as if she was on holiday. Putting an end to growing greed, hatred, and death spreading across the world was more than a full-time job. If she could, she'd work it in.

Chapter Twenty-Two

ONCE MEARA STEPPED onto land, she barely got to take a breath before the horn moved in her bag. It trembled and pulled. A glance downward revealed the bag pushing outward as if a live beastie might be inside. The superstitious might claim she was possessed and a demon was doing its best to get out. She pressed her hand against the bag, pushing it back to her body. "Stop it."

"Stop what?" John looked up from checking his mooring ropes.

Meara flushed a little at being caught talking to an inanimate object. Her brows furrowed as she tried to decide if a magically created instrument might actually have an intelligence of its own. It did know they were near its other part. Still, that could be yet another spell meant to help her, the seeker. Oops, she hadn't answered John. "It's Nole, the dog." Since he was sitting right beside her there wasn't much she could complain about. "He was scratching."

"Dogs do that."

She held up her hand. "Thanks for the ride."

He grinned. "Take care. Do try to see Aunt Mary. Green roof. By the parish church. Lamlash."

"I'll try." She smiled and gave a final wave before heading up the road. The worn path leading away from the water forked. Which one should she take? It was still early, and no one was about. She'd let the horn decide. Turning to the left, she took a step only to have the bag pull to the right. It looked like they were going right. John told her the island was ten miles long. Let's hope she didn't have to walk the entire ten miles to find it.

Neat cottages lined the road. Many of the windows were open to the morning breeze. As she passed one, the windows opened out and the owner pursed her lips when she caught sight of Meara and Nole. Even though the woman didn't speak, her look conveyed her aggravation at having the two of them on her lane. Nole was thin, and she hadn't gotten all of the burrs out of his coat, but he looked about the same as most dogs she'd seen. He had the look of a water retriever, which made sense since he turned up near water. Well, that meant it was her who turned up the housewife sour and all.

There would come a time when she'd shed Ronan's cast-off clothes and take a proper bath. She might even find a comb to run through her hair. It would be nice to appear civilized as opposed to a vagabond. Right now, her appearance worked in her favor. People kept their distance. In the beginning, she'd started out as a green girl with long, red curls. Now she was a disreputable looking boy with a dog.

As for the curls, the hatchet cutting job she did on them did little to tame them. They had grown out some, but she took to them last night in the woods and hacked away some more. The matted mess she burned in the fire forebore no resemblance to her former curls. Most of the sisters had been eager for her to cut her hair, certain that the flame color demonstrated the sin of her mother. Sister Gabriella told her they were simply jealous. If the sisters were still living, they'd be happy now with the state of her hair. She ran her fingers through the short length and remembered Jane's words about most people seeing what they wanted to see. It worked.

After all the excitement and danger she'd experienced previously, today was merely a walk with the horn part exerting a pull whenever she tried to turn the wrong way. Hand lettered signs dotted the road with arrows pointing the direction to various villages. They got all the way to Whiting Bay before the sun reached its zenith. Along the way, she noticed signs for The Holy Isle. What was the Isle? Wasn't she already on an island?

Right between Whiting Bay and Lamlash stood another sign for the Holy Isle, and the horn pulled in that direction. Of course, her parents would pick the most inaccessible place to bury it. There was no ferry waiting to take her over, either. She didn't have a coin to spare for it, anyhow. Any money had to be saved for the train. It apparently didn't matter to the horn that continually pulled her to the edge of the shore. "Stop it! I can't walk over there."

Nole glanced at the water and trotted off. She expected as much. Somehow, she got the notion he had been sent by faeries to be her companion. Eleanor had told her once that the small faeries would often hitch rides on hares, birds, and the occasional dog. It had been nice to have some companionship on the ride over here and the walk. While some folks might not care for her appearance, the dog made her more ordinary. Now he was gone.

A sharp bark drew her out of the self-pity she was falling into. The sound had come from the direction of some tall reeds. Meara broke into a jog, worried that Nole may have got himself into a spot of trouble. The black dog poked his head out from the reeds and barked again. Instead of running to meet her, he stayed in his position. He had to be stuck.

Using her hand to part the thick reeds, she disturbed a cloud of stinging insects she batted away. Why didn't magical protection ever extend to the mildly uncomfortable, but not truly dangerous situations? After slapping her arm and waving her hand for what seemed like forever, she turned her attention to Nole. He stood in water that reached his belly and beside him was a boat with oars. She pressed her hand against her chest.

"Good boy. You must be a retriever or maybe a finder. That is exactly what we need." She waded into the cold water. "You'd think it'd be warm, but no." The boat was caught in the reeds. The owner may have hidden it there or it may have escaped on its own. Nole scrambled into the boat and took a seat in the bottom as if acquainted with boating. She gave another hard tug to get the reeds to give up its bounty. Finally, they did and sent her tumbling into the water and muck.

"Ugh." She lifted one hand covered in silty mud. Odds were she couldn't look or smell any worse. Good thing she hadn't bet on it. She pushed herself up and noticed the bag levitated just the slightest from her body. Was it because it didn't want to be coated with the foul substance or it was feeling the pull of its other part? Whatever it was, she needed to get to the island.

The fall had jolted her arm. Her boards had hit the mud hard, driving the jolt up her arm. It ached and throbbed, probably how broken bones were supposed to feel. It would be wonderful to have the use of both arms again. She wasn't even sure how she could row a boat, but she had to try.

After a few attempts, she got herself upright while Nole sat in the boat and barked encouragement. Great. She wanted a dog, why? Companionship. That's the problem with companionship, it didn't always work out the way you planned. She pushed the boat out of the reeds with water getting deeper until it reached her thighs. Beside the wooden rowboat, she could clearly see the tiny isle.

Now that she was in the water, how would she get in the boat? While using the ferry and a sailboat to cross water, she'd had no interaction with the crafts on her own, especially the getting in from the water part. When the sailboat capsized, at least she had someone to pull her aboard. A slight current tugged at the boat. If she didn't get herself into it, it would be eventually pulled from her grip. No need to waste what fate had so generously handed her.

She put her boarded arm in first, since it served no purpose in helping. Her fingers gripped the edge of the boat, and she tried to throw her left leg over the side. Instead of her leg, she managed only to get her mud-covered foot and ankle into the boat. Unfortunately, she could feel it slipping. Something grabbed at her pant leg and pulled. The boat shifted as Nole pulled her in bit by bit. The horn bag levitated too, adding to Nole's efforts. *Plop*! She landed in the bottom of the boat with a squish. Nole let go of her leg and shook his head possibly trying to rid himself of the awful taste.

"Appreciate the help."

Getting in the boat took about the last bit of energy she possessed. A few seconds rest wouldn't change the course of the future. A blue sky stretched overhead dotted with a few fluffy clouds that resembled lambs. One to her right could be a dragon in flight. The boat rocked as she named the various formations. It was moving. She sat up, trying to gauge where they were and what direction they were headed. Holy Isle grew large enough for her to see what she assumed were animals on the hill. White dots stood out from the green. Could be sheep, possibly goats. Whatever it meant, the place was inhabited. Good to know since someone might take offense at her digging holes on private property.

The horn bag trembled and pulled as they drew closer. If it could exert such a pull, she only hoped it worked as well to find the third piece. It didn't take too long for the boat to bump against the gravelly shore. Nole jumped out and grabbed the mooring rope. The dog must have had a fisherman owner to know what to do.

Meara got up, cradling her arm. It throbbed and ached more than it had before. Time was supposed to heal things, not make them worse. She stepped out of the boat. Once she did, Nole backed up, pulling the boat up a little more. With any luck, it would be there when they returned.

There were a few battered looking shacks that had seen their share of storms. A circle of blackened stones announced an extinguished campfire. Beside it stood a white-bearded goat who watched her with a curious expression.

"I hope your owner doesn't mind us visiting."

The goat cocked its head as if listening. Flattening her hand, she used it as a sun shield to look up into the hills. There was something up there. A building of some sort, but it looked rather tumbled down. This might have been someone's home until they decided on more gregarious companions than goats. As if on cue, the goat *baa-ed*, which resulted in Nole barking. If there was anyone here, they would know she was there by now. It was possible there were wild dogs, too.

In that case, they needed to get the horn and get going. Skinny Nole wouldn't fare well against a feral canine. The horn section danced about in its cloth bag until she started moving, then it pulled her in the directions she needed to go. The absolute strangeness of the situation had her shaking her head. Never would she imagine that she'd be off in another country with two boards strapped to her arm, trying to find an ancient relic while being led by another one. Laughter bubbled up in her, spilling out, and echoing a bit. She stopped and waited. Now would be the time for someone to demand *who goes there* or just show up with a shotgun. Both would make an impression, although the shotgun would make a stronger one.

A rocky hillside faced her, and she didn't relish the idea of going up. The goat scrambled up it with ease, and Nole followed, leaving her behind. Her head hurt so bad it felt like lightning bolts were flashing inside. The bag jiggled so hard against her belly she was sure the horn would jump out. Thank goodness she'd buttoned the top of the bag.

"Hold on."

One step at a time while leaning forward should work. A walking stick would help. A quick survey determined all the kindling and broken limbs must have fed the fire on the beach. The rocks shifted as she stepped on them, making her glad of the worn work boots. She slipped a little, swore, and caught her balance. Mother Superior would be aghast at her language while Eleanor would have chuckled. So many different people in her life in such a short time.

Meara managed a dozen or more steps without sliding backwards. A grassy stretch was her reward. It was still an ascent but a little less challenging. They reached a plateau where the crumbling buildings were. It had been something hundreds of years ago. Before she could even contemplate what, the bag jerked, and the outline of the horn showed as it pushed at the cloth.

"I'm moving." She couldn't blame the horn one bit. It was doing what it was meant to do. It must be unnatural for the horn to be apart. Its central goal must be to become one again. She swerved around the boulder, wondering where the mysterious second part might be. Would things not work out if she found the third part first? It was neither here nor there—just a thought—as she stumbled toward a green stretch littered with stones and broken crosses.

It was a graveyard. Not unexpected. Where you had people you usually had a graveyard. Would her parents be so bold as to bury something in a graveyard? Was that sacrilege or something? One final strong tug took her to her knees. A weathered cross had something written on it. Her fingers traced the letters as birds called in the background.

"Rest in peace. I. B. Horn," She read.

How come no one ever noticed that? It would take someone knowing where the horn was buried to pay attention. Religious protocol forbade digging up anyone who had been planted there. She knew I. B. Horn wasn't a person, but would anyone else?

The horn shook as she dug with one hand.

"I'm doing the best I can. A shovel wouldn't be refused." As none were coming, she used the cross that had marked the spot. She had to stop and take off the bag since its constant jiggling was getting on her nerves. "You're going on the ground, and if you can help in any way, please do," she told it, not that she expected any actual help.

A breathy, musical blurt came from the bag. How could that have happened? Dirt crumbled and spilled away as the second piece of horn worked its way up from the ground. It tried to blow. Only a squeak came through the dirt packed inside. Whatever container it had been in must not have lasted. She took the second piece of the horn, which was longer and narrower, and tried to scrape the dirt out from both ends. The dirt stuck in the middle, she managed to dislodge by hitting it against her leg. She placed it next to the second piece and waited to see what would happen.

The two pieces inched their way toward each other, rose, then screwed together in mid-air. If that wasn't impossible enough, a musical bleat sounded. Though stronger than the first one, t it wasn't quite the sound she expected after being assured it would put an end to the fighting. That third piece had to be the secret, and the way it had been explained to Meara, the chosen one had to blow the horn, which would be her. The horn sounded again. The tone improved somewhat. So far, this had been relatively easy, but a new thought occurred to her. What if the horn could be heard and whoever was looking for it—for her—could recognize what they were hearing? It would be the same as lighting a beacon fire.

She grabbed the horn and put the bell-shaped part against her shirt "No more sounds. I know you're probably happy to see each other, but we have to keep the music to ourselves until we find the third part."

The instrument pulsed in her hand as if agreeing or possibly disagreeing. She could only hope no one had been listening for it. Although she knew better.

Chapter Twenty-Three

HER ORIGINAL PLAN included catching the ferry back to the mainland. She hadn't taken into account how hard it would be to make it back to the main island. Nole and Meara pushed out the boat and jumped in when the tide came in to give them an extra boost. The boat danced on top of the rising tide, then splashed down in the water. What should have been so simple ended with the boat rocking in a trough between waves. They weren't going anywhere. Using the paddle left in the boat, she dug into the water on her right side, turning the boat left. Another strong pull and the boat turned again, turning in circles.

The lamb and dragon clouds came together and made one dark storm cloud right above the boat. "How am I going to make it back?" She plucked at her shirt and added, "It's so hot."

A nearby splash caught her attention. Nole's dark head showed above the water. "Are you deserting me once you saw how hopeless it is?"

The boat started to move. The rope used to tie the boat up was pulled tight as Nole held on to it and swam for their lives. When they reached shallow water, Meara scrambled out, trying to reduce some of the burden. She pushed the boat back in the reeds where she found it. All she had to do now was get to the ferry, fast.

The ordeal had left Nole exhausted. He collapsed on the bank with his tongue hanging out. He was probably too tired to pant. The poor creature needed fresh water, which she had, but wasn't sure how to give it to him. After pawing through her knapsack, she found a cup—not very big. It could work. She poured water into the cup and held it out to Nole, who gave her a grateful glance before slurping it up. Meara poured some more and watched the tired animal made short work of it. It didn't look they were going to make it to the ferry.

They might make it to Aunt Mary's, though. With any luck, she'd be as kind as John and maybe feed them. Yes, she certainly hoped the woman was generous. Just the mention of her nephew's name to Mary might be enough to get them a cup of tea and a scone. Nole would need something more substantial. She didn't feel like looking for berries and nuts. On a small island like this there probably wasn't that much and what they had would have already been picked over.

Even though the path to the town wasn't that far, with a third of her weight in mud clinging to her and squishing in her boots, every step was a herculean effort.

Keep going. She was sure if she chanted the mantra in her head or aloud it would help. Probably in her head because speaking would take too much work.

Her personal thundercloud moved on leaving the bright sun beating down on her. Had she heard Scotland was cooler than England? That couldn't be. She was suffocating. At last, she spotted the spire of the parish church. "Almost there."

Meara wasn't sure who she was reassuring—herself or the dog. "Green roof. Did he say something about a dragon?"

Two women circled around her. One clicked her tongue. "Another of Mary's strays. Don't know where she finds them."

Mary, that was the name she needed to remember. Green roof. The buildings kept going in and out of focus. It was hard to decide which one had a green roof. Two elderly ladies in matching aprons and caps popped out of twin doors. They hurried in her direction.

"Oh, my dear, take my arm. You're ready to drop."

It was hard to know which arm to take. She tried to grasp one, then the other, and finally felt something solid under her fingers. The woman led her up a neat stone path outlined by flowers. Meara knew she should say something. What was it? "John, John sent me."

"Oh, that would be like him. He has a heart softer than mine. Did he say anything else?"

He had. She couldn't remember. "I...I forgot."

"No worries. We'll get you inside and sit you down on one of my wooden kitchen chairs."

Anything that had to do with kitchen was good. They passed through a rounded doorway into a home that smelt of lavender and apples. An indignant bark meant Nole had the door shut in his face.

"My dog." She couldn't afford to lose her companion and so far, he'd proven his worth more than once.

"I didn't know. Let me sit you down and I'll look after your pet."

Not feeling capable of speech, she allowed the slight woman to push her into a chair. After that, everything went black.

A PERSISTENT NUDGING finally forced Meara to open her eyes. Anxious brown eyes gazed into hers, then a long pink tongue swiped her face. "Nole."

Hearing his name, he blessed her with two more good licks. A woman she remembered briefly before a descent to the floor bent down to look at her.

"Your pup has been worried. I've been a tad, too. Tried to clean you the best I could. Got your boots off. You should be twenty pounds lighter without them." She gestured to Meara's clothes. "I sponged off the front. Couldn't do much about the back. If I can get you to sit up, you need some liquids."

Using her good hand, she managed to wiggle in an upright position, bracing her back against the wall. "How's this?"

"It will work for now." She bent and handed Meara a cup of tea.

It had cooled off and was tepid to the taste. Just as well because she gulped down the sweet liquid. Mary took her cup and placed a sandwich in her hand. Food! Nole sat beside her but had no real interest in the sandwich besides a cursory sniff.

"Don't be sharing your food with the dog. He ate and ate. It was as if he'd never eaten in his life. You two been on the road long?"

Mary assumed the two of them had been together for a while. "Can't say for Nole. I just met him today."

"What should I call you? The tag on the dog you just met today reads, Meara. That can't be right."

Well, she had her there. Was it too late to tell her a pretend name? "You can call me Mark."

"Now, why would I want to do that unless it is short for something like Marcella."

"Could be." Her teeth sunk into her bottom lips as she considered what to do. "Might as well call me Meara."

"Are you running from the law?" Her thin brows knitted together, and she placed one fist on her hip. "I'll not tolerate any law breakers in my home."

"You'll have none. No, I haven't broken any laws." Maybe stretched a few. That she'd keep to herself. As for whatever those squirrels did, that was all them.

A chair squawked as Mary dragged it across the floor and set it beside Meara. Taking a seat, shehe placed her fragile hand on Meara's brow. "Some fever. Not as much as before. I put some yarrow in your tea to help with it."

It was hard to fight the temptation to push her hand away. Growing up in a world without physical touch could cause her to over-react to the smallest stroke. "It was weird. I could barely walk or see."

"Eat. Drink. I'll get you some water. The flush on your cheeks tells me dehydration but it could be a reaction to the infection."

"What infection?" She had a clue something was up with her

arm, but she needed to be clear just in case another part of her body decided to play tricks on her.

"Your arm." She stood ready to retrieve more food and water. "John must have mentioned I was a nurse in the Crimean War. With an infection like yours, they'd just cut off your arm."

"No!" It might not be working too well. Still, she wanted to keep it. "Can I do something about it?"

Mary gave her a long look before smiling. "I'd say you've done just about enough going through God knows where and getting filthy. Who knows what you might have contracted. Let me go get my herb basket."

Meara shuddered, imagining microscopic bugs crawling all over her. She used her good hand to brush them off. Her hostess returned with a large basket hanging from her arm and started sorting through it. Picking out muslin bags with writing on it and the occasional jar. She sat them on the nearby table. Mary held up a jar and spoke.

"First off, a hot bath. I may not have much in modern medical supplies, but I do have plenty of herbs. I'll make you a tincture of cat's claw that might ease the infection. I'll throw in some ginger and cinnamon, too. It will help with the taste and the infection. For your bones, I have comfrey and rue. I have a salve I made from arnica that should help you."

The names of the different herbs flew by her as Meara focused on the word—bath. How long had it been since she'd had a real bath as opposed to washing off in the stream? It had to have been back in Ireland at Aunt Erin's home. That had been months. No wonder people were avoiding her on the street. She'd found the second part of the horn. Surely, that should deserve a celebration. A bath sounded like one to her. "I'd love a bath. Do you think I can have one and get down to the ferry before it leaves?"

Mary broke off, considering the jar in her hand and assumed a stern look. If you left this minute you might make the ferry."

That meant no bath. She placed her hand against the wall and struggled to stand. Her attempt left her off balance, causing her to slide back down the wall.

"The fact John sent you to me meant he already knew how sick you were. He has a sense about those things. Look at you, as puny as a newborn kitten. Never got to finish what I was saying. If you leave now, you might make the ferry, but the infection will spread through your body. Since you're on your own with no one to care for you, I expect you to be dead in a month. Maybe less."

Dead. Even though death was an eventuality, she hoped to put it off for a bit longer. "Why would I be dead in a month?"

"Look at how weak you are. Would you be able to find food and water and care for yourself if flat on your back with fever? Doesn't take a medical expert like myself," she pressed her palm to her chest, "to see you're in a bad way. How long have you been living on the land? Months? A year?"

If Mary thought she'd been living out in the woods for a year, she must look bad, indeed. The sad reality was she was this bad off after days, not months. "I, ah, long enough."

"My advice is for you to heal. Give your body time to recover. Whatever it is you need to do can be done when you are well."

Could Braeden and Billy wait until she was well? She doubted it and shook her head. "I need to go now. I don't have time to wait and get better."

"Calmy dooney and use your noggin. You told me you were not running from the law. Even if you were, it is unlikely that the law would find you here. Leave now and you'll end up face down somewhere. Allow your body to heal and your color to return. Once you're tiptop, you can move much faster. Could be at the end, you could use some vigor as opposed to dropping on the floor again."

No one knew what the end entailed. It would be lovely if it was just as easy as today was. She knew better. By leaving her friends, she was hard to track, but that bit of horn blowing at the cemetery may have given her away. Her teeth snapped onto her bottom lip and worried it as she considered the possible outcomes. Whatever was chasing her didn't want her to succeed. If she stopped for a moment, would it leave her alone or catch up with her? What if—an idea started to take form. "Your nephew, John. You say he has a sense about things."

"Aye, that he does." Mary pulled another packet out of the basket and placed it on the table.

"Would he be able to sense if someone had bad intent and not ferry them across?"

"That he would. He's done it more than once, too."

Curious. "How does he do that?"

"He has a sense of who is waiting for him. If it feels bad, he doesn't bother to board his ferry. The bad sort might even ask him when the ferry is leaving, and he might say the wrong time or that it isn't running today."

Made sense. Her evil following was especially clever. Hadn't he used Toby and fooled them all? Could have been because he was a shapeshifter. She hadn't learned much about his kind. "What if this person took his ferry?"

"That would be bad." Mary agreed and continued to sort. "We had some young hooligans do just that. John has the motor locked down when he isn't using it. It takes a small key to open it. The hooligans took the ferry and pushed off thinking it was all a simple matter of getting from there to here. They soon found themselves adrift with the current. John and a few other lads had to rescue the boys. A lesson learned for them."

There might not be any crossing at this time. She knew so little about her nemesis. Was it even flesh and blood? It made use of fleshy bodies, so maybe it did need a ferry. "I will stay until I'm better if that is okay with you."

Mary slapped the table and cackled. "I thought I was going to have to arm wrestle you to get you to stay. I would have won, too.

I'll get started on heating water for your bath."

Bath. It sounded glorious. What could a day or two, possibly three hurt?

Chapter Twenty-Four

DAYS SLID INTO weeks and weeks into months. The broken arm had long since healed and no longer troubled her. Little bothered Meara. Her life was a contented one. Mary and she had developed a good relationship. She helped the elderly woman with her medical practice, gardening, and feeding the birds. Even Nole put on weight and took on the appearance of a pampered pet as opposed to a stray. On the isolated Isle of Arran, the war was more of a rumor most tried to ignore. There were things Meara felt she wasn't remembering, but had little concern over in her contented state.

The summer sun warmed her exposed neck, as she cut herbs in the garden while Mary deadheaded the flowers. A frantic husband rushed in the yard and pleaded for Mary's medical help. The woman agreed to go immediately and gave Meara instructions to follow and what to bring. The raspberry leaf and Black Cohosh would bring on the labor pains. They might not be needed to judge by the anxious look of the future father's face. Those herbs, Mary had in her bag, but she was out of catnip. That would have to be picked and brewed into a tea by Meara. After picking a handful, she went to look for the tea kettle.

Normally, it hung on the knob, but was missing. Peculiar. Meara rooted around the cabinets without any luck. Finally, she resorted to using a stool to search the higher cabinets. The higher she got, the more it sounded like music was being played. It had to be the church folks practicing for Sunday service. It didn't bode well that whoever was playing kept repeating the same flurry of notes, though by Sunday, he might have the entire song down.

When she opened the last cabinet, a blast of sound almost knocked her off the stool. Inside was a wiggling bag. Should she touch it? Had a varmint in search of food climbed into the cabinet? A musical tweet sounded from the bag. Goodness, it must be a bird. She carefully took the bag by its top and carried it outside to release the bird.

Once outside, she opened the bag. Nothing happened. When she peered inside, she saw a horn of sorts and drew it out. Her fingers tingled as she did so, and her memory returned.

It's time to go.

Where had her past gone to? How had it faded away? Where had the message come from? Better yet, why now? She'd been happy with Mary, believing as most folks that she was a shirt tail relative who had come to help the elderly woman and was glad of it. People usually smiled when they saw the two of them together. How was she introduced?

Since the population was small, most stayed with first names or titles such as Nurse Mary or Nurse Helper Meara. A few had even started calling her Young Mary, too, though the gutsy nurse had never married or had children. The days had all been similar with the usual chores and an occasional medical emergency. It shouldn't be too unusual that they'd faded into one another. Still, she often felt as if she was repeating something she had done before but couldn't remember doing it.

When she touched the horn, she remembered everything. Ten minutes before she couldn't even remember winter or when she had shown up at the place. Scenes from almost drowning in the sea, to running with Rosemary, to a parade of squirrels crowded her mind. Each memory forced its way in. Vivid, violent, and determined to be, reminding her of all she'd forgotten. An urgency built inside of her making her restless and wanting to break into a run. It was time to go.

First, she took the catnip to Mary. It would have to be brewed there. It was a short jog to the laboring woman's house. On the way, a few neighbors greeted her warmly, and she returned the greeting, explaining she had no time to talk. She did have plenty of time to think. How had she forgotten about her mission? Was this a trick by a pursuer? It was a good one since she never had a suspicion of what was happening to her until the horn called to her. Mary and she had settled into an easy life together. They took walks, attended church on Sunday, took tea together every morning and midafternoon. She enjoyed hearing Mary's tales as a nurse and her work behind battle lines. Was the war even happening? Had she missed her chance? Maybe she had not even been needed? Could everything be just a fevered dream?

With the horn bag strapped crosswise against her body, the vibrating assured her it was very real. When she arrived at the house, she didn't bother to knock. Instead, she strolled in and announced herself. "It's me, Meara. I'm here."

"Good. Bring me the catnip tea right away," Mary called out from the other room. A deep moan accompanied her order.

"I will, but I have to brew it first. I couldn't find the teapot. Do you know what happened to it?"

There was silence, then another moan, which propelled Meara into action. Obviously, Mary was too busy with the new mother to answer. She set aside the cool water to add to the tea once steeped. Once done, she delivered it, and waited while the woman drank. Here, so far away from the mainland, almost all the medicines were herbal. Not only were traditional medicines hard to get, they tended to be expensive, too. Almost anything could be delivered via a tea.

Meara watched as Mary encouraged the mother to drink the tea. There was silence in the room as the woman drank and the cup was handed back to Meara. "Do you need my help?"

"Not right now. Labor takes a while. You could make dinner. I don't think Martha," she angled her head to the woman in the bed, "is up to doing it."

It was a familiar drill, and despite Meara's confusion and growing concern, she applied herself to caring for the patient. Mary and Meara had arrived at many houses to treat sickness, deliver babies, or ease the transition to the other side. The one thing they all had in common was families had to eat, as did the medical help. Few people ever paid Mary with money. They often brought her produce, a chicken, firewood, or whatever they had a surplus of.

Bread and a hearty soup would serve. Most larders would have the makings for that. Since it would take the bread longer, she started with that. As she stirred, she considered the breadmaking skill. How had she learned it? The convent cook guarded her kitchen jealously—so it hadn't been there. She put down her spoon to knead the dough. Odd how she remembered simple things such as making bread, but had forgotten her quest. Her body remembered many things she had learned, but her mind didn't. Peculiar.

The dough sat in a greased pan on top of the stove as Meara started on the soup. What would have made her forget? A bump on the head? Maybe. Her nose crinkled as she considered just how long she'd forgotten. Didn't seem likely. Someone or something could be making her forget. The most likely candidate would be her nameless nemesis who often seeped into others to do his dirty work. No one had threatened her or had been mean to her since she came to the island.

Still, she was here and as far as she knew the war raged on.

Footsteps had her turning slightly to see who it was. Mary smiled at her. "Something smells good."

So typical of her friend, quick with praise even when she didn't deserve it. Meara held up a turnip. "I'm only cutting vegetables. I haven't made the soup, yet."

"It must be the bread."

Meara's shoulder went up in a shrug. "It hasn't even risen, yet.

Not sure what you think you are smelling. It might be someone else's dinner wafting on the breeze." When she turned to face Mary, the horn clanked against the stove, drawing attention. "Is the war still going on?"

"It is. I figured you know as much since you've discovered the horn."

"You'd be right. What I want to know—" Meara started, but her friend interrupted her before she could finish.

"I know what I did was wrong." She wiped her hands on the apron wrapped around her waist. "It didn't start out that way. I just wanted you to get better."

"I am better. I'm not sure I understand." She picked up a carrot as she considered Mary's demeanor. Living as they did, she'd had plenty of time to know the woman's moods and expressions. Sad, happy, tired, even mischievous were all familiar ones, but this one puzzled her.

"Well, ah." Mary pulled at her collar. "It started with you being near death and trying to go finish your task. I told you rest was what you needed. You wouldn't listen. The only thing I could think to do was to give you a calming tea for forgetfulness. Usually it's something I use for heartbreak. It helps when a woman has been left by her beau choosing another or by dying. It's not something I'd advise someone to take for a long time, but it helps in the short run. You were going to die if you ran off without allowing your body to heal. John knew that, which is why he sent you to me. As a nurse, my job is to heal. It's an oath I swore."

Tea. That was it. Even though she liked the tea, Mary had urged it on her every day, sometimes twice a day. "I must have been healed for a while now."

"True." She picked at her apron, avoiding Meara's gaze. "I liked having a constant companion. There's been plenty of people who drift through my home and leave as soon as they are better. I knew you'd be gone as soon as you remembered. That's why I hid the odd horn and anything else that might cause you to remember."

Meara's hands went up to her throat. All of her necklaces were missing. Wouldn't she be a sitting duck without her amulet? Surely she could be sensed easily. Then again, maybe a person had to be close to do that. Could be since she had no clear memory of who she was, she existed only as a ghost of who she used to be. Didn't ghosts have memories, which led to their haunting places? She wasn't even a visible spirit, then. Everything that identified her had been removed.

"Where is my amulet? My locket?" A tear formed in her eye as she realized all that had been taken. "It was the only tie with my mother."

"I realized someday you'd remember and want your things. I kept them. Try to understand." Moving close, Mary held out her hand to touch Meara.

Meara stepped back. "I'd appreciate the return of my things before I leave. What made you keep dosing me with that tea every livelong day. How could that be right?"

"It's not right. I'm not proud, but I was lonely. We worked so well together. Maybe in time, I'd have lessened the dose and stopped it eventually, hoping you'd agree that we'd had a happy time together and would want to stay."

Words she needed to say were not coming easily. Instead, Meara wrestled with growing anger over being drugged for so long, as well as being deprived of everything that should have been protecting her. From the amulet to the protection ring Aunt Erin had made her, nothing did any good hidden away. Even the Tarot cards and the pendulum would have provided some guidance. What had happened to Rosemary? Jane and Ronan? With the war still going, were Billy and Braeden still alive? What about her dreams? She couldn't remember any. Had her mother and father tried to speak to her? "I can't even remember dreaming at night."

"Everyone dreams." Mary's voice cracked a little on the last word. "Because of that, I may have added a sedative to your late afternoon tea so you'd sleep soundly."

Who was this woman she had loved as a surrogate grandmother? Here she thought they had a close, loving relationship. Was any of it true? Maybe any strange girl could have tumbled in the street outside the door, and she would have done the same. Not everyone had the need to travel on. Someone else may have stayed without being drugged.

It was hard to gaze at Mary, knowing what she had done. "You even took my dreams from me."

"No!" She held up both hands as if holding off the accusation. "I may have helped you forget your dreams. I never stopped them."

Fearing she might throw them in frustration, she put down the carrot and knife. "How is that any different?"

"I love you. I took care of you." She wrapped her arms around Meara's stiff body. "That should count for something."

"It does." Her anger melted a little. She did love Mary, despite the woman's actions. "All the same, I have to go. I'd like to have my belongings back."

"You will just as soon as we deliver this baby." A long moan from the bedroom had Mary releasing her and hurrying to see her patient.

Six hours later, they welcomed the newest resident to Lamlash, a dark-eyed boy with a thatch of equally dark hair. The proud father thanked them numerous times as they packed up to leave. He pushed a small money pouch into Mary's hand.

"I know most folks give you something they have. It might not necessarily be something you need, either. I figure you could always do with a bit of coin. My wife and son are priceless. I can't pay you what you deserve, but here."

Mary managed a tired smile and wrapped her fingers around the bag. "Treasure your family."

Geese honking was the only sound on their walk home. Most of the words had been used up between them. Nole welcomed them at the garden gate with a joyous bark.

Dropping to her knees, Meara gave the dog a hug. "Sorry I was gone so long. I would have taken you, but a woman in labor could probably do without a barking dog."

"I'll miss Nole, too," Mary said with a tiny tremor to her voice.

The dog could stay. Meara almost offered but knew better. Nole would go wherever she went. When she asked for companionship, she received Nole, and on the same day she met Mary. What if Mary had been meant to be her companion? The stuff in the tea was sneaky, but it could have been fate. She hated that so much time had passed. Still, if she had left when she wanted to, she would never have made it. What if fate kept her there, so she'd be strong and ready to go when she could? It was something to consider. It made her less resentful toward her friend.

Instead of saying anything, she embraced Mary, hoping to convey what she couldn't say.

Mary hugged her back and spoke. "I always wanted a daughter. If I had one, I was going to teach her to be brave. Show her how she could survive as a lone woman in a man's world. In some ways, I pretended you were my daughter, and I did show you what I knew. You are brave and determined to go alone in this world. Somehow, I have a feeling it will be all right. When you're less angry with me, think about visiting."

She rested her head on top of the smaller woman's head. "I'll be back if only for a visit. Only, I'll make the tea."

"I'll let you." They both chuckled and the three of them went inside for the night.

There were a few hours left to the day, and Meara spent them getting ready. She took a bath since it could be her last for a while. Her hair had grown out some, and she debated about cutting it. No matter how brave she was, a woman alone still gathered unwanted attention. Mary trimmed it for her, insisting she didn't have to look like a ragamuffin. After the haircut, Mary brought out the laundered clothes and boots Meara had worn when they first met, along with her knapsack, knife, and necklaces. She placed the amulet and locket around her neck and felt a tingle and an immediate weight.

She pawed through her knapsack and found the ring Aunt Erin had made and put it on. With each item donned, she felt more like herself. With the last ferry for the day gone, it would be morning before she could leave. With any luck, she'd sneak out before Mary awoke.

The woman lifted one eyebrow as if divining her thoughts. She pushed a nightgown at Meara. "I know you'll do your share of sleeping in the woods, but there'll come a time when you'll get to use a bed. For that, you'll need a nightgown. I was working on this one for your Christmas gift. Good thing I finished it early. It has the yellow Scotch Broom flower you like so much on it. You can remember Arran when you wear it."

"I'll think of you and Arran when I wear it. It's always good to have a bit of civilization with me."

"Good." Mary tried for a cheery grin that wobbled some. "Don't go thinking you'll sneak out on me without a decent breakfast. I'll pack you and Nole a lunch, too. Don't go saying you don't need one, either."

That she hadn't planned on. If she learned anything from her adventure, it was eat when you could, because you couldn't be certain when your next meal was coming. "I won't."

Meara's plan was to go to her bed and go through her knapsack to get ready for tomorrow. She would soon. Right now, she'd spend time with Mary. "Have you ever told me about when you were a girl?"

"I told you about when I was a nurse."

"Before that, when you were just a girl, what was your life like? Did you have any dreams or goals?"

They sat in the kitchen as Mary recalled her girlhood from long ago, smiling at things she hadn't recalled in forever. It was an easy time of shared camaraderie and fond laughter, a fitting way to say goodbye. Meara knew there'd be a leave-taking in the morning. This time was more about forgiveness and friendship. Meara didn't want to leave on a sour note. It was hard to explain why she was no longer mad since she didn't understand it herself. Tomorrow she'd start her journey again, and she'd be ready.

Chapter Twenty-Five

A BIRD TRILLED outside the window. Meara had come to think of the little petrel as an alarm clock of sorts. On this day, she'd been awake for a while, considering what route she should take. Back to England for sure, which would be south with an eye peeled for a train station. Since she had her Tarot cards, which had survived a dunking in the water, she could put them to use. Closing her eyes, she considered her question and shuffled the cards.

The first card she pulled was a Six of Swords. On the card, was a woman and child in a boat being rowed to the other side. There were six swords in the boat with her. It was clear change was involved, along with travel. Her fingers gripped the card as she held it up to her face, searching for the markers Grandmother Biddy had taught her. They were on top of the water, but not in it. Whatever emotions were involved she could control them. Everyone had their backs showing with their faces toward whatever would come. She was leaving the past behind. There was blue sky on the other side, hinting at a better future. There were also six swords in the boat if she should need them. It was a fitting card. Too bad it didn't tell her where her father's farm was.

Uncle Simon mentioned receiving a letter from someone from Beacon, Wales, that told about Fulmen's death. The farm could be in Beacon or close by. Someone also might have ridden to the next town and posted it. If she drew close enough, she could ask. Even though it had been years, folks should remember villagers on the rampage, a Druid killed, and his pregnant wife escaping through the woods. Most should feel enough shame never to mention it, but then there were those who liked to talk. If all else failed, the horn she carried would pull her to the rest of it.

The clank and clatter of pans meant Mary was up. Nole rested his head on the bed and watched her with his liquid eyes. He'd need to go out for a final run in the garden and possibly a fast game of chase with the neighbor's cat. The big yellow cat next door would take a turn at chasing Nole, too. It amazed her that creatures so commonly referred to as enemies could get along if they chose to, which was more than she could say for mankind in its current state. The smell of sausage and tattie scones got her moving toward the kitchen with Nole following along.

Even though it might hurt Mary's feelings, she'd have to bypass the tea. Fool her once was understandable. Fool her again and they might as well call her the village idiot. "Morning," she called out as she passed Mary at the stove to let Nole out.

"Morning," Mary replied and handed her a pitcher. "I figure you could get us some water since I doubt you'll trust anything I might serve you to drink."

Rather than reply to the inference, she grabbed the pitcher and followed Nole out. They had several barrels in the garden to collect rain. Fresh water could sometimes be scarce on an island. That's why her bath of the night before had been such a luxury. Most of the time a basin and a cloth served. When she re-entered the kitchen, Mary had placed the kettle and a tea tin on the table. The unspoken message was she could brew the tea.

Without making any comment, she rinsed out the kettle before filling it up. The noise had Mary glancing up from the skillet. "So, you're going to forgive me a little?"

"Looks like it."

"I don't blame you for being upset. Anyone would be. Most wouldn't have passed the night with me. I'm glad you did. What are your plans?"

Grandmother Biddy's words came back. *Trust no one.* Well, she'd certainly failed at that one. Did Grandmother mean not to trust her own relatives? Uncle Simon had come to England to find her. Ronan, Brigit, and Aunt Erin helped her find the first section of the horn. There had been a few brushes with folks and the shapeshifter calling himself Toby. It would be best to misdirect, which would be a fancy way to say lie. "I guess I'll go back to Hogstead where I'm from."

Mary raised an eyebrow. "I didn't think you were too fond of the place."

It made her wonder what she'd said. Drinking a steady diet of forgetful tea made things a little hazy. She could have talked about Hogstead until she forgot about it. "It's not the town as much as I told my sweetheart that I'd wait for him when he went off to war."

"That's a different story, then. Is he a good man?"

"Yes, he is. Braeden chose to fight before they started conscripting men." No need to add he did it partly to get away from Adelaide's machinations, which made him sound flimsy as opposed to patriotic.

"Be safe. Don't take chances. If I had a weapon, I'd give it to you. Your knife is better than anything I have. Since you've gotten proficient with the herbs, I packed a few for you. Tucked in some peppermint for belly problems, and it reduces fevers, too. Included yarrow, which helps with wound healing and anxiety. There are a few others, too. Not sure how you plan to get by, but you know enough to do general nursing."

Meara measured the tea into the china pot as she listened. She savored the aroma. Good black tea was hard to find. Most of it was shipped to the troops. When you considered the Tommies were far from home, they should at least have a drop of tea. She and Mary had been drinking various leaves, usually peppermint, some chamomile, and raspberry, which made it easy for Mary to sneak something else in. Nothing else smelled like Earl Grey tea with its hint of bergamot. She'd only had it a few times, but it was enough to make an impression.

After the tea steeped, breakfast was served. Mary and Meara ate without much discussion, each lost in her own thoughts. The ferry came early so there wasn't too much time to waste. "I'll need to get going. Nole and I have a few miles to walk."

"John will be expecting you. I sent a message with one of the fishermen who was heading that way. He'll wait for you. Hope there aren't too many on the ferry who'll be upset by waiting. Shouldn't, as I'm sure people have waited on them a time or two. Let's say our goodbyes inside. I don't care for everyone knowing my business."

Meara could empathize. No sooner than the news would be out about her departure, than some would feel obliged to tell Mary she'd been taken advantage of. Never mind the hard work Meara had put into helping her hostess. People would forget with her leave taking all she had done. Sometimes, relationships weren't meant to last forever. It hadn't been easy leaving Eleanor when she and Rosemary fled England. Still, it would be hard to say goodbye to Mary.

No use putting off what had to be done. "I appreciate all you've done for both Nole and me. I'd offer to let him stay if I thought he would."

"Aye, that would never work." Mary clucked her tongue. "That one is your dog through and through."

"It appears that way." She stood and shouldered her bag. "We might even have to run a bit to make decent time. Appreciate the meal. Feel bad leaving you with the dishes."

She shook her head slowly. "Don't. It will give me something to do. Before you go, I have a blessing for you." She cleared her throat. "I wish these things for you. Someone to love, work to do, a bit of sun, a bit of cheer, and a guardian angel always near."

The tender sentiment choked up Meara a little, but she swallowed the emotion before it got the best of her. The woman in the boat on the Tarot card may have been sad at leaving, but she knew the change would be for her own good. It was a positive card that she'd hold onto. There were no promises. Life could change day by day. Her motto would be she could only worry about one day at a time.

"Thank you. That was lovely." She embraced Mary, and Nole made his goodbyes by nudging his hostess. The hug went on a little longer than planned. Finally, she loosened her arms and turned to the door, holding one hand up in farewell. Others might have had more to say with flowery speeches, but Meara didn't trust herself not to cry. It was best just to go.

She left, closing the gate behind her. Nole understood her mood and walked quietly beside her instead of his usual dashing ahead. Mary determined he couldn't be too old since he had no white in his muzzle, had all his teeth, and a great deal of play in him.

It's the right thing to do.

Surprisingly, she recognized her mother's soft voice. "I know it is. I still feel bad about leaving, even if everyone must be so disappointed in me for spending so much time on Arran."

It was as it should be. Timing is very important when you blow the horn. You couldn't arrive any earlier.

"I thought once blown all men would put down their weapons." She could testify to its magic. It certainly could find its other part.

I thought the same when we buried it. I've had plenty of time to observe mankind. It saddens me how people can be so cruel to one another. The thing that is obvious to me, isn't to the living. Your time here has allowed hearts to become weary of war. This should work in your favor.

The reassurance her parents' comments usually provided was missing. Maybe it was because she hadn't heard her mother in such a long time. One of the villagers waved at her as she passed. She waved back, not bothering to stop and made no reply to her mother. Even though she was on her way out, it would do Mary no good to have folks say she'd harbored someone who was off in their head and talking to herself.

The ferry was up ahead with John leaning against a pole, talking to another man dressed in a fishing slicker. It could have been the man who carried the message. John saw her and waved. "Here comes my fare."

The man joked he should get to work and headed to a small boat tied up near the pier.

Nole ran ahead when he spotted John. He raced around the man, barking his glee.

She was a little less vocal about seeing the amiable ferryman.

When she neared, he teased. "Who might this be coming along with Meara's dog, Nole?"

"You know."

"The voice sounds familiar." He scratched his head as if confused. "Couldn't be. You're cleaner and probably a stone or two heavier than who I am thinking of."

"A stone, not two stones," she corrected. "I certainly hope I am cleaner. I'm not sure I could have got much dirtier."

"Aye." John agreed and opened the gate for her to board. She winked as she got on, letting him know she knew he spoke the truth.

He gathered the mooring ropes and hopped back on before the ferry could drift away. As a good-sized man, he had a fair leap. "It would help if I had a helper waiting at each end. So far, no offers."

"In time." She put down her bag to root through it for coin. "How much do I owe you for passage?' Her fingers curled around the money bag at the bottom of her knapsack. She pulled it upward. It felt heavier than she remembered. Thinking Mary had put in the recent money she earned from her midwifery had her smiling.

"No money. The coin you gave me last time will keep you in ferry rides for years. Went to Aberdeen in the winter to see Kelly Ann's folks. There's a coin dealer there who gave me a generous price for it. I count myself blessed."

"It was obviously meant for you."

"I like to think so." He moved over to the motor and started it, adding a little pulse to the rocking the water already provided. "I'm glad you spent some time with Mary. She may have fattened you up, but you've done a world of wonder for her. I appreciate your staying as long as you did. Surprised, actually."

No need to mention anything. She shrugged. "Your Aunt Mary can be insistent."

"That I know."

The morning sun glinted off the water and picked out the shape of trees on the opposite shore. From here, it was tranquil. *Wait.* She was the woman on the Tarot card. Instead of a child, she had a dog. They were both moving on to the next stage of their life. Grandmother Biddy would remind her this moment was confirmation she'd picked the card meant for her. Always good to know. It made her wonder what you did when you picked a card that wasn't right. How would you know?

The ferry nosed toward the shore as John scurried to turn off the motor. Afterward, he grabbed one of the heavy mooring ropes and threw it at the sturdy pole hammered into the ground. The big loop hung in the air, then dropped down onto the pole.

"Hey-o." He grinned, opened the gate, and flipped out a short walkway made of a couple of boards to span the gap between the water and the land. Meara walked over it while Nole followed more slowly, staring at the water. Before he could make a definite decision, John scooped him up. "I certainly wouldn't want you going off without the pooch."

"Thanks. We're off on our adventure."

"Good luck to you."

Meara smiled and waved while adding mentally that she'd need all the luck she could get. Nole bumped up against her leg as if seconding her opinion. The adventure begins. Somehow, it sounded better that way.

Chapter Twenty-Six

LUCK WAS WITH her on the early days. They managed to hop a freight train heading to England. They were okay for a while in a train car that must have held horses. There was hay left behind, along with the smell of horses. Meara and Nole found a clean corner on the side with the door. It worked well. Whenever the railroad guards peered in to check for freeloaders, they weren't seen unless they did a thorough job. Most didn't. Few even bothered to slam the door until one shut it and latched it from the outside.

For a few panicked moments, she was sure they'd die in there. Still, they had water and some food. The rocking motion lulled Nole and Meara asleep. They made it to Manchester before someone decided to check the cars again. The rattle and slam of the doors announced an inspection coming their way. Meara had her knapsack on and her cap pulled down, ready to jump out when the door opened. Nole growled as the sound grew closer, flattened his ears, and settled into a half crouch. The employee shouted at someone as he opened the door and had his head turned away. When Nole hurtled through the opening with a snarl, the man stumbled back. Turning sideways to fit through, Meara jumped to the ground and ran, following Nole. There were a few shouts and a chase that broke off almost as soon as it started. While riding the train for free might be frowned on, no one wanted to apprehend anyone with a vicious dog.

Those were their salad days. By day twenty-two on the adventure and she expected to be farther. Walking everywhere took time, especially when they had to hide whenever she heard a carriage or an automobile. The cars, however, were rarer due to the lack of fuel. This they found out when they ended up meeting a woman walking home after deserting an empty car. Nole befriended her, and Meara felt rather peculiar, lurking in the woods like a monster from children's tales.

It turned out the woman driver had a father in a key position, which allowed him the privilege of a car and fuel. Apparently, it hadn't been as much fuel as the daughter had thought. They kept her company until she made it to her father's office. Anticipating it probably wouldn't go well for her, they left as fast as they could. Nor did she like being in the confines of the city that kept her from any natural help she might get from the faeries or the animal kingdom. On the way out, she saw a couple of soldiers shuffling by on crutches. A second look had her checking to make sure it wasn't Braeden or Billy.

"What are you looking at?" one of the soldiers jeered. "Haven't you ever seen a cripple?"

"I have. Sister Lazarus used a cane. I wondered if any of you were someone I knew."

"We're no one. Nobody knows us now. People look the other way instead of doing us the courtesy to look us in the eyes."

She wanted to deny that people did that. How would she know? "I was wondering if you knew a Braeden Douglas?"

The bitter one gave a negative shake while the other looked thoughtful and asked, "Do you know what unit he was in?"

Even though they promised to write one another, she never received that information. "All I know is he joined almost at the beginning. We promised to write." She shrugged her thin shoulders. "I move around a lot."

The bitter one ducked his head to peer under her hat bill. "Will you look at that. It's a girl. See what this war has done. It has our women dressing up like men. Damn Huns!"

Meara could have explained the Huns had nothing to do with it. She changed her opinion when she considered the bombing and her mission. The war changed all their lives in some fashion. She waited on the quieter one to speak.

"I think I do remember a Douglas." He held his hand up to his head. "About this high, brown hair. Came from somewhere with a swine name if I remember correctly."

"Hogstead." The name came to her automatically.

"That's it." The man nudged the other one. "I knew the name sounded familiar."

"When did you see him?" It meant Braeden was alive or at least living when he was seen. Her heart skipped a beat at the news.

"It's been a while." His eyes rolled upward as he considered. "Not sure how long ago. Time is difficult to track at the front. With all the shooting, mortars, and grenades going off, half the time I wasn't even sure I was alive. There was no way to know the difference between night and day. It was smoky and almost impossible to breathe all the time."

It sounded horrible, but he hadn't answered her question.

The other one picked up the conversation. "It was hell, pure and simple."

"Walter, you don't talk to a lady that way."

"Figure if she can wear pants, she can hear the truth."

"All right, boys." She held up one hand, hoping to delay an argument. "I can handle the truth. Where did you see Braeden Douglas?"

"Field hospital. He was there because he was gassed. When I saw him, he was being shipped back. He could be at one of the convalescent centers set up around the country. There is even one here."

"Where?"

"I can show you," The taller soldier with the kind eyes offered., His friend grumbled.

"I don't want to walk that far. I'm not a tour guide."

She held her hands and waved them slightly above her waist. "Don't go to all that work. Tell me the direction and I can find it."

"I wouldn't feel right allowing a lady to traipse around the town on her own."

"It will be fine." She forced a smile to reassure him. "I've traveled through Ireland, Scotland, and Wales. I'm sure I can handle Manchester."

She could tell the man was reluctant. He told her the address and made her repeat it back twice. "Thank you."

She had no clue where the streets he mentioned were. Someone had to know. If she asked enough people, she would find it. Could it be so simple that she'd find Braeden in a hospital bed close by? She tried to not to skip as she rushed off. No reason to be excited. If he was back, it didn't mean he was waiting to see her. It had been over two years since they were together last. The girl he kissed goodbye no longer existed. She'd been replaced by a harder, more cynical version.

It took her a good thirty minutes to find someone who knew where the streets were. The war had done a great job of relocating everyone and few people were natives. Instead of arriving at a hospital, she found herself at a library. At least, it had been a library. There was a plywood sign with poorly printed letters announcing a soldier convalescent center that didn't fully cover the larger library sign. The ARY stuck out making it read Centerary.

The front door was open to catch a breeze as she approached. A doctor and nurse complained just inside the door about their lack of supplies.

"We have no aspirin. None." The nurse said. At least Meara assumed she was a nurse. She had a large white apron wrapped around her body and wore a high, white hat that made her look more like a sister than medical personnel.

The bearded man, with a stethoscope around his neck, shook his head. "I can't believe we don't even have the simplest of medicines.

How are we going to deal with fevers and inflammation?"

Even though she hadn't been invited into the conversation, she waded into it anyhow. "Have you tried arnica for inflammation? Yarrow, especially if mixed with peppermint, can bring down a high fever."

The man arched his eyebrows. Meara wasn't sure if inserting herself into the conversation offended him or the use of herbs.

The nurse, however, accepted her suggestion with a smile. "I remember grandmother using those. Sometimes, if I had a headache, she put a couple drops of lavender oil on a handkerchief and have me lie down in a cool, dark room"

The doctor gave a dismissing sniff. "I'm sure you're going to tell me it cured your headache."

"It did. There's no reason to look down on the old ways if they work."

It would have been hard for anyone to look more skeptical. "At the risk of returning to the dark ages, where do we find these miraculous herbs?"

The nurse shrugged her shoulders. That was Meara's cue. "I have some in my bag."

"For which you are going to charge me an obscene price. Forget about it. I don't buy the medicine. I only use what they send me."

"Oh, no, I wouldn't charge. I spent a good part of the last year working with a nurse from the Crimean War."

The nurse leaned forward to hear better. "Those nurses were the trailblazers."

"She must be a hundred years old." The doctor added a sniff to the end of his statement.

Meara didn't know Mary's actual age. "No. She's in great shape—and practically takes care of everyone on the isle. There aren't any fancy medicines, which leaves her growing her own herbs. It works very well. Just before I left she did a delivery using catnip tea for pain. She used cohosh to bring on the labor, I think."

The doctor gave her an interested nod. "I'd like to see your herbs and you can explain how to use them."

Meara slipped off her knapsack to root through it while the nurse moved closer. The herbs were in muslin bags that she placed on the counter. "This is what I have. Mary gave them to me before I left just in case I got sick. Didn't happen, so I have plenty left."

"This would be useful. How do you use them?"

She ended up not only demonstrating how to make tea out of the herbs but helping the short-staffed facility distribute them. Usually, she started every conversation with a patient with a question about Braeden. None of them had any information. The next soldier had his head wrapped in bandages, including one over an eye. She asked again. Instead of the usual response, he flashed a smile before he spoke.

"You spend your time asking after Braeden. Nothing for your old pal, Billy O'Dell?"

The voice startled her. It was so out of place here. The Billy she knew belonged on the water or his ironically christened horse, Wind Racer. The single eye and smile she recognized. "Billy! Is it really you?"

"What's left of me." He managed a lopsided grin. "Where's everyone else?"

She shrugged. "I'm clueless. We got separated shortly after you were taken. Rosemary was so devastated at your loss she opened the entire bottle of the forgetfulness potion."

"Ah, how is my Rose?"

Hadn't he heard her mention the four of them had separated almost a year ago? "I wish I knew. Last I saw her, she didn't know any of us. She could remember the basics such as cooking, driving a wagon, and delivering a right hook. She even knocked around a ne'r do well Ronan befriended."

"She shouldn't have to do that, I should have been there."

"You weren't. More's the pity. How have you been?"

His hand went up to his bandages. "See this. My only battle wound, and it is a doozy. Fellow soldiers used to call me lucky and indestructible since I never took a bullet. Never got thrown around by a mortar or a grenade. No matter where I went, nothing happened to me, until a month or so ago. My luck ran out the best I can figure. Still, I'm alive. What are you doing now? Still on that quest?"

Did he forget it was a secret? She whipped around to see who might have heard. The bed to his right was empty. It must have been recently vacated because the covers were mussed. On the other side, the man laid prone with his eyes closed and his mouth open. Either he was asleep or dead. Meara had no desire to find out which.

To forestall any more inquiries, she put out her flat palm. "This isn't the place. The answer is no. Is there still a war going on?"

He sucked his lips and nodded. "Still happening as far as I heard. Information is slow to get around. I've wondered more than once if the war was still happening. We might be out there killing each other after all the big wigs shook hands and went home."

"Still on is what I hear, too." She was about to add more, except she caught sight of the nurse bustling her way."

"Good news!" The nurse beamed in her direction. "If you can go out and find more herbs, brew them, and help treat the patients, we can pay you a small stipend."

"How much?" She could use the money. Her small cache of coins grew smaller with everything being so expensive. Even Nole's soup bone cost her plenty.

Although, it might not be as easy as she might think finding the herbs in war times. Most families knew a little herb lore and were probably collecting what they could.

"Two pounds per week."

Billy shook his head. "Not enough, considering you have to buy the herbs. You need a place to live. Then there is food."

It had sounded like a lot to her, and she had almost said yes.

The nurse, aware that her extra help might vanish as fast as it came, pressed her fingertips together. "There's a cot back in the storage room you can use. It used to be for the night porter. He left. You could eat here free and save money."

Billy grimaced. "It's no treat."

It was sounding better and better. Sleeping on a cot beat sleeping on the hard ground. "There's my dog. In fact, I better go take care of him. He's been waiting for a while." As she turned to go, Billy commented.

"A dog would lift everyone's spirits."

The nurse pursed her lips as if considering the matter. "Maybe. I'm sure the doctor will regard it as a flea factory. You might be able to keep it in your room. The cook could save scraps for your dog."

"That could work." She started to make plans even as she spoke. Two pounds per week was a decent amount. If she ended up buying herbs, that would cut into it. First, she'd have to see what she could find on her own before what she brought ran out. "I'll take it for now. My plans don't involve putting down roots. I was on my way home."

"Hogstead?" Billy inquired. "Do you think Rosemary may have returned there?"

She hadn't meant Hogstead. It had never been her home, just a place where she existed and at the end, hardly even that. It was more a place she had to flee to keep on living. "It's possible. I know Jane and Ronan were well aware that was where she was from."

"I'd love to visit when this is all gone." He touched his bandaged eye. "Do you think Rose would mind? Me not being my usual handsome self?"

"You'll be even more dashing. Maybe with an eyepatch like a pirate."

The nurse who stood nearby echoed her agreement. "Keep in mind, you'll be a war hero. What woman wouldn't love a war hero?"

Possibly one who couldn't remember, but no need to add that. One day at a time, she reminded herself. Today, she found Billy. No telling who she might run across tomorrow.

Chapter Twenty-Seven

B ATTERED SOLDIERS WHO were far from home welcomed the medicinal teas for healing their bodies. What they welcomed more was Nole's evening stroll through the beds after the doctor left, which healed their spirits. The black dog accepted being called a variety of names from King to Blackie, recognizing the men missed their own furry friends.

The faeries assisted Meara in helping her to find the right herbs, but the cooler breeze and the falling leaves hinted at autumn and it was soon past time to go. Meara stayed on, reluctant to leave Billy on his own. His father had no clue what had happened to his son and had probably returned to Ireland. It wouldn't be long before Billy would be asked to leave the center. He could walk, and his wound had healed. There wasn't much more that could be done for him. The battle that had put him in the center had taken his left eye. He'd taken to wearing a black eye patch and pretended to be a pirate. It wasn't too hard to see through his jovial façade to the frightened man underneath.

Billy being scared wasn't right. He was probably the most fearless of all of them—possibly next to Jane. Her traveler friend hadn't been fearless. It was more like Jane did the scary thing because it needed to be done. Billy, on the other hand, hadn't believed in bad things happening to him. It had worked for him for the most part.

Meara went back to her room, and checked her backpack, which was bulging with the food supplies she'd added to it. The center food was similar to what they served at the front and barely edible.

On the upside, it kept well. She saved the tins of mystery meat the soldiers nicknamed the contents due to not knowing if it was beef, pork, or kangaroo. She doubted it was the latter. Her hand rested on Nole's head, and she whispered, "Soon."

She'd already informed the staff she needed to get home before winter. No one questioned her excuse. It was the only practical thing to do. Now all she had to do was make her goodbyes and head out while it was still daylight. With any luck, she might catch a ride with a farmer heading in the right direction.

When she entered the ward, the nurse hurried toward her and shook her hand. "You are a kind person."

Well, she liked to think she was but was uncertain what brought this on. A casual survey of the beds showed many had left, possibly due to the herbal teas and positive canine interactions. More than a handful had died. A few more had their families show up with the intentions of giving them extra special attention at home. She felt bad about Billy. He had no one. The man in question stood by his bed in his clean uniform, clean-shaven and crisp looking. There was even color in his cheeks.

"Thank you. I hate to go and leave you with all the patients." When she tried to release the nurse's hand, she held on and gave a little extra squeeze.

"I'll miss you. I know the men will miss Nole. We all have places we need to go. It was so gracious of you to take Billy home with you."

Wait. Did she mention taking Billy home with her? She wasn't going directly home. First, she had to crush out the evil that caused the war. Second, she had to take her father's farm back. It might take some legal wrangling, force, or faerie magic. Billy gave her a little finger wave, possibly aware of the information being conveyed. The nurse gave a final pump to her arm.

"You are a wonderful human, and I'm happy to have met you. Not many would take a poor, orphaned soldier home with them.

Especially one with his terrible affliction. Always keep in mind he fought for Mother England."

The hand mangling ended when the nurse dropped her hand.

"What affliction?" Meara found herself asking. Many a soldier sported an eyepatch. Billy wouldn't be the only one.

The nurse leaned closer, cupping a hand around her mouth to shield her words. "Surely you've noticed he's Irish. Told me just his mother was Irish. Still, most would hold that against him."

Not sure how to reply to such blatant discrimination, Meara widened her eyes as if surprised by the news. "People are people. Guess I'll go pick up my person, and my dog, and hit the road."

Ironic that her pretend destination she told Mary ended up being a true one. She wouldn't stay long, just long enough to find a spot for Billy and she had one in mind if all worked aout as she planned. Meara's intention was to keep to the woods, but she soon discovered a wounded soldier got plenty of free rides, which made the trip much easier. They even got one ride all the way back to Hogstead. As strangers, they asked directions to Rosemary's home. Directions were grudgingly given, and one man insisted on going with them. He complained about it being a peculiar farm with only women on the premises.

As they approached the farm, she could see a wagon in the field along with figures around it. They'd led a horse that bore some resemblance to Hercules pulling something. The people picked something up off the ground and threw it into the bags wrapped across their bodies.

Their self-appointed escort muttered, "Potatoes. Her father used to grow corn and wheat. Rosemary comes back with that witchy Irish woman, and they plant potatoes."

"Make sense," Billy commented, making his accent a little more pronounced. "Especially considering you have women bringing the crop in. Less work. There's no waste with potatoes, either, not like with corn, which is about ninety percent stalk. Smart lassies are what

I call them."

The escort yelled to the women in the field. "Hello, there. I brought you company."

Both Meara and Billy waved as the women moved closer.

Their escort hollered again. "I'll be glad to take them back if they're not wanted." His expectant face conveyed his feelings about their arrival and glee about helping them on their way. His grin drooped a little as Jane climbed the fence.

"Meara, you're alive!" She ran and wrapped Meara in a hard hug. "Good to see you, too, Billy."

"Not feeling the love," he quipped. Before he could say anything else. A shout stopped him.

"Billy!" A woman ran full tilt at the fence and hopped it as the last minute, showing she had done such a maneuver several times. "You're back," Rosemary ran up, then skidded to a stop.

"Is it the eye?" Billy asked. "Or should I say the lack of one?"

"No." She shook her head. "Paul told me not to get my hopes up. You might have taken a wife while you were fighting in all those foreign countries. You could have forgotten me."

"No one could forget you. Now, where's my proper welcome?"

Rosemary walked into his open arms with a sigh and placed her head on his chest.

They stayed that way for a few minutes until Billy spoke. "Who's Paul?"

Rosemary turned in his arms and pointed to the escort who was halfway down the dirt path. "Him. He's been asking me to marry him ever since my Dad died." She waved her hand in dismissal. "The farm's mine. It's mine to work and look after my mother. Jane helps."

The four of them were finally back together. It cheered Meara immensely. There was so much hugging and talking at once that Nole tried to get in on the action by squeezing between bodies and barking. An older woman, who resembled Rosemary walked up to the fence and whistled to get Nole's attention.

"Look, Rosie. Samson is back."

Rosemary stepped away from Billy. "Mother, it's not Samson. He died. Remember?"

The woman looked slightly confused and shook her head, murmuring to herself. "So much death."

"Look, mother, my friends have arrived."

The woman gave them an up and down survey. "A one-eyed soldier, a scrawny boy, and a dog that looks like Samson."

Meara pulled off her hat and ruffled her hair. "Don't you remember me? I used to live with Eleanor?"

Rosemary's mother pointed in her direction. "You're dead or should be. Eleanor's house in the woods burned down. Most say the women were inside, but no bones were ever found. That's when the trouble happened—when you showed up. This used to be a quiet village."

"Mother." Rosemary put her hand on her parent. "I think the sun is getting to you."

"I know what I know. Adelaide Douglas told me."

The name was a knife shoved into Meara's heart, especially paired with the Douglas surname. Seeing her expression and guessing at the cause, Rosemary spoke in a rush.

"She married Grayson, not Braeden."

"Oh." What a relief, but she hadn't come to Hogstead for Braeden. "Did he—" she stopped, dreading the answer.

"Make it back?" Rosemary finished it for her.

A quick bob acknowledged her desire to know. Grandmother Biddy would remind her it was always better to know than not know. At least she knew Braeden hadn't married Adelaide. She wouldn't have wished that on anyone. "Yes. Did he?"

"He's here. At least in body. He's not the same man who went away. Heard he was gassed. Not sure what that means. He keeps to himself. Never comes to the village. Wouldn't even have known he was back except Adelaide couldn't wait to tell everyone." She wrinkled her nose and grimaced. "The hateful wretch told everyone she picked her husband well since Braeden is broken. Whatever that means."

Rosemary's mother interrupted the conversation. "I never brought you up to say such mean things."

Before Rosemary could add any more objectionable descriptions to everyone's favorite female to hate, Jane gestured to the field. "The potatoes won't harvest themselves."

"You're right." Rosemary agreed. "Mother, you go rest. I'm sure Meara and Billy will help."

"We will." Meara and Billy answered together, then laughed as they headed for the fence.

"Is that Hercules?" Meara pointed to the field where the horse stood, unmoving.

"No other horse would stay in the same place while all the humans deserted the field."

Her boots sunk into the dirt as she followed the others. Everyone was accounted for except Ronan. Jane, despite her general attitude toward Ronan, always had a soft spot for him. If she hadn't said anything, then it must mean her cousin was dead, he was missing, or somewhere else. It felt like the elephant in the room. "What happened to Ronan?"

Jane turned one hand on her heart. "You don't know?"

What could have happened to her cousin when the four of them managed to stay whole—mostly? Her cousin had the gift of charisma and a handsome face. That should have been enough to keep him safe, but they were living in dark days. "No. Tell me!"

"He's in Cardiff, Wales, with his da, your uncle."

"Uncle Simon is back?"

"He is."

"Why are they in Cardiff?"

"Your uncle had a lead on the farm your da inherited."

A sudden booming roar shook the ground. Billy reached for Rosemary, who shouted to be heard. "What was that?"

Jane glanced up at the blue sky. "Odd to be having thunder. There's not a cloud in the sky."

"It wasn't thunder." That much Meara knew. Here she thought everything had been so easy. The horns she carried strapped across her body trembled and shook. It was hard to determine if they were excited or scared. She knew what she was. "It's the opening volley. We need to prepare."

Chapter Twenty-Eight

LIGHTNING FLASHED, AND thunder rumbled, shaking the boards on the aging barn. The doors stood wide to let in the last bit of daylight. The clouds had moved in fast. They planted a pole to show where they left off on the harvesting before hurrying Hercules from the field. The old horse must have known something was up. He trotted to the barn instead of his usual slow walk.

Rosemary stood at the open door, staring out at the sky. "No rain yet. Peculiar weather. We seldom get lively storms like this."

A crackle of lightning caused Rosemary to jump away from the door. "That was close." She peeked back out the door and gasped. "It split one of the apple trees."

Jane chafed her arms as the wind whipped into the barn, tossing hay around. "It's all a big show." She turned to address Meara. "No need to worry."

No need to worry? She couldn't even believe her friend could say such a thing. She gestured to the trees waving in the wind. "Look at that!"

Sharp pings sounded on the metal roof. Rosemary moved closer to the door. "It's hailing. I can only remember one hail storm other than this."

Billy joined Rosemary and angled his head toward the field. "Good thing you went with potatoes. This would have ruined your wheat crop."

"Jane used the Tarot cards to decide on what to plant. Wheat had a bad outcome."

Hearing her name, the taciturn traveler smiled and held up her hand. "Ask me what I found out with the cards about our final adventure?"

Hearing it described as the final adventure didn't bode well. It sounded as if they would all die. "What card did you pull?"

"Six of Wands. Sometimes called the Six of Rods. It deals with the unseen spiritual forces. The card showed a proud woman carrying a wand, bearing the victory laurel wreath. She was surrounded by five seated companions with wands."

"You think this predicts success." Even though she'd been basing many of her decisions on the cards or the pendulum, she had her doubts. How could a piece of pasteboard predict the future? "Grandmother Biddy told me that the cards could predict possible outcomes. The cards show options that are only possible when the individual provides the action component."

"Exactly." Jane slapped her hands together. "I used another deck to confirm. Same card. Only this time instead of a wreath, there was a long horn being blown to announce victory. The person blowing the horn could have easily been you."

"I don't know." Everything felt so up in the air. In the beginning, everything was so clear-cut. Gather the pieces of horn, assemble them, blow the horn, and the world goes back to the way it was before. While she knew there was opposition to peace, she never considered the sacrifices her friends would have to make. Billy and Braeden were both back from war. Did she really need to do anything else?

The shutters flew open, startling the chickens. It could have been a sign, or it could be the wind. Weather happened, even peculiar weather. She went to the open shutters that allowed more wind to force its way into the barn, frightening the chickens and causing the milk cow to moo in distress. At least she could close the shutters. When she managed to grab a hold of the banging shutters, she noticed two figures outside. Despite the weather, they stood still holding one another's hands, and their clothes and hair didn't flap in the wind.

The bearded man gave a slight nod while the red-headed woman smiled. It was her parents, together at last. She heard their voices in her head, and she'd glimpsed her father in a dream. This was the first time she'd seen them together. Instead of latching the shutters, she held on while the wind tugged at them waiting for her parents' message.

Sorcha spoke first. *My daughter, you would not have been given this task if you were not capable.*

"My friends. What about them?"

They, too, are capable.

Her father lifted his hand as he spoke. *Daughter, this is your battle, and it is not your battle. You are the arms and legs to complete the mission. All of us who care about goodness, peace, love, and nature, it's our battle, too. You are not alone. There are thousands around the world joining you with their intentions and psychic powers.*

"How can we draw on their powers?"

I'm glad you said we as opposed to I. The wheels are already in place. People are coming together. They don't necessarily know why. We need a ritual to inform them. We have forty-eight hours in which to accomplish this, and I want you to take Braeden with you.

Her father had to be joking. "Not Braeden. He just got back from the war. From what I heard, he's not only physically damaged, there's some spiritual injury, too."

More the reason he has to go. He is the sixth. He needs this. It will be both the sacrifice and victory he needs.

Meara remained unconvinced. Sure, she wanted Braeden to get better, but at what cost? How could you have both sacrifice and victory? The words contradicted each other. "Isn't there another way? Another person? What about Uncle Simon?"

Everything is already in place. The tools you need await you. The people are on their way. It's all up to you. You can do what you were fated to do even before we knew of your existence. Or you can choose to do like so many others and allow evil to thrive by doing nothing. You've come too far to do nothing.

She had come so far. The images of her parents grew translucent, allowing the trees to show through them as they dematerialized. She could still hear their voices. *Remember we love you and will always be with you.*

Their voices faded away. She took a couple of deep breaths mulling over their instructions, pulled the shutters closed and latched them. Rosemary called out from her place near the front.

"A rider is coming!"

Billy peered out into the wind-tossed landscape. "What fool would ride in this weather?"

"It's Braeden." Even his name surprised her because she knew what she knew on a much deeper level. Everything had already been set in place. It wasn't just her. It was everyone she knew. Jane drifted closer and put a cool hand on Meara's arm.

"It's time for the ritual."

"At least one of them. I have a feeling we might need a series."

The horse and rider came through the open barn door. A hat and slicker concealed his face, but she knew, even before he dismounted. He removed his hat and placed it on the saddle revealing a face aged more than three years could account for. His cheeks were lean and stubbled while his eyes remained weary and watchful. Braeden turned slowly, surveying all the faces until he saw hers.

"Meara."

All this time, she wondered how she'd feel when she saw him again. There had been doubts, thinking perhaps what she had initially felt for him was just a young girl's fantasy. It all fell away as she ran toward him. "Braeden!"

She ran into his arms and covered his face with kisses. There was a boom outside, then the rain came, buckets of it splashing hard on the ground, melting away the hail. His arms came around her and held her tight as he whispered.

"I was so afraid. I made it back only to find you gone. There were rumors about you dying in a cottage fire. Adelaide changed the rumors to say you started the fire. I knew you wouldn't have done such a thing. I always knew you wouldn't have left unless you had no choice. Still, I worried how a woman alone could survive." He dusted a kiss across her hair, then backed up.

"I dressed as a boy at one point."

Braeden ruffled her hair. "The world has gone mad if they thought your sweet face was male."

"It worked from a distance. I wasn't talking to too many strangers. I was fortunate to find friends along the way." She gestured to Billy and Jane.

He held out his hand to Jane who shook it, saying, "You are as Meara described you—and more."

"Did she speak of me often?" he inquired with a grin.

"When she did it was with great passion. Didn't you see her when you were fighting for England? Hear her voice?"

His eyebrows lifted. "I did."

"As I said, with great passion."

Even though she always wanted the best for Braeden, calling it great passion might have been an overstatement. Sometimes, she was so conflicted about how she felt. Her goal had been for them both to survive to explore their attraction to one another.

He entangled his fingers with hers. "I'm glad. When I came back and you weren't here, there was no purpose to my life. Somewhere in the back of my mind, I felt you were alive, and if I waited long enough, you'd return to see Rosemary. I waited. When I heard Paul had escorted strangers to Rosemary's farm, I had to come and see for myself. So I did."

She gave his hand a squeeze and turned slightly to face Rosemary and Billy. "This is Billy. We met him when Ronan drove the horse and wagon into the bay."

Both men shook hands before Braeden turned back to Meara,

and said, "That must have been horrible. I'm only sorry I wasn't there."

"It was mild compared to some of the other things that happened. I'm glad you're here because we need to talk about you being the sixth of the Six of Wands."

"Not sure, I understand."

"You will." Jane nodded in the direction of his horse. "You'll want to unsaddle her and get her comfortable before we start. It will take a while."

Chapter Twenty-Nine

THE HAY BALES were arranged in a circle as they prepared for the ritual. Rosemary had taken her mother into town for a function that included making bandages for the war and gossiping, although not necessarily in that order. Jane held up a candle.

"I'm not so sure about this with all this very burnable straw and hay."

"Good point. I have an electric torch that still works, or we could use a lantern."

The water sloshed out of a basin as Jane placed it in the circle. "We could use both. I'll light the candle to sterilize my knife. We'll need that. Do you want me to lead the ritual or do you want to do it?"

Meara replied, "You can. Still, there are things I need to say."

The sound of hoofbeats sounded on the muddy pathway. Jane placed a pheasant feather in the east along with a bell. "That must be Rosemary and Billy returning."

It wasn't. Billy and Rosemary had used a wagon. Meara drifted to the door where Braeden stood watching the two horsemen. "Expecting anyone?" he asked.

"I wasn't expecting anyone, when you showed up."

"Should I ask if there is anyone you're not expecting?"

Her heart gave a leap at his slow smile. There was something here. If it was love, she hoped there was enough time left to discover it. "Probably just about everyone in the world. With my luck, I wouldn't be surprised to see the Kaiser rolling in."

The horses slowed near the house.

"Hello, the house!"

She recognized Ronan's voice. "Over here!" She waved her arms to grab his attention.

"Meara!" Both men rode into the barn. Ronan dismounted first and hugged his cousin, hard. "Did you find the second part of the horn?"

"I did. That part was easy. Remembering to return was the tricky part." Nole barked adding his two cents. "I picked up a companion, too."

The older man got off his horse and turned to greet Meara. The familiar smile she knew. Her uncle was one of the few people to smile at her before she left the convent. Smiling was considered partly vanity and mostly frivolity by the nuns. If a sister smiled, that meant she wasn't concentrating on the depravity of the world.

"Uncle Simon!"

"Meara, at last." He opened his arms as she hurled into them. "I'll never forgive myself for thinking you'd be safe at a convent while I ran up to London. Something tweaked my spirit, but I told myself all would be well."

"It wasn't your fault. It was fate. Even though I may not have liked some of my adventures, it had to happen to get me here. I'm sure Ronan told you about the horn."

"He did." He cleared his throat, ridding himself of the catch that might have signaled he was choked up about something. "Sorcha would be the one to get involved with the fae. I'm sure Fulmen had a part in it, too."

"Yes. You're in time for the ritual. It will start once Rosemary and Billy return. We are the six from the Six of Wands."

"I'm not following." Uncle Simon dropped his embrace and rubbed one hand over his beard. "What ritual? What's this about wands?"

Before she could explain, Ronan strolled over and slapped his father on the back. "It's been a long trip from Wales, especially with my da complaining about not having an automobile. Still, he has news that will make everything easier on you. Not sure what your ritual might be. There might not be any need for it."

The shutters flew open again. Meara gestured to them. "My da disagrees. We need the ritual because evil exists. We need all those with pure hearts and strong wills to help. I think you'll agree the war has to stop."

"It will." Ronan added, "Wars always stop, eventually."

Braeden, who had been quiet during the entire exchange, swiveled away from watching at the door. His voice, strong and charged with emotion, carried. "How long will the war last? Will it be another hundred-year war? At what cost? Already England has used her youth to stop the Huns without any success. Not only is your uncle doing without the convenience of an automobile, the common people are managing without food staples or even medicine. Everything goes to feed a war machine that will not be sated. There are children without fathers, wives without husbands, and parents without sons. How long should we wait for this to stop?"

An awkward silence reigned as Ronan looked from Meara to Braeden. Finally, he put his hand out. "I'm Ronan Cleary, Meara's cousin. I don't think we've met."

"We haven't." Braedon shook the offered hand. "Braeden Douglas, embittered war veteran and Meara's fiancé if she'll still have me."

"Now there, that almost makes us family. I may have talked out of turn. Overlook my bold tongue if you can. All I want is things to be easy for my cousin since she has been through so much." They both dropped hands.

Braeden delivered a hearty slap to the leaner Ronan's back. "I want the same. There's some business with evil we must handle before we can get to the easy stuff. After that, it may be clear sailing, or at least, I hope it is. As for the bold tongue, you remind me of my own brothers who never temper anything they say. So, what took you to Wales?"

Ronan glanced back in his father's direction. "Do you want to tell it, Da?"

"I would. First, I'm thankful my seat is not moving." He perched on a nearby hay bale. "The story of Fulmen's inheritance is a bloody one. I'm not sure Meara has relayed it. My sister, Sorcha, married Fulmen. They moved to England and scratched out an existence until a relative he barely knew left him a fertile farm. I'm not sure of the details or if Fulmen even knew the man well, but there was a legal will that gave the farm to Fulmen. Thankfully, there was a copy of such will recorded. More about that later.

"Turns out some in the town of Beacon thought they'd get the farm. This part isn't very clear. Not sure if Fulmen's relative had said something to give them such an idea. It could be people speculated on the man dying and leaving no will behind. In that case, squatters could have taken over the place unless a relative showed up to toss them off. It took a while for Sorcha and Fulmen to get the news and discovered a squatter had taken residence before they even buried the owner. Fulmen had to pay for a lawyer and a constable to evict the man. Apparently, he was a persistent sort and instead of being red-faced about his nefarious actions, he was determined to get back the farm he had so briefly inhabited. He stirred up bad feelings about Fulmen. To anyone who would listen, he talked about Fulmen doing animal sacrifices and hinted that their children might be next. His claim for why Fulmen got the farm instead of him was black magic. One night, he got some of the local boys drunk enough that storming a man's home and terrifying his pregnant wife seemed like the thing to do."

Simon shook his head before continuing. "At my age I should be used to what one human will do to another. Still, this tale turns my stomach. They stormed up to the place. Some had torches, a few knives, and a couple of pitchforks from the tale the locals repeat. They call it the curse of Fulmen.

"Anyhow, Fulmen must have intuited it because he made Sorcha dress and escape through the woods. When the mob arrived, Fulmen went out to reason with them, but they'd hear none of it. There was fisticuffs, and it was then that Fulmen died. Some say he stumbled and hit his head on a rock. That's the generous version. Others say the squatter hit him from behind, but Fulmen turned, saw his attacker, and cursed him as he lay dying."

The thought of her father being brutally killed made her shudder. Braeden wrapped his arm around her and brought her close to his side. Jane held up one finger.

"What was the curse?"

Simon scratched his head. "You do realize this is hearsay. There is no proof. Fulmen cursed the man to never have a happy day on the land. Crops would fail. Livestock would die. No woman would consent to be the squatter's wife. At night, he would not sleep because he would be bedeviled by all the evil he had wrought."

"What happened to the squatter?" Braeden asked the question Meara wanted to ask.

Uncle Simon placed a finger by his nose. "It's said he hanged himself. Still others implied there were those in town who decided he should be hanged for his actions. After the evil deed, nothing in the village was the same. There was a taint on the town due to a handful of participants. The townsfolks tried over the years to make things right. Even searched for Fulmen's wife without success. No one ever made the mistake of trying to take over the farm. It stands vacant. Roof needs fixing on the house and the fields are full of weeds.

"The locals were happy to see us because they wanted a blood relative to lift the curse that lingers on the land. I told them that you were alive and would take over the farm, which pleased them to no end. I got the papers right here." He tapped his jacket pocket.

At one time, living on the farm had been her secret dream. She wanted something to call her own, a place to belong. Now, the idea of living somewhere where her father was killed didn't appeal. "I appreciate all the work you went to. I believe I will have to visit the farm, but I'm not sure I could live there. What if I came face to face with someone in the market who was there on that horrible night?"

Uncle Simon coughed and held up his hand for time as Ronan handed him a canteen. "Road dust has a way of getting into your throat. Your Wales and England is more dusty than dear, old Ireland. Anyhow, I thought to ask about that. The squatter is dead. The five men involved quietly left town, just in case whoever helped the squatter on his way might visit them. The people really want you to come. You'll be a savior of sorts. It will give them an opportunity to make up for the evil done to your parents."

"No one can do that." Meara shook her head violently. "A cord of wood or a round cake won't make up for growing up without parents."

"I agree." Simon fixed her with a somber stare. "Think about Fulmen."

"I am."

"He'd want you to have the land."

The shutters came unlatched and banged. Her father had waded in on the discussion. "I think he would, too. I will look at it."

"That's all I can ask."

The sound of a wagon in the distance meant it was time to get the ritual going.

ONCE EVERYONE WAS in the barn, they shut the doors. Uncle Simon volunteered to be the guardian, although they didn't expect any interruptions from the natural world. Rosemary had talked to her mother's friend, who agreed to take her for a couple of days. The excuse given for the absence was a wedding in Wales. Rosemary tacked on it was a friend's wedding since it would be expected for her mother to attend a relative's. Come morning, they'd all be headed to Fulmen's farm to unearth the final piece of the horn. With a single blast, the madness that had overtaken the world would end.

Even though Jane had agreed to do the ritual, Meara decided to speak first. She stood, taking time to look each person in the face. This voyage had taken a toll on each and every one of them. Jane sat with her hands folded, looking very decorous, when she was anything but. Her wise traveling friend had left behind her family, her tribe, her identity. Her gaze moved on to Rosemary, always an adventurous spirit. The first to join the journey. She'd lost her memory for a time and briefly her sweetheart while protecting Meara. Then there was Billy, just as gutsy as his love. He, too, left his country and oddly ended up fighting for another. He gave an eye and possibly more on the killing fields.

Here she thought she'd had a hard time of it. What had she lost? Early on, she was denied the privilege of having two parents and being raised in a home with love. That was beyond her control. Family would have been nice. Even knowing about her Irish relatives would have been a gift. She smiled at Ronan, not knowing what sacrifices he'd made since she saw him last. He definitely had more experiences to recall. Possibly, he'd entertain at a local pub in a future evening with his traveling tales. Then there was Braeden.

On his account, she was blameless. She hadn't urged him to join the army or to travel with her. Whatever happened to him in battle was on his head. But was it? She held his heartfelt regard, knowing whatever the man had done, he did it in the belief it would make a life for them. Not sure what he expected the war to be, but it was much more. His harsh, rasping cough echoed through the barn, a clear indicator of some of the damage the war had wrought.

Meara held her hands out. "I expect you all know why you are here. We have to find the last piece of the horn."

As she related the information, the horn bag bounced and jostled against her body, causing her to grip it to keep it in place. It, too, was ready to be done with the chase. "Anyone who doesn't want to be a part of this, I understand."

Jane tried to interrupt. "Meara, there has to be six."

"I know." She nodded her head to let her know she hadn't forgotten. "Jane pulled the cards. It's a Six of Wands, possibly meaning victory and triumph. I believe if six is our number, then six people will present themselves." She held her hand high. "I'm going."

"Don't even think of leaving me behind," Rosemary announced with two balled fists on her hips.

"That goes for me, too. I'd like to send an end to this tale." Billy added, then wrapped his arm around his Rosie.

Jane cleared her throat. "No question about me going. It was foretold back in Ireland. This is my mission as much as it is yours."

"Blood sticks with blood," Ronan said.

Uncle Simon spoke from his place at the door. "Well said."

She came to Braeden, not knowing if she could ask such a thing of him. He hadn't a clue about the dangers. When she came to him, she was ready for his refusal.

He stood. "I could not call myself a man if I let you leave without me. Nor can I take a chance of not seeing you again. If I were the type of man who sat on my bum while you were in danger, I'd not be able to look at myself in the mirror. Tell me what to do. I'm going."

This was the man she knew from her dreams and visions. He'd be an asset. Meara took her seat beside him on the same hay bale as Jane rose to speak.

"We're up against some powerful evil. One reason it has grown is because good people chose to do nothing. They sat at home, behind closed doors, wringing their hands, talking about how bad things are.

"That will not do a powerful lot of good. Meara had told me there are those who will join with us in spirit." She touched her temples. "They may give us knowledge, experience, strength, and possibly vision of things to come. We can use their help. First, we will make a sacred circle."

Jane held up her knife in one hand and the bell in the other. The crystalline ringing of the bell filled the barn. Braeden cocked his head as she went around the third time swinging the bell. Before Meara could say anything, Jane did as she finished her circuit.

"Three is a sacred number. We create the circle, so we can remain protected as we conduct our ritual. The bell ringing drives out low spirits that would meddle in our affairs. We'll now call the elements to assist us. Meara, air. Ronan, fire. Rosemary, earth, and Billy, water, of course. I'll call on the Goddess Danu to assist us."

Meara stood. "Air, even now you rage and dance outside the barn. Hear me now, we call on you to assist us in the name of all that is good."

There was a fierce moan as the wind swept across the land. The barn roof rattled as if it would come off. Simon held onto the doors that wanted to fly open. Then the wind grew softer until it could be heard no more. It was Ronan's turn.

The lamp light shadowed his features as he spoke. "Fire, all consuming, you represent warmth, passion, energy. Fill us so we can be like you and burn through the obstacles set before us. Welcome."

No fires or sparks occurred, which was good. Billy took his turn. "Mother Water, how I miss you. Your call is constant. We cannot survive without you. On this night, be with us and enable us with your mighty power. So, mote it be."

This caused an eyebrow lift from Jane. Their chance-met helper may know more about the old ways than he let on.

Rosemary rose and stomped with her booted feet. "Awake Earth. Always faithful. Always true. Come to our rescue." She clapped her hands twice. "Make it so."

They turned to the center as Jane's voice rose and fell, beseeching the Goddess Danu. "Precious, powerful Danu. Creator of the isle and your people, the faeries. This night we labor to restore that which once was. Even though we are children of those who deceived you, we ask for your wisdom, your sight, and your power, to restore that which has been broken. Let us be your tools. Let us blow the sacred horn for you. Hear us, Great Danu."

A patter that sounded like stones on the roof sounded along with the screech of a seagull. Jane closed her eyes and whispered loud enough to carry. "She is here. She send her bird as token." Jane stepped out of the center, joined the circle, and held out her hands.

"We'll hold hands and visualize white healing light filling the room, covering Hogstead, encompassing the United Kingdom. Everywhere we can think of, there will be white light."

They sat in silence imagining a world without war or hate, a healed planet. Meara could feel the hands gripping hers and the energy zooming around the circle. After a while, Jane spoke again.

"Call in the helpers."

Different names were shouted. Most she did not know. She heard Grandmother Biddy and was sorry she had forgotten to call her.

"My mother, Sorcha. My father, Fulmen."

We are here.

There came another quiet time when everyone had shouted all the names they knew and sat trying to think of more. Jane held the knife in the lantern light. "Two is better than one. Three is better than two, only when you can be of one mind. We must work together, not apart. To accomplish this there will be a mix of our blood. It will allow us to call on one another without words to relay messages when we are too far away. Each of you will slice your thumb with the knife. We will come together in the middle and rub our thumbs together. Each person must rub their thumb with the others. This only works for a short time. I can't guarantee how long since I have never done this before. I always remember Grandmother Biddy advising people not to waste time."

She gestured for everyone to come forward into a tight inner circle. Jane sliced her thumb less than an inch and handed the knife to Meara. Each person cut their thumb and held it to the other five, chanting.

"Flesh to flesh, blood to blood, bind me tight to the other. Let me see from their eyes. Let me hear with their ears. Let us work as one. So, mote it be."

There was a terrible rattling of shutters and doors as they pronounced the last word. It knew. It sensed they were here and was doing its best to disrupt whatever they were about. The lantern blinked off, and they stayed united with their thumbs touching. Energy flowed through them. There was a sharp bird cry, an eagle. Suddenly, Meara found herself outside flying through the night darkened skies. Then, just as rapidly, she found herself back in her body with her thumb smarting.

The voices erupted around her as each person explained where they had been and what they had seen. One had run with a nearby fox. Another saw with a horse's eyes. The stories varied. Apparently, they would not be united with one another, but with nature.

Uncle Simon walked toward them with a match. "Let me light the lantern. Erin complains about my pipe smoking. At least I always have a match on hand." He re-lit the lantern, and they stared at each other in awe, knowing they had shared something unexplainable.

Jane held her hand up for attention. "Let's try small things to see if we can control this new ability. Without control, it is not useful. Rosemary think of a tune, and we'll see if we can pick it up."

After a few seconds, Billy gave his beau a quixotic look. "Really? That one?"

Meara listened, and she could hear music commonly played at weddings, although she didn't know the name of the tune. They got that one, then went on to experiment with several different examples. It got faster the more practice they had.

"Enough." Jane declared, "It's time for a protection spell."

"I'm all for that," Rosemary stated. "The more, the better."

They stood in line as Jane drew a pentacle on their foreheads with her finger. The protective symbol would shield them from harm. Meara turned to Jane and did likewise.

Simon had stood in line for the protection ritual but looked like he had something to say. He waited, then inhaled, holding both hands, palms out at chest level and spoke. "Irishman are known for their gift of gab. Part of it is probably because we realize the power of the spoken word. Another part is we just like to hear ourselves talk. I'd like to bless all of you. May you walk and never tire. May you eat and never hunger. May your problems be few. Your burdens shared. May your pillow be soft and your sleep sweet. Your waking sweeter."

He dropped his hand and waited a few beats. "Where are we bedding down? We need our sleep to get an early start in the morning."

Early start in the morning made it so much more real. Only hours to go. Either they triumphed or they didn't. At one point, Meara felt compelled to go to her father's farm, but now she didn't. Was her desire due to wanting to have something to call her own? Could her longing for land be leading them away from where they needed to be? If only she could have a clear sense of knowing. The horns trembled when they were near each other. They were fair to dancing tonight. What if they were moving away from the horn and not toward it?

Chapter Thirty

THE FULL MOON beamed into the room, touching on the dresser, the lamp, and the basin in Rosemary's room. It was a simple bedroom with a few pegs for coats and hats. A rag rug kept the floor from being too cold. A nearby bouquet of late roses on the dresser scented the air.

A snore signaled Rosemary was asleep. It was hard to tell with Jane. The woman already had suspicions because Meara refused to change into her nightgown. Her excuse was she wanted to be ready to go in the morning and not to waste any time dressing. It earned her a disbelieving look. It made her wonder if Jane could now read her mind due to the blood mixing. Then again, she could just be nervous due to her part in saving the world.

Mother, Father, she mentally called, not risking speaking aloud. *What can you tell me about the horn? I'm heading to Wales in the morning. Is it in Wales?*

Not Wales. I knew I couldn't leave my most precious possessions on the farm where those ruffians would destroy it. I sent the horn with your mother.

Her father didn't even know where it was. *Mother, where is it?*

That was a horrible time. It feels like just yesterday, I was running for my life and your life. I had that horn banging against me. A couple of times, I almost dropped it. I owed it to Fulmen not to be so careless with it. Before I got to the convent, I decide to bury it.

The pain and anguish in her mother's voice was as if she was reliving the night. "*Do you remember where you buried it?*

Outside the convent.

Close? Like a couple yards or more like a quarter of a mile?

I can't tell you for sure. I wasn't thinking straight. Every step felt like a mile. I saw the sign for the convent and decide to bury it before I got there. It has to be near there.

She'd never seen a sign. Wait. One of the sisters said something about taking the sign down after your mother came there for sanctuary. Mother Superior didn't want any more beggars or their git. The sign was long gone. What can I do?

Go to the convent and work your way out from there. The horn sections will recognize their own.

It sounded easy and was close. She could do this while the rest of them slept. As for her nemesis, if he had been listening, he assumed they'd leave tomorrow and head for Wales. All she had to do was slip out tonight and find the horn. It wasn't where anyone expected it to be.

Her foot found purchase on the floor as she tried to slip the rest of her body out without making the floor creak. Almost there, she gave a little roll, then slid to the floor. Someone murmured in their sleep as Meara crouched by the bed. No one woke.

She'd made a point of leaving her boots on the porch, so she could slip them on tonight if need be. The dance the horn sections did convinced her the third part was close by. All she had to do was find it. If she found it tonight, no one would be at risk. Her hand went to her amulet that felt slightly warm. There might be some danger involved. Maybe she should call down a flock of owls if needed. The important thing was to protect her friends. What type of person willingly marches her friends into danger?

Not her. The safest was for them to be at home asleep in their own beds. She reached the porch with no issue and slipped on her boots. The men had elected to sleep in the barn, which meant no four-footed conveyance for her. She glanced up at the moon in its rounded glory.

At least that worked in her favor. She stood looking across the fields, getting a sense of direction what she should head. The horn bag she kept strapped to her body moved, pointing west. That answered that question. Even though the muddy fields would slow her down and leave clear evidence of where she went, if she was quick, everything should be done before her friends awoke for the day.

A black shadow came around the house and greeted her as soon as she stepped off the porch. Meara froze. She had expected some push back from the giant evil, but not so close to Rosemary's home. A cold nose and a swipe of the tongue revealed that the shadow belonged to her loyal canine.

"Nole," she said his name, wondering how she'd get him to stay. While he could be courageous, he wasn't necessary obedient when she needed him to be and tended to do things when he wanted to. Only now and then did it work out that they wanted the same thing at the same time. He'd have to go along. She'd never succeed in making him stay. Her efforts would only wake everyone else up. Maybe he'd get bored with a long walk in the dark and return on his own.

She checked for her needed supplies. Knife. Had it. Electric torch. Had it, too. Holy water, she tucked into her shirt. Uncle Simon had stopped by a sanctuary to get it on his way here. He wasn't sure if it would work, but he felt it couldn't hurt. Before they went to sleep, her uncle had taken off a necklace he wore, explaining he'd received it from a shaman on his travels and placed it around her neck.

Like Rosemary, she believed she could use all the help she could get. Still, someday, she'd like to lay stuff aside for a while and give her neck a break. Nole and she made it over two fences before another shadow caught up with her.

"Where are you going?" Braeden asked as he fell in step with her.

"Go back. I don't want you here."

"The sneaking out in the night was my tip off to that. Are you heading out to Wales on your own?"

Even though he looked like Braeden, he could be a shapeshifter. "I'm going to visit Eleanor. It is the least I can do since I am here."

He grabbed her arm and shook it. "Are you sleep walking? Eleanor left when you did, and there is nothing left of her cabin."

"Would you leave my arm alone? I had to check to make sure you weren't a shapeshifter."

He dropped his hand. "Convinced yet?"

"Yes, all the more reason for you to go back."

"I need to protect you. What if you wander into a fairy circle and aren't seen for another seven years or more."

"No worries there. That's just people badmouthing faeries. Why would peace-loving folks want much to do with us?"

"You got a point. I never bought into the changeling thing, either. Why would faeries want human babies?"

"That's what I mean."

They discussed the accepted old wives' tales about faeries and why they couldn't be true until they got to the woods. Even during the day, it held a feeling of menace. Now they'd have to walk through it in the middle of the night, knowing something might attack them. She pulled out her electric torch and switched it on.

"A torch. That must have cost a crown."

"Found it. Have you've been in the woods lately?"

"Yes. As the village's resident hermit, I spend a great deal of time in the woods. It made me feel closer to you. Let me have the light."

"I'll hold onto it." She heard his snort but chose to ignore it. He was a bit like Nole. She couldn't stop him from coming. Her goal was to accomplish what she came for at all costs. Right now, she didn't know what the costs might be, which is why she chose not to bring her friends along. Nole dropped his nose to the ground as if he smelled something. It was probably a rabbit or another citizen of the woods. You couldn't smell horn as far as she knew.

A loud roar sounded, and a large beast ran straight for them. Braeden shoved her aside as he crouched to meet the beast while

Nole issued his own threat. From her prone position on the ground, she knew there was no bear, wolves, and certainly no lions in England. "It's an illusion."

Braeden glanced back at her. "Take cover."

She pushed to her knees, then feet. "It isn't there. There was a part of the forest like this, where you had to ignore everything and keep going. I had no clue it had spread this far."

"How can you be sure?"

Nole gave a final growl and charged the beast, jumping right through it.

"That's how."

She never mentioned where they were going, hoping by doing so, it would prevent any informational leaks. It was hard to know what was known by her nemesis. He could just be patiently waiting for her to uncover the complete horn, swoop in, and take it. If that were the case, she was betting no one would be left alive to tell the tale.

There were several more illusions that they walked through. Even Nole was starting to ignore the angry bears, the knight on horseback with a pointed lance, and the angry boar. Although the last turned out to be real and sent Braeden and Meara up a tree. Nole was smart enough to make use of his black coat to hide. They came down after the coast was clear with Meara holding onto the light. The horn bag pulled her in the direction it wanted her to go.

Braeden tried to take her hand once, but she pulled it away. For some reason, she felt it was a ploy to get the flashlight. She wondered why she didn't feel the same way about Braeden as Rosemary felt about Billy. Once they were reunited, they didn't let go of each other. Here she wouldn't even hold Braeden's hand. Something was off, but she couldn't say what. "Do you know where we are going?"

"Why don't you tell me?"

Yeah, he'd like that. The thought popped into her head. She couldn't be sure where it came from.

Can't be trusted. She was starting to get that feeling, too. "It's more fun if you guess." She managed a girlish giggle.

"It's not fair. Give me a hint." He laughed and made a grab for the flashlight, which she foiled by changing hands.

"Think of where we first met." Any man who was devoted as Braeden claimed he was would remember their first meeting.

"Was it here in the woods?"

Meara turned off the flashlight and moved off the path. Her fingers encountered a tree, which she hid behind. She couldn't risk going too far, because he could track her by sound. What shapeshifter was it this time?

There was a sound of snuffling and limbs breaking, and she thought of the boar they'd avoided earlier. Whoever he was he was good, had her physical-self fooled, but her physic-self wasn't buying it.

"Come on, sweetheart. Let's not play games. It's too late for that. I know every girl romanticizes the first meeting. Men don't. It's the girl, not the place that matters."

His voice was warm and teasing. Not the voice of someone determined to find the final horn section and had just been tricked by turning out the torch. He'd be mad. Of course, if he were smart, he wouldn't let it show. She pressed up against the tree trying to make herself invisible. *I need help.*

Even if someone was awake to hear her message, it would take a while for them to arrive. She needed something more immediate. *Faeries, I need your help. Remember, I'm on your mission.*

There was a click and a beam of light. Did the Braeden lookalike have a torch all along? The light moved away from her and was followed by running footsteps. "There you are my red-headed trickster. Who's playing games now? Are you leading me around with your electric torch beam?"

The beam moved slowly away with the look-alike trailing and yelling out what he assumed would be romantic sayings. Why would anyone want to be called a red-headed trickster? It was little better than red-headed stepchild. Soon she could move. Whoever had the flashlight was heading toward the pit, a natural sinkhole formed by too much rain. Most people knew where it was and avoided it. Real Braeden would know. She heard a yell as he fell and she popped out of her hiding place, running down the path in the dark.

He might be too far away to see. Then again, he probably just shifted to his natural shape, which could be goat-like, and scampered out. All she had to do was get close and the horns would do the rest. Last time, one practically pulled the other out of the ground. Imagine what two could do? The sounds of rushing feet and heavy breathing made her push harder until she tripped over a root and dropped her torch. It would have been easier to find the torch if it were on. Whatever was behind her would catch up with her if she took time to look for it in the dark. Indecision gripped her. She'd not find her way out of the woods without the torch. Before she could push up, the beast was on her—licking her face. Nole.

Once she found her light, she stood and allowed the horns to guide her in whatever direction they pleased. Off the path, the ground was bumpy and choked with sticker bushes that often caught her clothing and sometimes her skin. It was twenty years ago that her mother buried her piece. Things had changed since then. Along with the sign vanishing, the path must have grown over, too. She couldn't imagine a nine-month pregnant woman making it through here.

The horn bag vibrated and bounced, letting her know she was near. With this journey, ninety percent done, she realized she hadn't brought a shovel. There was only so much she could have done to prepare to sneak off alone raising suspicion. A shovel placed by her boots on the porch would have been a giveaway. Almost done and all her friends remained safe.

She stumbled into a sunken area, and the horns sections went crazy. It might be taking a chance, but she switched on the torch. It was a flat mossy strip with no trees or bushes. The moss could have been a path at one time. She knelt when the horns pulled the hardest. To resist would take more effort than she had.

Knowing the horns would do all the work, she opened the bag. The two sections snapped together and made an out of tune bleat, which was enough. The other piece came ripping out of the ground and attached itself. Complete, they made a melodious sound, but the work wasn't done until a human mouth blew it. She reached for it, glad she let the others sleep. Maybe no one heard her panicked cry for help.

"You make me laugh."

It was a voice she'd hoped never to hear again and chilled her blood. Adelaide lounged against a tree somehow more glamorous than ever. While the war had been hard on some women, it had been more than generous with her. She couldn't be here. Yet, there she was.

"The odd, little orphan girl is going to save the world. Nice dream. It is a dream. Just like Braeden loving you. That's a dream, too. It's all been a dream. I married Braeden. He always wanted me. He flirted with you just to make me jealous."

She found herself transfixed as Adelaide crept closer to her and the horn. Part of her accepted she wasn't real, another part listened and squirmed as Adelaide spun her hate-filled stories. The horn shook in her hands, even to the point of pushing itself closer to her mouth, which Adelaide must have seen.

"You can't do it. You're a failure who will never amount to anything."

That gave her the push she needed. Meara pushed her lips against the horn and blew. The first sound was raspy and weak. She blew again as the tone grew stronger. On the third blow, a loud clear note rose in the night and a streak of light lit up the night sky.

Adelaide gave an indignant scream and faded away, leaving a lean, shadowy creature behind. It grew leaner the longer she stared.

He snarled. "What you looking at? I would have thought if your greatest fear was a spiteful blonde, you'd be easy to outsmart. I was wrong. I could have used you on my team. There's one thing I need to do before I leave."

Lunging at Meara, he was blocked by a giant, snarling Nole. The shadow man stumbled to the ground as he grew even smaller. "Your parents don't play fair. Even with them dead, I still can't win." His voice grew higher as he grew tiny.

Then he faded away under Meara's eyes. The horn she just blew also disappeared. She glanced at Nole who had returned to his ordinary size. "You better not fade away on me, too."

"Never. I'll be with you forever."

Did the dog just talk or was she dreaming, as Adelaide had suggested? A commotion in the nearby undergrowth, along with lantern light, and several of her friends calling her name brought her out of her reverie.

"I'm over here!" Meara braced her hand against a nearby tree. Her legs trembled after the fact, making it hard to stand. She gave up the attempt and plopped down in the dirt.

Braeden was the first to break through the brush. Was it the real Braeden?

He lifted his lantern high. "I should have known you'd go off on your own. I knew the day I saw you at the market you were no regular girl."

She reached for his hand and felt the reassuring tingle. "You have no clue how right you were."

Epilogue

THE LATE SUMMER sun bathed the entire farm in a golden glow. Laughter and screams came from the direction of the creek where she'd last spotted the children. No telling what those rascals were up to, especially with the addition of the Cleary cousins and Rosemary's twins. It was a recipe for mischief.

The back door slammed as Jane and Rosemary exited, carrying the tablecloth and dishes.

"Over here," Meara waved when the two gazed in confusion where the table used to be. "I moved it."

"By yourself?" Jane asked with arched eyebrows.

"Mostly. There may have been some faerie help. You know how it is here."

The three of them laughed as they smoothed the tablecloth over the table and set it for a meal. Meara added the candles she had waiting in the shade. "I think we need flowers. It's been ten years since I moved to the farm. It's a celebration."

"There's many to be picked. Take a look." Rosemary gestured to the surrounding area that was thick with colorful wild flowers and climbing roses.

"You're right. Everything looks so good. I think I'll leave them where they are."

Jane nudged her. "After the horn blowing, you went a bit daft. Declaring you wanted nothing to do with the farm or Braeden, for that matter."

Leave it to friends to bring up subjects best left alone. Meara shot one hand through her hair. "That feels like a hundred years ago." She held out her hands as she spoke. "You never saw the shapeshifter. He looked like Braeden, sounded like Braeden up to the end when he called me a red-headed trickster. Then, there was Adelaide or what I assumed was Adelaide." It made her shudder.

"She was a right, fine wretch." Jane grimaced. "Here, I never met her. Just heard talk about her, which was plenty. If I had met her, we might have gone a round or two."

Rosemary patted Jane's bicep. "My money would have been on you to take her out in one. In some ways, I'm grateful for Adelaide."

"What!" Meara stared at her friend as if she had never known the woman. "She never spared her malicious tongue when it came to you."

"That I know. Her malicious tongue had me leaving Hogstead and joining forces with you. We had a grand adventure."

"I'm sure you weren't saying that at the time, especially when we were running or almost drowning."

Rosemary smirked. "There were moments, I agree. We got through them." She placed a hand on her hip as she continued. "Let me finish. I never got to what I wanted to say."

"Go ahead." She pointed to a smaller table underneath a spreading shade tree. "I'll work on the children's table."

"Don't put a tablecloth on the children's table or at least not one you like. Anyhow, if I hadn't left Hogstead and Ronan hadn't driven into the Bay, I would never have met Billy."

"I'll give you that." Meara agreed and spread an oil cloth over the smaller table. "What has Adelaide done to benefit me? She's been nothing but mean to me. Three years ago, we decided to attend the Douglas family reunions back at Hogstead. Mother Douglas is old, and Braeden misses his brothers. The reunions have been painful affairs with Adelaide bragging about how important she is every live long minute."

"Aye," Jane stopped in mid-action of putting child size plates on the smaller table. "Did she stop the war?"

"That one would start a war," Rosemary commented, then carried the tray with the flatware over.

"Can't say I stopped the war, although suddenly Germany wanted to have peace talks. It may have been the horn, or it could have been they'd used up all their supplies and wanted out."

Jane and Rosemary shouted together. "It was the horn!"

"You two." Meara smiled to herself, thankful to have her friends visiting. "I never heard anything about how Adelaide did me a favor."

"Not a favor." Rosemary wrinkled her nose. "By being her usual self, she drove you here. You didn't want to live in Hogstead, and you had a farm here already waiting."

"I considered going back to Ireland to stay with my relatives."

"That you did," Jane agreed. "Even though Braeden and you weren't the huggy-kissy pair that Rosemary and Billy were—there was a spark."

"Mighty small spark." She shook her head. "That was one determined man. When I had no use for hand holding, he came and helped me clear the farm land to get it back in working order."

"Aw," Rosemary placed her crossed hands over her heart. "Only a man in love would work that hard."

"I came to see that, eventually." It took a while. A little over a year passed before she quit quizzing Braeden on things he should know.

Finally, her mother showed up to knock some sense into her, explaining she and Meara's father had specifically picked out Braeden for her. They'd even engineered the first meeting and hoped nature would take its course. If her parents approved of him, they'd know better than anyone else who he was. She wasn't up on shapeshifters, but she did know evil could not flourish on the farm. The squatter swore the land was cursed but was blessed for the right person.

The man in question appeared. He came up behind Meara and wrapped her in an embrace. "Everything is looking beautiful, including you, wife." He nibbled on her neck making her giggle. "I told the boys I had a lovely whiskey we might open."

"I'm sure you did. Bring out six glasses so we can all toast."

"That, I will." He headed toward the house as Billy and Ronan joined their wives under the trees.

Billy still sported an eye-patch. The current one had an eye drawn on it. He pointed to it. "It's me own design. I figure why not have fun with it. You probably heard we sold the farm in Hogstead. I took over Da's ferry business in Holyhead. He never went back to Ireland after the Easter riots. We were—"

Rosemary interrupted. "We bought a pub that we renamed the One-eyed Pirate. It's going to be a nice place where you can get a decent meal. Not another smoky dive like the waterfront taverns."

"Sounds like you two have been busy," Ronan commented. "Are you going to teach the twins how to work a ferry or how to run a pub?"

The proud father spoke, "Little Billy has sea faring blood in him and takes to the water. Jimmy, on the other hand, loves to cook. He even made a dish for today."

"Impressive." Jane agreed with a nod. "I think our two will follow in their parents' steps."

Meara knew that Ronan had taken over farming the family land. Would being a wife and mother keep the quixotic traveler busy enough? "Is Esmeralda turning cards for the local market?"

"You'd think." Jane grinned. "It's my Ro who had the gift with readings. Esmeralda is out in the fields with her da. She had a way with animals, too. No one was sadder when we bid Hercules goodbye. So, what about you Meara Douglas? Getting any more visits from your da and mam?"

She shook her head once again, wondering about the lack of visits. "They don't come by much. It's been…" She had to think about it. "...not since little Rosie was born. I feel them on the farm, though. It's like they're a part of it. As long as I'm here, they are, too."

"How about the townspeople?" Rosemary inquired. "You were afraid they'd treat you bad."

Braeden exited the house with a bottle and glasses on the tray. Obviously hearing the question, he answered. "My Meara is a local heroine. Once we put the farm to rights, the village prospered." The whiskey chuckled as it splashed into six glasses. Braeden picked up one and held it aloft. "So, let's toast to the six of us. The willing five and the headstrong one."

They each picked up a glass and clinked it with another before swallowing the peaty whiskey down. Meara placed her glass down and raised an eyebrow. "I assume you meant yourself when you said the headstrong one."

"Whatever you say, dear." He winked as the rest of them laughed.

When the laughter died down, there was a noticeable lack of sound from the creek area. The birds still sang, and the evening insect chorus was warming up. "Where are the children?"

Four muddy bodies came around the corner at a run and shouting.

"We saw a faery!"

"Faeries!"

"A right lot of 'em!"

Rosie, equally muddy, followed at a walk. She pretended to be bored and yawned. "The farm is named Faerie Lights Hill."

THE END